W9-CEJ-232

The Kingdom
of
Christmas

The Guardian of the Mountains

By

The Snow Spirit

Cameron Smith Publishing
Available from Amazon.com, CreateSpace.com, and other retail outlets
Available on Kindle and other devices

Copyright © 2014 Kate Shawcross (The Snow Spirit)

Illustrations Copyright © 2014 Thalia Evans

The right of Kate Shawcross and Thalia Evans to be identified as author and illustrator of this work respectively has been asserted by them in accordance with the Copyright, Designs and Patents Act 1988.

All rights reserved. No part of this publication may be produced or transmitted in any form or by any means, electronic or mechanical, including photocopy, recording or any information storage retrieval system, without permission in writing from the author or under licence from the Copyright Licensing Agency Limited.

The moral right of the author of the work has been asserted.

www.thesnowspirit.com

Second Edition 2015

ISBN-13: 978-1503027626

Map of The Kingdom of Christmas

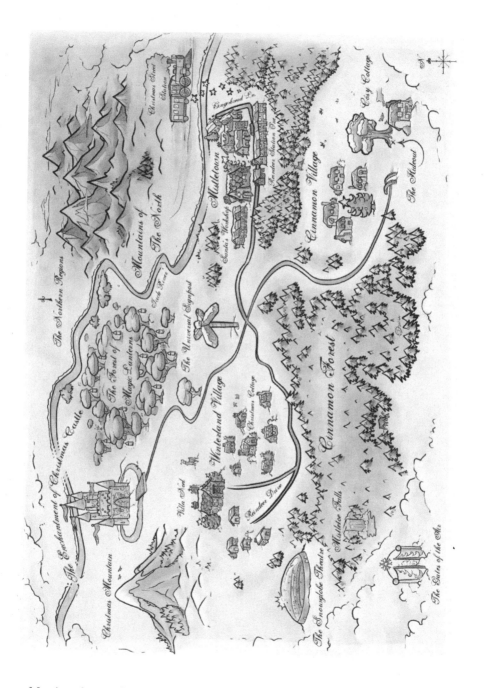

Map in colour and character profiles also available on www.thesnowspirit.com

Contents

1 - The Night Before Advent

It was November 30th in The Kingdom of Christmas - the date of the annual Christmas concert at the Snowglobe Theatre - and Rudolph was running late. He had decided to visit Earth that afternoon to see how preparations were coming along for the Christmas Season. He should have been back by 7pm, in fact, he shouldn't have been there at all; but Rudolph being Rudolph, and his mind often easily distracted, there were now only 20 minutes to go until the concert started, and he was flying as fast as he could towards the North Pole.

He shook the clouds away from his pink jumper and pushed on ahead into the night. He hoped that the Elves and the Snowflakes were behaving themselves. They were always kept apart at events like this. Rudolph personally blamed that missing book, *The Testament of the Snowflakes*, but then again there were other issues driving their rift.

Rudolph reached into the brown satchel about his waist and quickly showered himself with an extra helping of gold Reindeer dust – the dust that enabled him to fly. Then, as the clouds dispersed, a white plain featuring two large ice caps came into sight.

'I'm nearly there, Christmasdudes,' he said, flying down between them. As he did so, he showered himself with a smattering of pink Reindeer dust - the secret key to The Kingdom of Christmas - and a whirlwind rose up beneath him.

'I hate this part,' whimpered Rudolph, shutting his eyes and curling himself into a ball.

He was then squeezed through a tunnel of dense cloud and, without warning, he shot through a trap hole at the other end and landed on a little pink cloud in The Kingdom of Christmas.

'What a ride!' he exclaimed, shaking the vapour from his antlers.

As his vision returned, he now took in the sight of the Kingdom sparkling magically in the winter's evening. To the northwest, Christmas Mountain glowed with its familiar pink tint, whilst just in front, the Snowglobe Theatre bustled with the folk of the Kingdom, all queuing up for the concert. In the north, The Enchantment of Christmas Castle – home to The Spirit of Christmas – stood grand and impressive and paved the way to Winterland Village – home to the Elves, the Reindeer and Santa. The Forest of Magic Lanterns – mystical abode of the Snowflakes – was lit with shimmering silver lights especially for the occasion, whilst below, Cinnamon Forest - home to the Woodland Creatures – sparkled with magical fireflies. Rudolph sighed sentimentally before sweeping his eyes across to the northeast, to where the Icicle

River marked the edge of the Kingdom, and the Mountains of the North loomed eerily in the distance. The Mountains were an old enemy of the Kingdom and housed an evil Guardian who had been locked inside them for over 10 years. True, he was no longer a threat, but there were still times when he could be glimpsed on the Mountain ledge, and the thought of this caused Rudolph to shudder involuntarily. Suddenly, however, he was brought back to his senses, as much as Rudolph ever could be brought back to his senses, by a sharp kick to his rear hoof.

'Rudolph, where have you been? The Reindeer have been looking for you all day,' exclaimed a glistening female Snowflake, or Snowbelle to be more precise, who now looked down at him crossly as he sat on the cloud. She had blonde, fluffy hair, large, sparkling wings, and was dressed in a white, sparkling tutu.

'Oh, hey there, Clarinda. I didn't think they'd need me today. I've been to Earth to see the Christmas lights being turned on. Wow, it was Christma-pretty! How much time have I got before the concert starts?' asked Rudolph eagerly, as he dusted the vapour from his fluffy jumper.

'You've got about 15 minutes, Red Nose,' came a voice to his right. 'Don't worry about it too much though. We're running late ourselves. We can always try and stall things a bit if you'd like?'

Rudolph looked up, rather startled, to see the Queen's son - Prince Michael - on a flying snowmobile, his brown hair and eyes prominent in the moonlight. His twin sister, Princess Sarah, was seated next to him – her blonde locks and blue eyes equally striking.

'Hey, Princey, hey, Sarah, how are you both so late?' asked Rudolph, scratching his head in confusion. 'Aren't you playing *Hansel and Gretel* 1 in the second half?'

'Yes, but we had an Adventuring Class down at Camp Christmas,' replied Princess Sarah, adjusting her pigtails. 'It's so that we can learn to be a good Prince and Princess. Of course, we couldn't leave until *someone* had fully completed the adventure. The stars forbid that we should leave a minute sooner.'

'And quite right too, Sarah. I hadn't finished the task. If we're going to learn how to be a good Prince and Princess, we're going to do it properly,' declared Michael, before turning his attention to Rudolph. 'Do you want to latch onto the back of our snowmobiles, Red Nose? They're pretty fast, you know. We can get you to the Snowglobe in no time!'

'Oh, no thanks, Princey. I've gotta go back to my house first! I've got a prop to fetch for the surprise opening, and I'm sure every Christmasdude is guna love it!' exclaimed Rudolph, as he was about to

---

1 *Hansel and Gretel*, by The Brothers Grimm, published 1812.

jump off the cloud.

'You're attempting *another* surprise opening?' asked Clarinda crossly, as she pulled him back up by the tail and cringingly remembered his string of surprise openings from last year. 'Rudolph, you don't have time to do a surprise opening. By the time you get to your house it'll be time for the concert to start.'

'Oh, I can't open without it, Clarry! The entire show depends upon it! Besides, I'm a celebrity, remember! I can do things better than other Christmacreatures.'

With that, Rudolph leapt off the cloud and flew east, in the opposite direction of the Snowglobe, towards Winterland Village.

'Christmas help us! I wonder what it's going to be this year,' vexed the Snowbelle, shaking her head.

'Well, whatever it is, I'm sure it'll be entertaining,' added Michael, amused. 'But don't worry. We'll get word to the other Reindeer. See you later, Clarry. I hope you make it to the show in time for the pantomime.'

Prince Michael and Princess Sarah also set off to get ready, veering in the opposite direction to the red-nosed celebrity.

Meanwhile, at the Snowglobe Theatre, Blitzen, the head Reindeer, was showing the folk to their seats and was trying to clear the entrance as quickly as possible so that he would not keep Her Majesty waiting.

'Alright, just go straight ahead now. No pushing,' he ordered, as crowds of Bunnies, Badgers, Elves and Snowflakes bustled past.

The Snowglobe Theatre featured a crescent-shaped stage at the front, lit by fireflies, and was covered by a large glass dome from which glitter, bubbles, Elf Pops and chocolate drops all fell alternately onto the seating area below. There was a large glass door on the side, which was currently open for the creatures to enter on foot or by flight, as the case may be.

'Woohoo, look at this,' cried the little triplet Bunnies from Cinnamon Forest, as they tried catching the pieces of glitter that fell from the glass ceiling. They were so excited by the display that they almost knocked their younger brother over and caused the line in front to surge forward.

'Alright now, young Christmacubs, no pushing, or you'll cause a case of Christmas dominos,' declared Blitzen, as he eyed the quartet sternly. The Bunnies, who went by the names of Patch, Hopper, Carrot Top and Bunnyflower, were certainly a strange mix. Patch was a white Rabbit with black feet, a black tail, black ears and a rather large black patch around his left eye; Hopper was pure chocolate brown, with a tendency to jump up and down a lot when he got excited; Carrot Top was a chubby Bunny and was an undecided mix of white and grey, with a rather unfortunate tuft of orange hair on top of his head and an even more unfortunate tuft of orange hair for a tail. And then there was

Bunnyflower, who was the bonniest little Rabbit you have ever seen. He was as white as snow, with big black eyes that looked larger than ever as he now stared up at the mighty Chief Reindeer.

'We're sorry, Mr Blitzen, Sir,' said Hopper, who was still jumping up and down and could barely contain his excitement.

'Who's playing at the show this year, Mr Blitzen?' asked the slightly overweight Carrot Top, as he tried to catch the little bubbles that now fell from the ceiling.

'Well, let's see. We've got carols from the Snowbelle Quartet, Christmas songs from Elfis and the Elf Pops, and for the first time this year we've got rock anthems from the Rockin' Reindeer Group. Now the Queen is already here, so do try to be quick about it.'

'She is? Well, where's she sitting?' asked Patch excitedly. As he scanned the theatre he descried a floating Christmas cloud with the Queen seated amidst it, waving gracefully at the excitable Christmas folk down below. She had alabaster skin and long, blonde hair that trailed behind her like rays of the sun. She was dressed in a red velvet dress and clutched a sparkling crystal ball that glimmered magically beneath the fireflies – it was the Altra, source of all her magical powers.

Patch was especially chuffed that he had caught a glimpse of her and reached into his pocket for a star-shaped Wish Biscuit.

'I wish for a banner to wave at The Spirit of Christmas,' he declared boldly.

With that, there was a flash of light, and a white, sparkling flag with the words *Long Live Queen Krystiana* appeared in the air in front of him.

'Oh, wow!' gasped Bunnyflower, whose eyes had grown wide with delight. 'Hey, let me try one.'

'Well now, Christmacubs. I'm afraid you're going to have to put your Wish Biscuits away and take your seats!' After all, there were still a great many Christmacreatures trying to get in behind them, and some of the Snowflakes had started flying in order to cheat the queue.

'Oh, ok,' chimed the Bunnies, as they bounced off towards their seats.

'And don't forget to put your seatbelts on! Alright. Next up. Keep moving,' continued Blitzen, as the folk of the Kingdom surged past him.

The queue quickly filtered out, and Blitzen now made his way hastily towards Comet, who was selling Christmas corn and Elf Pops in the front row.

'Comet, have you seen Rudolph? He's presenting the show tonight, and so far there's no sign of him.'

'Sorry, Chief. Haven't seen him all day. He didn't come into the station either.'

'That's right. He didn't show up for work – again! Well this is just getting to be ridiculous. The show starts in 10 minutes,' remarked Blitzen, tapping his hoof loudly on the glitter-covered floor.

'Do you think we should start looking for him?' asked Comet, as he handed a bag of green and red Elf Pops to a little Hedgehog from Cinnamon Forest.

'Well, I think we should at least be prepared if he doesn't show up. I can't believe that Reindeer, really I ......'

'Ho Ho Ho. Good evening, Comet. Good evening, Blitzen. Both looking forward to the big concert?'

'Santa,' they beamed, as they now saw their Boss neatly attired in his usual red suit.

'I'm sorry, Santa, but I'm afraid there's a bit of a problem,' said Blitzen in his most authoritative voice. 'Rudolph's.......'

'.......Not here. Yes, I know! I just ran into Prince Michael and Princess Sarah. Apparently he's got another surprise opening planned.'

'Oh, Christmas crackers, not another surprise opening,' gasped Blitzen, placing his hoof over his eyes. 'Can't that Reindeer just surprise us by showing up on *time* for once? What has the great idiot got in store for us *this* time? A gigantic bubble gum to carry us off into space?'

'Well, whatever it is, Chief, it can't be any more of a disaster than the giant snowball he showed up in last year,' observed Comet, chewing on a Carrot stick. 'It wouldn't even fit inside the theatre. And then it took us 4 hours to tunnel him out.'

'Yes, and don't forget the giant Christmacocktail shaker that he.....'

'Hey, Blitzen,' came the voice of Prince Michael suddenly, as he and Sarah appeared in the air above, hovering on their snowmobiles. 'You're not having a grumble about old Red Nose again, are you? He *did* promise that he'd be here.'

'Oh, I have no doubt that he will be here, Michael, it's what *time* he'll be here worries me,' replied Blitzen, growing impatient. 'Did he give any indication as to what the surprise might be?'

'Sorry, Blitzen- he just said he wanted to make amends! Go easy on him though. I've got a feeling it's going to be a good one,' added the Prince with a wink.

The Prince and Princess then left, before Blitzen had time to enquire further, and headed backstage to prepare for their own roles in the Christmas Pantomime.

'Well then, see?' added Santa, forcing a smile. 'The Prince says we've got absolutely nothing to worry about. Perhaps we should take a bough out of his holly bush and trust in Rudolph's abilities.'

'*You* take a bough out of his holly bush and trust in his abilities,' said Blitzen, taking out his Christma-caller. '*I'm* going to ring Vixen backstage to organise a contingency plan just in case.'

Vixen was currently seated backstage in the company of the Rockin'
Reindeer Group and promptly answered his own Christma-caller.

'Hello! I'm afraid you're guna have to speak up cos it's a little
Christmacrazy in here.'

'Vixen! It's the Chief. I'm afraid you may have to open the show.
Rudolph's not here yet and apparently he's attempting another surprise
opening!'

'Aw, what?' barked Vixen, who almost dropped the Christma-caller
in annoyance. 'The guys are still tuning up. Why the baubles is he doin'
one of *those*? He botched it all up last year.'

'Yes, well according to the Prince and Princess, he feels he needs to
make amends,' explained Blitzen, tapping his hoof on the floor.

'Oh crackers,' grumbled Vixen, rolling his eyeballs. 'Ok Chief, I'll get
the band to tune up faster. He ain't here in 5 minutes, we're openin' for
him.'

'They're giving him 5 minutes,' reported Blitzen concernedly, as he
closed his Christma-caller. 'You know, if he wasn't a Reindeer, I think
he'd be a clown.'

Santa nodded and looked around. The seats were full, and hands,
paws and hooves were clapped as the Snowflakes sent magic sparks
from their fingers up into the air like fireworks. Some of the Snowflakes
had even reduced themselves to the size of fireflies and flew closer to
the stage to get a better look. Of course, their ability to fly meant that
they didn't have to wear seatbelts.

'Come on, Rudolph, you can do it,' whispered Bunnyflower, peeping
between his paws as the anticipation became too much.

'Do you think he's guna show?' asked Hopper, looking all around the
Snowglobe which was absolutely littered with glitter.

'I dunno, Hopper. Maybe he'll get stuck again.'

'Yeah, maybe they'll need a giant firework to get him out like last
year.'

'Whoa, you guys, you guys, what is *that*?' asked Carrot Top, pointing
up to the sky just beyond the Snowglobe to where a strange-shaped
object now came flying directly en route towards them. All four Bunnies
fixed their gaze, and the entire theatre soon joined them, becoming
completely awestruck at what they now saw.

A gigantic gingerbread house – most fitting to the theme of the
pantomime – was floating towards them, mobilized by a hefty
showering of Reindeer dust, with Rudolph seated in pride of place
amidst the chocolate chimney.

'Good evening, Christmasdudes,' cried Rudolph, waving a sparkler,
as the audience continued to gaze at him, completely spellbound.

'Good Christmas, I don't believe it,' uttered Blitzen in astonishment, as the fact that Rudolph had even shown up clearly amazed him.

'Raise the ceiling! Raise the ceiling!'

The Elves raised the roof and the house floated in just in time, allowing Rudolph to pirouette comically out of the chocolate chimney.

'Alright, it fit. Good evening, Christmasdudes,' cried Rudolph, as the sparklers on the stage arch lit up, and a small piece of the gingerbread wall fell away. 'Oops. Oh well, at least I made it inside this year, he he.'

'Alright, Red Nose,' cheered Michael from backstage. 'Your best Christmas surprise yet.'

'Ok now, party gang. Put your hands and paws together, cos we have got a Christma-crackin' show for you tonight,' declared Rudolph, as he looped the loop across the stage.

The crowd began clapping and cheering as Blitzen and Santa took their seats and the glass door to the Snowglobe slid shut.

'Ok now, Christmasdudes. Fasten your seatbelts, cos we are ready for Christmas blast off.

Are you ready?'

'Ready.'

'Are you steady?'

'Steady.'

'Then three, two, one, gooooo!!!!!!!'

The curtains on the stage were raised as the Rockin' Reindeer Group began to play. Glitter, sweets, snowdrops, chocolate drops – all came showering down from the roof of the Snowglobe as it lifted itself off the ground. The concert was set in motion as the globe rocked back and forth and the night took on a whole new magical dimension for the creatures of this Christmas Kingdom.

'Well, that's it then, I suppose. Old Red Nose has set the tone for the season,' announced Michael the following day, as the children returned to the castle parlour after their morning lesson.

'It'll be the best Christmas we've ever had, I'll wager. My letter to Santa's done, I'm ahead on my Princehood programme, *and* our father's coming home from travelling the universe in exactly 12 days. What could possibly be better than that?'

'Yes, of course, Your Majesty. That is exciting,' replied the children's nursemaid, Dora, who was in fact an elderly female Elf (Felf) from Winterland Village. She was short and stubby, with dark hair and pointed ears, and her shoes curled up at the toes in a typically Elfin fashion. 'Why, you haven't seen your father in almost a year.'

'Yes, I know,' continued Michael excitedly. 'I can't wait to hear the tales he's got for us about how he spread the joy of Christmas to the far off regions. You know, I plan to do something similar myself one day, Dora. It's so brave of him too, what with our father being human and all. Did you know that humans have less protection against magic than any other creature in the universe? Sarah and I are lucky on that count because we are also half spirit.'

'Hey look, look, everyone. The Guardian's back. He's standing on the ledge again,' came Sarah's voice from the balcony, as she peered through a spyglass.

'Oh, I don't believe it,' exclaimed Michael, suddenly running out onto the balcony and snatching the pocket spyglass from her. The morning was clear and bright, and far across the Icicle River in the east, the Prince could just about descry a black, shapeless mass standing on the ledge of the Mountains, supported by what appeared to be a crooked walking stick.

'Good golly, he's holding his Staff! - Get back inside, you big maggot. What are you doing out here? There's nothing in this Kingdom for *you* to take, so why don't you stop obsessing over it,' cried the Prince cockily, as he cupped his hands over his mouth to enable his voice to travel. As his words travelled across the air, a slight flash of yellow could be seen within the darkness of the Guardian's hood, and Michael was ready to start a second round of jeering when Dora marched out onto the balcony.

'Michael! What is the matter with you,' she cried, pulling him by the ear and marching him back inside – indeed for a little Elf she could really be quite feisty! 'Do you *want* to anger the Guardian of the Mountains? He is this Kingdom's greatest enemy,' she added, ushering Sarah inside too and locking the glass doors.

'But he's locked inside the Mountains, Dora. Our mother locked him inside, herself. He can't *do* anything to me. The furthest he can walk is to the edge of that ledge, and his own magic Staff doesn't even work anymore,' protested Michael, snatching another quick peek through the spyglass. The black mass now disappeared inside the Mountain, leaving the ledge eerily clear.

'Yes, Your Majesty, he *is* locked inside, but that is *not* an invitation to taunt him, young sir. You wouldn't throw rocks at a lion-monkey in a cage now, would you?' asked the Elf, now looking seriously at the young Prince and crossing her arms.

'Well, I would if he was coveting *my* Kingdom,' declared Michael, raising his eyebrows with resolve.

'Well then, I'm sorry to say it, Your Majesty, but there's a streak in you that needs a curbin', and you'll need to work on that in your Princely classes,' scolded the maid rather crossly, as she now busied herself tidying the parlour. 'When an enemy is defeated, that is not an invitation to continue defeating it. And by the way, Your Majesty, it's not just *your* Kingdom. You share it with your mother, your father and your sister, remember?'

'Yes, Michael. We are both the future rulers, don't forget,' added Sarah, sitting on her own seat which was also shaped like a sleigh, but with a small lantern overhead.

'Yes, thank you, pigtails, but that's beside the point when it comes to the Guardian,' responded Michael quite haughtily. 'He hates our Kingdom, therefore I hate him. And FYI, I don't understand how it's possible for anyone to hate Christmas.'

'Will you tell us the story again, Dora?' asked Sarah, sitting next to the busy little Elf. 'It makes me feel safe.'

'Oh yes, do tell it again, Dora. I'm with Sarah on this one,' added Michael enthusiastically.

'Very well then,' said Dora, putting her duster down with a sigh. 'But only if you stop snatching glances through the window.'

The children did so, and now sat up like bright-eyed young Rabbits as Dora related the tale.

'About 11 years ago, before you children were even born, a pedlar appeared in The Kingdom of Christmas. No one knew what creature he was - his face and body were covered by a black cloak and hood that he said he wore to hide a hideous disease that ate away at his skin. Whether this was true or not, no one knows, but this seemingly poor pedlar turned up at the castle door one night bearing a wooden stick which helped him to walk. He said he was cold and hungry and that he needed shelter for the night. The Snowflake guards were suspicious, but your kindly mother took pity on him and gave him a chamber, on condition that he did not enter the North West Tower, for indeed, that was where she used to keep the Altra.

The pedlar agreed and disappeared into his chamber at sunset. Late that night, however, the Snowflake guards awoke to discover the pedlar in that selfsame North West Tower, trying to steal the Altra so that he could attach it to his walking stick. It transpired that this was actually not a walking stick at all, but was a magic Staff known as the Staff of Evil, and when joined to the Christmas Altra, it would become the most powerful weapon in the universe. Well, your mother responded immediately, and had the pedlar locked inside the Mountains of the North, placing a powerful spell on them so that the pedlar could never break free. She also bound the powers of his Staff, so that it could only ever regain its force if it was joined to the Altra.'

'But, of course, that will never happen,' interrupted Michael, snatching a quick glance at the Mountains to see that the ledge was still reassuringly empty. 'I mean, the spell our mother placed on the Mountains is unbreakable, is it not? The Guardian is doomed to stay there forever.'

'Yes he is, my child! As are the Snow Wolves who also live there and who, we believe, have since become his followers. But we must never be complacent about it and continue to remember why he is there,' added Dora, looking at the two children in earnest.

'And the Guardian's identity?' asked Sarah in curiosity. 'Did they ever find out who he is?'

'I'm afraid not, Your Majesty. The Snowflakes believe he is an Elf. We Elves believe he could well be a Snowflake. Other creatures, including your mother, believe he is a Fairy from the neighbouring world of Alendria, but nothing has ever been proven,' said Dora, with a mysterious lilt in her voice. 'His identity is blocked by a charm too difficult to unravel.'

'Well, whatever creature he is, he's a nasty piece of work. And if I had a catapult, I'd pelt him on a daily basis.'

'Oh, good Christmas, you're not *still* going on about the Guardian of the Mountains, are you, Michael? I've told you to stop launching snowballs at him. We've had enough problems from him in the past, without you trying to exacerbate them,' came the voice of the Queen, as she now walked through the door in the company of two Snowflakes.

'Mother,' beamed the two children, as they rushed to greet her. 'Mother, are you having a meeting in here? Dora's just been telling us all about the night the Guardian came to the castle,' cried Sarah, holding her mother's hand.

'Yes, and about how you believe he's a Fairy from the world of Alendria, the dirty villain,' added Michael, chipping in.

'Oh! Did she tell you how Elves are merely servants and aren't really qualified to talk about the historical and political matters of the Kingdom,' retorted Hansen, the male Snowflake, as he strode haughtily over to the fireplace.

'Now, Hansen. There's no Christmacall for such rudeness,' warned the Queen, before turning her attention towards her darlings. 'Now children, I would love to hear more about your morning, but I must talk with the Snowflakes. Off you go now. And no more aggravating the Guardian!'

'Oh alright, Mother. If you insist,' said Michael with a sigh. 'Come on, Sarah, last one to the castle gardens is a melted snowman.'

Sarah was soon up and racing her twin brother out through the door into the garden.

'I hope you don't mind me telling them stories about the Guardian, Ma' Lady,' said Dora, as she poured some Christmas Coffee for the Queen and tried her best to ignore the Snowflakes.

'Oh no, Dora. It's important that they know what happened here. I just don't like Michael drawing attention to himself too much where the Guardian's concerned,' stated the Queen, smoothing her dress neatly.

'Oh, I'm sure he'll grow out of it. Is there anything else I can get for your meeting?' asked Dora, again bristling slightly as she looked at her rivals.

'Yes. How about a nice dose of Elf-free air?' sniggered Hansen smugly, as he flexed his fingers. 'I hear that's got a pleasant taste to it.'

'Oh, crumbs to your rudeness,' snapped Dora, flopping her hair back as the second Snowflake, Loretta, smirked behind her fingers. 'Ma Lady, I'll be outside if you need me. Being next to these two makes me as tense as a Christmas cracker.'

The little Elf then looked indignantly at the two visitors, before walking past them and exiting through the door into the hallway.

Hansen too now smirked at the Elf's behaviour.

'Well, that was an amusing little display,' he remarked to Loretta, before pulling up a gilded seat next to the Queen.

'Oh, Hansen. Must you be so rude to the Elves?' said the Queen sadly, as she looked upon her royal subjects with an air of disappointment.

'I apologise, My Lady. I suspect that tonight's scheduled slalom race is bringing out the competitive side in me,' said Hansen half-heartedly. 'You know how seriously I take my role as team captain.'

The slalom race between the Elves and the Snowflakes – or rather between the Elfin Wonders and the Magic Lantern Marvels – took place every year on the first night of December and was one feature of a much larger affair known as The Festival of Christmas Mountain. The rivalry between the two teams was intense, not merely because of the wider rivalry that existed between the two races, but because the Snowflakes were renowned for using magic to cheat and consequently stole an unfair win at every slalom race, without exception. The Queen raised her eyes at Hansen and placed her Christmas Coffee on the table.

'Hansen, you are *always* rude to the Elves. It has nothing to do with the race tonight. Just because you Snowflakes can all fly and do magic, and the poor little Elves can do neither, that is no excuse to stick your wings up at them! Apart from which, I invented the slalom race as a means of expressing your rivalry in a friendly way. It was not meant to exacerbate it.'

'I am sorry, Your Majesty, but my sense of Snowflake pride sometimes gets in my way.'

'Yes, well maybe you could shelve it for a while. I mean, must this rift between you and the Elves continue? I would dearly love to see a day where we have mixed teams of Elves and Snowflakes playing. This Kingdom was, after all, founded upon the principle of free will and not fate, Hansen.'

'I understand that, Your Majesty, and I am exercising freely my superiority over the Elfin race. I am sorry if I offend you, but the word of *The Testament of the Snowflakes* is eternally binding. I am therefore as polite as my principles will allow. After all, who am I to question the universe's natural order?'

The Testament of the Snowflakes was an ancient book which allegedly named the Snowflakes as the greatest race ever created. The book had been lost for centuries, but the Snowflakes still believed in its ideology, much to the annoyance of the Elves who were belittled by its so called 'teachings'.

'You are a subject of the Christmas regime, Hansen, and tolerance would serve you better, I fear. You have no solid proof of *The Testament's* contents. Such bigotry can only lead to problems.' said the Queen, growing annoyed.

'Yes. Well there's no need to spoil the day by going into all that,' returned Hansen dismissively. 'It *is* the start of Advent, after all.'

'It would be better if it were the start of a new era,' said the Queen, looking seriously at the two Snowflakes. 'But we can speak of this again. For now I understand there is some business afoot. To what do I owe the pleasure of this visit?'

'To a letter, Your Majesty. It came via the North Wind this morning. It was deposited in our post box,' said Loretta, now coming to life again as she took out a silver envelope and handed it to the Queen.

'Ah wonderful,' smiled the Queen, opening the letter to discover that it was from her husband.

'Oh, my. I see it is from my husband, Prince Harcourt.'

Dear Krystiana, she read.

My work in the Northern Regions is taking longer than expected. I am currently in The Town of Flickering Candles, and I am afraid the Butterfly folk that live here will need a little more persuading. During the daylight when the candles are out, they are open to the idea of Christmas, but once darkness descends and the flickering candles are lit, I am afraid their perceptions, like the light, become unstable. I cannot see myself returning to the Kingdom until just before Christmas Eve. Please pass my apologies onto the children.

All my love and Christmas Wishes,

Harcourt, Prince of Christmas.

PS Can you believe that some creatures out here have never heard of free will!

The Queen then folded the letter and sent a piece of red ribbon along the North Wind to show Harcourt that she had received it.

'Well my – how backward can one get,' scoffed Hansen, picking up a silver biscuit.

'Still, it's a rotten shame. I had rather hoped the Prince and I could fit in a spot of skiing before the season got underway properly. But it was solely for the letter that we came. We shall see you at the Festival later.'

The Queen and the Snowflakes then parted ways so that the Snowflakes could have a token 'practice' session before the Festival that evening.

Meanwhile, across the Kingdom in Cinnamon Forest, Bunnyflower was about to make a surprising discovery. The incident occurred while he was out playing snowball with his three older brothers. The game involved two teams hitting a snowball back and forth without dropping it. If one team dropped the snowball, then the other team gained a point. Unfortunately, being much smaller than his brothers, Bunnyflower wasn't faring particularly well and was costing his team mate, Carrot Top, a great deal of Christmas points.

'Jump higher, Bunnyflower,' whined Carrot Top, as he watched his brother miss the ball for the fifth time in a row.

'Ha ha! 5 Christmas points to us,' cried Patch, as he marked the score in the snow. 'You two play like a pair of she-cubs.'

Bunnyflower scowled rather crossly. 'I don't play like a she-cub. You're hitting it really high.'

'Hey, don't blame the shots,' yelled Hopper, as he bounced up and down ecstatically. 'We're winning Christmas fair and square, and you know it.'

Bunnyflower scowled at his brothers. He would need the assistance of a miracle to win this match, or at least a dramatic spurt in growth.

'Ok, now for the next shot,' cried Patch, as he held the ball up in the air. The clearing in which they played was quite small and a long way from Cinnamon Village, where they lived. A dense forest surrounded them on every side, and one clumsy shot and their snowball could be lost forever. But Patch now drew back his right paw and hit the snowball towards his brothers.

'Get ready, Bunnyflower, here it comes,' cried Patch, as the ball came hurtling towards the little Bunny. Bunnyflower crouched down to the ground and pushed himself up into the air, as high as he could manage. But even though he stretched his paws out as far as they would go, the snowball was still too high for him to reach, and it skimmed past his ears and flew straight into the dense forest behind.

'Oh, Bunnyflower, *now* look what you did,' scolded Carrot Top, as the ball disappeared from view.

'Hey, that's still another point for us though,' cried Patch, as he picked up the stick and marked yet another Christmas point in the snow.

'I'm sorry, Topsy,' whimpered Bunnyflower, hanging his head sorrowfully. 'I just can't jump that high.'

Carrot Top, as the youngest and largest of the triplets, always somehow ended up on the losing team and pulled a jib at his youngest brother.

'So, who's guna get the snowball?' asked Hopper impatiently. 'I mean, it shouldn't be me cos I'm on the winning team.'

'Yeah, and it shouldn't be me either cos I've been scoring all the Christmas points,' seconded Patch with a stiff nod.

'That's unfair. You were the one who hit it in there, Patch,' complained Carrot Top in annoyance.

'Hey, I didn't make up the Christmas rules,' stated Patch, crossing his paws.

'Well, *I* can't go and get it! I can't bounce that fast,' said the slightly overweight Carrot Top dejectedly.

'Well then, I guess *Bunnyflower* will have to go,' announced Hopper, looking eagerly at his youngest brother.

'Wait, why do *I* have to go?'

'Because you're the youngest, Bunnyflower, and that's what the youngest always does,' declared Patch firmly.

'Says who?'

'The Christmas *rules*,' said Patch again.

Bunnyflower looked into the forest. Although snow covered, it was dark and uninviting, since the fireflies only lit it at night, and to the young eyes of Bunnyflower it now looked rather frightening.

'So I have to go in there alone,' vexed Bunnyflower, not fancying it at all.

'Mmmmhmmm,' nodded Patch vehemently.

'What's the matter, Bunnyflower? Are you scared?' mocked Hopper, who secretly didn't want to go in there either.

'No,' scowled Bunnyflower, twitching his nose.

'If you go in, I might give you a Christmas penalty,' encouraged Patch.

'Really?' replied Bunnyflower, his face now lighting up.

'Yep, really.'

'Ok'

Bunnyflower plucked up his courage and straightened his jumper before heading off into the forest to find the snowball. He couldn't be sure exactly where it had landed, but Patch had hit it in a straight line, so if he just kept bouncing he was bound to find it sooner or later. The snow here was fresh and smooth, and his paw prints were the first to tread in it. A few bits of snow fell from the surrounding branches as the robins fluttered by above him, but the forest was otherwise quite still.

'Have you found it yet?' came the voice of Hopper from somewhere behind him.

Bunnyflower turned around. His brothers were now no longer visible, and all the little Bunny could see were trees and bushes stretching for miles.

'Not yet,' he cried, as he set back onto his path and pushed further into the forest. He weaved his way through some rather prickly conifers, catching his tail on one or two as he did so.

'Ouch, that hurts,' he whimpered, setting himself free and pulling a few prickly needles from his tail. Then, as he looked up, he saw the snowball lying on top of a holly bush.

'I've found it,' he cried excitedly. He then bounced up to reach it, but as he did so, something very startling caught his eye. Behind the bush was a tiny clearing, hidden and completely removed from the eyes of the Kingdom. At its centre lay a small, purple purse that sparkled magically and emitted an enchanting purple glow. Bunnyflower had never seen anything like this before, and he was so intrigued that he simply had to have a better look. With a great heave, he crawled underneath the holly bush and clambered into the clearing. The purse sparkled even more up close, and as Bunnyflower untied its strings, he saw that it contained a multitude of small, sparkling purple stars. Tiny stars that seduced the Bunny with their mystique. But what could they be? He wondered at first if they were sweets, but being a greedy little Bunny himself, he couldn't for the life of him understand why someone would leave a bag of sweets uneaten in the middle of Cinnamon Forest. He looked again at how they trinkled, 2 and came to the conclusion that they must be some kind of treasure or charm. *Lucky* charms perhaps that someone had left there to help him win the game. Finding this idea very appealing, he closed the purple purse and put it inside his sweater pocket. He then picked up the snowball, and after a rather awkward shuffle through the holly bush again, he bounced back towards his brothers.

---

2 A word native to *The Kingdom of Christmas*.

3 - Villa Noël

Meanwhile, back in Mistletown, the Elves bustled around the workshop, wrapping and stacking the presents in between discussing tactics for tonight's slalom race. Two Elves in particular were so busy discussing tactics that they had abandoned stacking toys altogether and had drawn up a full-scale plan of action outlining how they would 'beat those smelly Snowflakes.'

'So you've got it all figured out then,' said Pretzel, who was unusual for an Elf in that he exceeded 3ft and had rather pointed features and a crooked posture.

'You Christmas betcha,' growled Grunch, who was the Wonders team captain. 'One dirty trick from those frosty Flakes and we're onto 'em.'

'That's the Christmas spirit, Cap'n! Now, what do we do if they try and trip us up again...?'

'Ho ho ho,' came the voice of Santa, as he joined the two Elves by the firefly-lit window. 'Everything alright with the new X-mas Boxes, Melfs? Not abandoning those little children on Earth for the sake of an old slalom race, are you?'

'Nah, Santa. We just wanna win is all,' replied Pretzel, as Grunch grabbed a handful of gingerbread men that hung down from the ceiling on liquorish red stalks.

'Well, I'm sure you're due a spot of Christmas luck,' winked Santa, as he too picked a gingerbread man from the stalk. 'Now then, I'm off to see Rudolph. It seems he hasn't shown up for work again today. No doubt the Papa Ratzi are preventing him. Will you be alright here without me?' asked Santa, looking thoughtfully at the Elves.

'Oh, sure thing, Santa. You can count on us,' Pretzel assured him, thinking that with their Boss gone they might fit in a spot of slalom practice on the workshop stairs.

With that, Santa shut the door and made a right onto the High Street, setting out towards Villa Noël, harbouring a strong suspicion that that's where the red-nosed Reindeer would be.

Outside it was a crisp winter's afternoon. Mistletown was dusted with a coating of soft, fluffy snow that picked up the lights in the shop windows and sparkled as it did so. A highly seductive scent of cinnamon laced the air and came wafting straight from Mrs Bunnie's Cake Shop, just down the street.

'Oh, jolly nice!' beamed Santa, as the scent tickled his nostrils.

Mrs Bunnie was the mother of Patch, Hopper, Carrot Top and

Bunnyflower, and was noted for her delicious, mouth-watering treats. Santa could never resist her goodies, and due to the proximity of her cake shop to the workshop, he sometimes found it very difficult to concentrate. Even now, as he approached her shop, he could not resist a quick peek through the window. Inside he could see that she was offering all kinds of seasonal treats. There were mince pies, gingerbread men, candy canes, chocolate cakes, jam cakes, mugs of hot chocolate with marshmallows and whipped cream on top, Christmas brownies, sugar-bread, cinnamon punch, chocolate stars, cream candy, Elf pops, Christmas cookies………oh, and of course, there were Wish Biscuits – the Kingdom's great delicacy. What with all these glorious treats before him, Santa's eyes were falling out of his head, and he barely noticed Mrs Bunnie, a jolly-looking Rabbit with a jolly, round face, wearing a jolly-looking apron, waving at him through the window before opening the shop door.

'Good Christmasnoon, Santa,' she chirped in a fluffy voice.

A few seconds passed before Santa realised that someone had spoken to him, and he had to prize his eyes away from the window in a most sincere effort to be polite.

'Oh my, my! Good Christmasnoon, Mrs Bunnie. I do apologise. I was just sidetracked by your cake collection in the window.

'Oh, not to worry,' she said, as she reached onto her counter for a handful of freshly baked Christmas cookies. 'Here,' she added. 'They're fresh out of the oven. Consider them on the house.'

'Oh, thank you, Mrs Bunnie. You're too kind,' said Santa, who was never one to turn down food.

'Nonsense. Have a good day now,' she chirped, before closing her shop door and returning to her baking. What with all this talk of food, the delicious smell of the cookies was almost too much for Santa to bear, so he began munching on them right away.

As he made his way down the High Street, he observed the posters in some of the shop windows. Mrs Prickles' Hair Salon was launching a new Christmas Cut for the approaching month. Through the window Santa could just make out Trixitail, the Squirrel, having her tail trimmed and decorated with all kinds of lavish adornments. A cluster of holly was tied to the top of her tail, accompanied by a spiralling array of red velvet bows.

'Oh dear,' chuckled Santa, with a mouthful of cookies. 'I wonder if she'll be able to walk with that lot on, let alone get inside her tree house.'

Across the street Mr Prickles, the Hedgehog who owned Prickly Bank, was encouraging creatures to invest more in his Hedgehog Funds. As it was nearly December, stocks were bound to go up.

Dress shops were sporting the new Christmas Fashions, and Mr

Bunnie's Bookie Bonanza had all the odds for who was going to win tonight's slalom race at the Festival between the Marvels and the Wonders. The odds currently favoured the Marvels, although supporters of the Wonders were still betting against these, regardless. Santa chuckled to himself at their enthusiasm as he finished his biscuits and dusted his suit clean of crumbs. To his left he could see Reindeer Station One, with its familiar red, metal doors and brown brickwork, quirkily decorated with murals of the individual Reindeer. The one of Rudolph certainly stood out more than the others - no doubt he had taken extra care to ensure that it did - and Santa shook his head as he now reached the edge of the High Street and the Universal Signpost, which marked the central most point in the Kingdom. He then headed west, down a little slope which took him into Winterland Village, where he soon found himself at Reindeer Drive and utterly blinded by the Christmas lights that came bombarding towards him from Villa Noël.

'Good Christmas, it's like being in Las Vegas,' chuckled Santa, marvelling at how much it contrasted with the basic wooden stables of the other Reindeer.

Indeed, the villa boasted a number of flamboyant features, including large, flashing letters on its roof, lit up with the most vivid colours imaginable, and spelling out VILLA NOËL. Every few minutes the letters changed colour and a different pattern floated across them. At the moment flakes of snow floated on a background of hot pink. Yes, it was still broad daylight - 3 o'clock in the afternoon to be exact - but Rudolph liked to let the Kingdom know when he was at home. A large electrical replica of Rudolph stood on the front lawn, its nose shining brightly, while a miniature train set could also be spotted chugging around the garden, with a cuddly toy of Rudolph seated in the driver's seat. 'Merry Christmas, Christmasdudes. And welcome to Villa Noël,' it chirped merrily.

As Santa drew closer, he spotted a large, rowdy crowd of Rats on the steps outside the front door.

'Oh dear, it's the Papa Ratzi,' he sighed, seeing yet another problem he had to encounter. The Papa Ratzi wrote for The X-mas Times and were as loud and pushy as they were ruthless and deceitful. There were at least fifty of them spilling over onto Rudolph's lawn, snapping pictures, manically scribbling and shouting questions at Rudolph, who stood on his doorstep proudly sporting a Magic Lantern Marvel's jumper.

'Rudolph, Rudolph, when will your next book be ready?' spat a Rat at the front of the crowd.

'Oh, probably sometime in the New Year,' smiled Rudolph. 'It's called **101 Ru-diculous Facts about Christmas**. Hey, you wanna take my picture?'

'Rudolph, Rudolph, are you looking forward to the Festival tonight?' lisped a particularly toothy-looking Rat from behind.

'Of course, Christmasdude. I always like a little '*Fes-ti-vi-ty*,' he replied, flicking his glasses to the beat of the syllables.

'Rudolph, Rudolph,' shouted a tiny Rat from the back. 'How do you feel about the fact that Vixen recently called you 'lazy, conceited and a fat waste of Christmas space' in an interview with the hit TV show *That's my Christmas Parcel?*'

'Oh, well uh…...'

'That's enough,' said Santa, as he pushed his way up the steps past the Rats. 'Show's over. Rudolph has to work now.'

'Santa, Santa,' began the Rats, at the excitement of this new spotting.

'Santa,' cried Rudolph, giving a huge beam and pulling him through the crowd. 'Hey guys, take our picture.'

An influx of camera flashes showered them, and more questions were hurled, but Santa quickly pulled away and turned towards the vulture-like crowd.

'Alright, alright, that's enough. Off you go now,' ordered Santa, pushing the Rats in the direction of the steps. 'Rudolph's had enough questions for one day.'

'But Santa, Santa,' snapped the Rats, as they busily tried to resist his efforts. 'What news have you got for us about the Festival tonight?'

'There'll be no news, I'm afraid, as long as you hang around here. Now, off you go,' insisted Santa, as the Rats wedged themselves out through the gates. 'Come along, Rudolph,' sighed Santa, as he pushed him inside and shut the front door.

'Uh-oh, is this cos I didn't show up for Reindeer duty again?' asked Rudolph, as he now scratched his back leg rather sheepishly with his front hoof.

'Well, as a matter of fact it is, Rudolph, but could we sit down somewhere?' asked Santa, feeling slightly awkward at having to reprimand Rudolph in the hallway.

'Oh, sure, sure. Here, come on through, Santa.'

Rudolph led Santa through the sparkling marble hallway, which was absolutely littered with trimmings, into his entertainment centre to the left. The room was large, to say the least, and featured a cocktail bar with the words **Rudolph's Christmacocktails** flashing above it, in none other than hot pink. There were hundreds of different coloured liquids placed on the frosted shelves, some of which Santa had never seen before, and a plaque on the wall next to them reading:

A Dashing Daiquiri

A Holiday Dancer
A Prancer Palaver
A Strawberry Vixen
A Frozen Comet
A Fruipid Cupid
A Creama Donner
A Christmas Blitzer
Rudi on the Rocks
A Snowbelle Sleigh Ride
A Flaming Elf

'Have a seat, Santa,' said Rudolph, pulling out a seat at the bar, the legs of which were shaped like Reindeer legs with small hooves at the bottom. 'Want a Christmacocktail?' he asked.

'No thank you,' replied Santa, looking at the list. 'Oh well, maybe just a little one,' he chuckled, making a small shape with his chubby fingers before perching himself on the Reindeer seat.

Rudolph picked up a few mixtures and concocted a cloudy blue and orange striped cocktail, which he slid across the table to his Boss.

'Ooh my, what's this?' asked Santa, looking half-excited, half-intrigued.

'It's my very own speciality,' announced Rudolph proudly. 'The Christmas Blitzer. I've named a cocktail after all the Reindeer, he he. You know, I really think I should open my own cocktail bar, Santa. What do you think?' he enquired enthusiastically, as he perched himself next to Santa.

Santa was busy sipping the cocktail though a spiral straw that had a plastic Reindeer clinging to it, and hadn't really heard him properly.

'What's that?' he asked, as a rush of flavour bubbled in his head and caused him to hiccup. 'Oh my,' he muttered, shaking his head as he finished the cocktail. 'Oh my, that was a strong one. Now then, uh, what in The Kingdom of Christmas was I saying, uh - oh yes, that's right. Rudolph, I'm afraid that the other Reindeer aren't too happy with you at the moment.'

'Hey, those Christmasdudes are just jealous,' snapped Rudolph, as he slurped the last few drops of his cocktail.

'They're not jealous of you, Rudolph. They are your friends and they would be a lot nicer to you if you made more of an effort as a Protector of the Realm,' replied Santa warmly.

Rudolph sighed. 'I know Santa, but I find patrolling the Kingdom to be a pain in the hooves. And Reindeer Station One is just plain Christmaboring.'

Just then, the large cuckoo clock on the wall struck up behind them, and out popped a flying Rudolph with a red shiny nose. '*Rudolph the red-nosed Reindeer. The time is now half past three,*' it sang. '*Rudolph the red-nosed Reindeer. You'll go down in history.*'

Rudolph merrily jigged his head to the tune of the clock, before straightening himself up as he caught the eye of the more serious looking Santa. 'Sorry, Santa,' he apologised, clearing his throat. 'Another Christmacocktail?'

Santa hesitated for a second, before allowing himself to be swayed. 'Oh well, go on then,' he chuckled. 'But look here, Rudolph, this is very serious. We need you to take your responsibilities as a Reindeer more seriously. Many creatures still get scared when they see the Guardian out on the Mountain ledge. One more Reindeer around the place could help to Christma-comfort them a little.'

Rudolph sighed as he picked up a Reindeer-shaped drinks stirrer. 'Ok, ok, I'll make more of an effort. But you know, that anti-Christmasdude gives me the Christmascreepies too, Santa.'

'He can't harm you, Rudolph. Just remember that,' assured Santa, who was pleased at least to hear a partial resolution from the celebrity.

'I know. I still get nervous when I think of him, though. Oh, here ya go, Boss,' said Rudolph, popping a highly ornate pink and yellow cocktail into Santa's hand, while he kept hold of a silver and red one.

'Oh my, my, what have I got here?' asked Santa, not quite knowing where to begin with this one.

'This here is a Fruipid Cupid,' beamed Rudolph proudly. 'And I've got me a Holiday Dancer. Well, Merry Christmas, Santa,' he toasted, as the two chimed their glasses together.

Santa slurped a few sips of his drink before his eyes went POP and a gurgle of fruitiness whizzed around his head. Rudolph's cocktail too was having some slightly unusual effects on him, as the minute he finished slurping, two large puffs of steam popped out of his ears and spiralled around his antlers.

'Wow,' he exclaimed, shaking his head a little in an effort to dispel the clouds of smoke. 'Well, that was different. How's yours, Santa?'

'Very tasty,' answered Santa, who was seized by the urge to wiggle all around the room. 'But I think I'm done for the day now. Thank you, Rudolph,' he said, once again shaking his head as the effects of the cocktail wore off. 'Now then, I think maybe it's time we made our way to the Festival. After all, it's getting on for 4 o'clock, and I'm sure the Woodland Creatures would welcome some help.'

'Sure thing, Santa. Just two seconds,' said Rudolph, as he jumped into a highly ornate leather seat situated at the far end of the room. He then pressed a red button and leaned his head back, as a large cloth attached to two metal arms slid out of the top of the headrest and lowered itself onto his large, red nose. The cloth made a great buzzing noise and moved backwards and forwards rapidly until his nose shone like an electric light bulb. Rudolph then opened his mouth and formed a huge grin so that the cloth could polish his teeth. The cloth lowered itself, and Rudolph's head rattled comically from side to side as his gnashers received a jolly good scrubbing. A loud PING was then heard, as the cloth stopped and disappeared into the headrest of the chair again, as though it had never existed.

'Alrighty,' said Rudolph, as he darted in front of his mirror and admired his own reflection. 'How do I look, Santa?' he asked, as both his teeth and his nose twinkled.

'Very nice,' remarked Santa, who was somewhat dumbstruck by Rudolph's rather bizarre set of contraptions.

'Ok then. Got any Reindeer dust?' he asked.

'Yes, just enough,' replied Santa, feeling for the little satchel tied around his belt.

'Well, hop on, Santa!' cried Rudolph, as he walked out onto the porch, shutting the large marble-stained front door behind him.

With that, Santa sprinkled Rudolph with the gold sparkling dust, and with a jerk they were off, climbing high into the sky towards Christmas Mountain.

Meanwhile, back in Cinnamon Forest, the game of snowball had resumed and the losing team was catching up, all thanks to Bunnyflower. It seemed that, with his lucky charms, he was able to jump higher and hit harder than he had done before. Indeed, they gave out a certain energy which made the little Bunny feel stronger, and they also gave him the ability to hover, so that at times he was practically flying. Patch and Hopper were greatly annoyed, especially given that they had no idea what had caused the transformation.

'Did you shower yourself with Reindeer dust or sumthin, cos you know you're not supposed to do that,' complained Patch, as he marked yet another Christmas point in the snow for the opposite team. It was now 5 all, and the first team to reach 6 points was the winner. One more hit from Bunnyflower and they'd lose the match.

'No. Do you *see* any pink or gold dust on me?' asked Bunnyflower, feeling rather chuffed at his new-found powers.

'Don't be such a party pooper, Patch. Just cos we're better than you,' boasted Carrot Top, delighted to be on the winning team for a change.

'Well, *you* haven't hit a single shot, Topsy, so don't go blowing your Christmas trumpet just yet,' snapped Hopper, who was getting ready to serve the snowball for the last time.

Bunnyflower crouched down ready to receive the ball and placed his paw in his pocket to feel the stars. As he did so, he felt a sudden surge of energy, and he prepared himself for his final shot. But suddenly he was distracted by a soft rustling in the forest behind.

'Wait,' he cried, jumping up in alarm. 'Did you hear something?'

Hopper sighed as he lowered the ball.

'What!' he asked, as his tail began to twitch.

'I heard something in the trees behind,' whispered Bunnyflower, now peering into the darkness of Cinnamon Forest.

Carrot Top moved closer to his younger brother, as his ears stood up on end. The rustling sound was then heard again.

'Hey, I heard it that time, too,' said Topsy, now looking afraid.

'It's probably just a robin in the trees,' added Patch dismissively.

'What if it's a Snow Wolf,' whimpered Carrot Top, who was suddenly seized by the urge to head back to Cinnamon Village.

Hopper sighed loudly. 'It's not a Snow Wolf, Topsy. They're all locked up in the Mountains. Now, come on.'

Carrot Top gulped. 'Fine,' he said, shuffling across the clearing and moving away from the trees behind him.

Hopper raised his paw back and hit the ball high into the air so that it now hurtled on course straight towards Carrot Top.

'I'm coming, Topsy,' yelled Bunnyflower, as he bounced into the air and hovered slightly as the ball came his way. But it was actually flying lower than he'd anticipated, so Bunnyflower threw himself to the ground with the force of two Rabbits, and with a swift hit he knocked the snowball back into the air so that it landed on the ground, bang, smack in the middle of Patch and Hopper.

'Hurray,' yelled Bunnyflower and Carrot Top, as they jumped up and down in the snow ecstatically. 'We won, we won. We are the Christmas champions.'

'Thank you so much, lucky stars,' whispered Bunnyflower to himself, as he felt for the purple purse in his pocket.

'You couldn't possibly have won. You were *losing* 5 minutes ago,' cried Patch, as Hopper pulled his face in a sulk.

At that moment, another rustle was heard in the forest behind them, but this time it went unnoticed by the Bunnies. Nor did they hear the branches of the holly bush, where just moments ago Bunnyflower had gone to fetch the snowball, shaken with frustration. In fact, all they could hear at this point in time were the sounds of defeat or victory, and they now headed back quite noisily towards Cinnamon Village to get ready for the Festival, with Bunnyflower still carrying the purse of purple stars in his pocket.

Christmas Mountain could not have been more unlike the Mountains of the North. It sparkled with a pink tint and consequently looked like a large mass of candyfloss. Because of the rivalry between the slalom teams, security at the Festival was very tight, and in order to get in, everyone had to undergo an inspection by the Snowflakes.

'Alright, you can go on through,' said one particularly tall and handsome Snowflake to a little Badger from Cinnamon Forest, slapping a silver wristband on his paw.

'Don't take it off. It's your proof that you got in legitimately. Next.'

Next in line was a little Elf, decked out generously in green and carrying a little green flag on a stick to show his support for the Elfin Wonders.

'Step up!' commanded the Snowflake sternly.

The little Elf stepped onto the inspection stool, looking up with beady little eyes at the Snowflake.

'Empty your pockets!' ordered the Snowflake. The Elf turned out his pockets to reveal two small bags of Elf pops.

'Elf pops in the basket!' said the Snowflake, callously.

'Bbbbbuuuu bbbbuuut,' stammered the dumpy little Elf.

'But nothing. No refreshments are to be taken onto the premises. There is plenty of food available for you to buy inside.'

The little Elf squinted and blinked a few times before reluctantly dropping his bags of sweets in the **No Admittance, Dangerous Objects** basket. The little Elf, now believing his inspection to be over, climbed down off the seat and proceeded to walk under the banner.

'Ahem,' said the Snowflake, folding his arms and standing impressively in front of the Elf so as to block his entrance. The little Elf looked up from his inferior position and gave a little smile, waving his banner in the most inoffensive way he possibly could. The Snowflake looked unimpressed.

'Banner in the box,' he commanded.

'My bbbbaaa bbbba banner?' asked the Elf, pulling it protectively towards his chest. 'Yes, your banner! It could be perceived as a weapon.'

The little Elf sighed, as his eyes welled up with tears. He quickly put the little banner inside the basket that was already overflowing with Elfin banner sticks. The Snowflake roughly slapped a silver armband on the Elf's dumpy little arm and pushed him through.

'Next!'

Next in line were Patch, Hopper, Carrot Top, and Bunnyflower, all neatly attired in Magic Lantern Marvels jumpers. Bunnyflower had taken extra care to place his bag of 'lucky charms' inside his pocket, and now hoped dearly that they would not be confiscated.

'Good evening, Christmacubs. Your allegiances are to be commended,' observed the Snowflake, as he looked approvingly at the Bunnies' silver jumpers.

'Oh, we love the Marvels,' enthused Patch excitedly. 'We wouldn't miss them for the Kingdom.'

'Excellent,' snorted the Snowflake. 'Ok then, cubs, jump up, one at a time.'

The Bunnies' inspections were brief, and their pockets remained unchecked, much to the relief of Bunnyflower, who was now able to take his bag of charms inside the fair.

'Alright then,' said the Snowflake, as he slapped on their silver wrist bands. 'Go on through. And don't worry about your banners,' he winked slyly.

'Hurray,' yelled the Bunnies, as they jumped under the sign into the Festival.

Inside, the Festival was truly a marvel to behold. The animals of Cinnamon Forest had certainly worked hard this year. There were goody stalls in every direction, and the air was laced with an almost tangible scent of cinnamon. Mrs Bunnie had a small cake stand selling the delights of her own shop. Cones of sugared almonds could be purchased, as well as mug-fulls of steamy Cinnamon Punch and Wish Biscuits. A small crowd of Elves could be seen enjoying a batch of Wish Biscuits, as magical POPS exploded in the air, showering gifts upon them. There was an entire Cinnamon Stand set up by Trixitail the Squirrel - who was still sporting her rather eccentric tail-do - which sold cinnamon cake, cinnamon doughnuts, cinnamon nuts - even the stand was made out of cinnamon bread and would be awarded to the biggest cinnamon eater of the night. Mrs Claus, who was shaped like a Christmas pudding herself, had a stand selling all types of Christmas puddings, along with a Christmas tarot stand where she gave Christmas readings from her own Magic Mixing Bowl. A giant ice cream cone stood at the entrance to the mountain thrill rides, and a sizeable crowd of Elves, Snowflakes and Woodland Creatures had already gathered outside, each with a little cup to scoop themselves generous helpings.

The fair had an eclectic range of rides. There was a large merry-go-round with Reindeer instead of horses. Rides with the real Reindeer were also available, and at this moment, Dancer was doing the honours, taking the Elves and the Woodland Creatures up around the mountain and back. A large Ferris wheel stood to the left of the fairground, lit up with magical fireflies from The Forest of Magic Lanterns. 'Pop the Elf', a shooting game where the aim was to hit a cork at the wooden Elf head, was a particular favourite with the Snowflakes, and as a consequence was causing a great ruckus amongst the Elves. The toboggan ride was very popular with the Elves, since they had a knack of travelling very, very fast. But the most popular of all the rides, judging by the size of the queue, was Ice Wars, a thrill ride built right inside the mountain. It was very much like a roller coaster, except that instead of sitting in a runaway train, riders wore ice skates and skated down a frozen track with steep drops, loop bends, sharp turns, snow showers and a few other surprises.

As the Bunnies entered the fairground, Bunnyflower became particularly fixated with Ice Wars. After all, with the strength endowed him by his lucky stars, he felt he could quite literally do anything.

'Oh, wow,' he exclaimed, looking up at the mountain. 'Can we go on?'

The triplets needed little persuasion, and within minutes they were standing near the front of the queue for this white knuckle, tail-raising attraction. The line was full of other eager Woodland Creatures, Elves and Snowflakes, all of whom seemed to become less enthused as they reached the top. Indeed, the mountain steepened with every climb, which meant one thing - the drop down was going to be gigantic. As they reached the top, a handful of Elves disappeared into the inside of the mountain just before the Bunnies.

'Wait here please,' ordered a Snowflake who was on patrol.

'Can't we go in?' asked Hopper, jumping up and down, and trying to see past the Snowflake to the inside of the tunnel where the ride began.

'Four at a time,' stated the Snowflake pompously, blocking the entrance. Hopper was still busy jumping up and down, while Bunnyflower discovered a way of sneaking a peak by sticking his head through the Snowflake's legs.

'Whoa, it's really dark and creepy in there,' murmured Bunnyflower, growing afraid.

'Hey, careful, Christmacub!' snapped the Snowflake.

A resounding scream was heard from inside the mountain as the Elves shot off.

'Huh! Did that come from in there?' asked Bunnyflower, his tail shaking and his stomach churning like a twister.

The Snowflake did not seem to have heard. 'Next four!' he barked, pushing them in, one by one, and blockading the entrance, or as the Bunnies now saw it, the exit. They were now inside a hollow cave, surrounded by ice. Screams could be heard echoing around the walls as the former daredevils plunged to their fate.

'Ok, Christmacubs, step right up,' urged the cheery voice of Donner. 'You know what to do?' he asked, looking vaguely amused by the four terrified Bunnies.

'Uh-uh,' answered Patch, shaking his head. He was now too scared for words.

'Ok, well, you put these ice skates on right here, and you stand at the top of the drop, behind the gate. I need you to bend your knees and place your paws on them. When I say 'Go', the gate will open and you'll start skating downwards. Got it?'

The Bunnies were now nodding out of fear, as opposed to anything else, and were having a great deal of trouble lacing up their ice skates due to the fact that they were shaking so much. Finally, they had tied them after a fashion, and all four lined up at the top of a black hole cut deep into the cave. A metal gate prevented them from going anywhere for the Christmas present, and Carrot Top felt that it was not too late to back out. The path was made of sheer ice, which meant that they were going to travel incredibly fast, and worse still - there was nothing for them to hold onto. As they stared down at the drop, all they could see was darkness. The drop appeared almost vertical.

'Ok then, cubs. You ready?' enquired Donner.

The Bunnies nodded, with the exception of Bunnyflower, whose eyes were stuck fast in front of him, as he placed one paw inside his jumper pocket and clutched onto his bag of charms.

'Alrighty then,' said Donner, as he pushed a metal lever forward. The gate in front of them slid across, and they were off, plunging 100 miles an hour down a 50 ft drop.

'Aaaaaarrrrrrgggggghhhhhh,' screamed the Bunnies, as their ears shot back behind them like pigtails blowing in the wind.

'Christmas crackers, I can't see anything,' yelled Patch, as they continued whizzing down the near vertical slope. They were in complete darkness and seemed to be falling forever. Then they hit the bottom and were immediately climbing another hill, this time not as steep.

'What!!!! We're going to drop again?' squealed Hopper, as they climbed the slope wildly.

'I think so,' screamed Patch, as they hovered over the summit of another slope before being plunged down at lightning speed.

'Aaaaaarrrrrggggghhhhh! I wanna get offffffffffffffffffff,' shrieked Bunnyflower, as his body shook with the motion of the drop. He was trying desperately to cling onto his bag of charms for fear of what might happen if he let go.

They hit the bottom again, only this time they were swung sharply around the corner into the heart of the mountain.

'It's really dark in here,' quivered Patch, as he reached out to hold onto one of his brothers.

'Get off, dummy, you can't hold on to me,' panicked Hopper.

'But there's no handle bars,' whimpered Patch, as they continued to swirl through the black cave.

'Hey look, what's that yellow glow?' cried Carrot Top.

'Aaaarrrggghhh! Snow Wolves!'

The animatronic Snow Wolves were now jumping out of the depths of the cave, and the track only swung around just in time for the Bunnies to miss them, even turning the foursome upside down and dropping showers of ice-cold snow on them. Then the cubs began to climb a steep slope within the mountain – the steepest one so far - and the ceiling was so low that the Bunnies were practically grazing their heads along it. They reached the top and were suspended there for a few moments.

'Well,' cried Patch, his eyes shut as tight as they could be, 'there's only one way out, and it's down this crazily long, black tunnel.'

'How long are they guna hold us here for?' asked Bunnyflower, as they rocked back and forth on the moving peak.

Then, without warning, a large Snow Wolf jumped down from up above, the platform tilted forward and they were flying down the final drop, causing a torrent of snow to fly up on either side of the track as they hit the bottom. The force of the drop caused all four Bunnies to fall over, and Bunnyflower's purse was abruptly flung from his pocket. Dazed and shaken however, none of the Bunnies initially noticed, as they were more concerned with the cheers that erupted from the surrounding onlookers.

'Wow,' cried Patch, suddenly beaming. 'That was amazing!'

'Yeah,' nodded Carrot Top unconvincingly.

The other three were still shaking, so Patch merely took this as an affirmation that they too had enjoyed it.

'Where to now then?' he asked, pulling himself up before taking off his skates and scanning the fairground.

'Oh, maybe the toboggan tra – uh, hey, what's that?' asked Hopper, as he suddenly spotted the purple purse in the snow nearby.

Bunnyflower blinked momentarily and thought that there must be *two* bags of lucky charms such as his, but on checking his pocket he found that it was empty, and suddenly jumped up in alarm.

'Hey, that's mine,' he shouted, as he made a dive for it. Unfortunately he was too slow, and his elder brother Hopper got there first.

'How is it *yours*, Bunnyflower?' he asked, holding the purse up high so that his younger brother couldn't reach it.

'I found it in Cinnamon Forest earlier. It must have fallen from my pocket. Give it to me!' cried the little Bunny, as he jumped up and down, desperately trying to catch it.

'You found it in Cinnamon Forest. Well, let me see then,' said Hopper as he untied the strings and peeked inside.

'Wowwwwwwwwwwww,' he cried, his eyes full of excitement as the purple purse now glistened seductively. 'Patch, Topsy come and see.'

The brothers jumped up immediately and accidentally knocked Bunnyflower over once again.

'Purple *stars*,' remarked Patch, knitting his eyebrows together. 'They look like *sweets*.'

'What are they *for*?' asked Carrot Top, scratching his head confusedly.

'They're lucky charms,' insisted Bunnyflower, who had managed to pick himself back up and was now trying to grab the purse strings. 'Give them back, I saw 'em first.'

'Bunnyflower, these aren't lucky charms,' declared Hopper, holding the purse up even further from his brother.

'How do you know?' asked Carrot Top, looking bemused.

'Cos lucky charms don't glisten like this, dummy,' replied Hopper, as a bright purple dust now trinkled across the purse. 'Besides, they've got some kind of energy around them. Lucky charms don't have that. They're giving me extra strength. They must be magic of some kind. And look, they're making me hover,' added Hopper, as he now floated in the air for several seconds before landing back on the ground.

'Is *that* how you won the game of snowball earlier?' asked Patch, raising his eyebrows and looking suspiciously at his younger brother.

'No,' scowled Bunnyflower, now looking quite ashamed.

'Huh! It *so* is. Christmas cheat,' accused Patch, poking his tongue out.

'Hey, cubs, do you think if we *eat* them they'll make us stronger?' asked Hopper, as his eyes now became fixed on the bag.

'Maybe,' mused Carrot Top, liking the sound of this.

'Yeah, or maybe they'll make us fly,' added Patch perceptively. 'I mean, look at them. They're making you hover just holding them.'

'Yeah, but we're not supposed to fly, Patch,' said Carrot Top worriedly. 'Only Santa and the Reindeer are allowed to fly, remember? They're really strict about it.'

'I know. But it'd be Christmacool if we could,' continued Patch naughtily.

'Oh, I don't know, Patch,' continued Carrot Top, vexed. 'We could get in a lot of trouble. Besides, I thought only gold Reindeer dust made you fly.'

'Yeah, normally it does. But these stars look pretty powerful. They look like they can make us do *anything*,' urged Patch with large eyes.

'You think so?' asked Hopper, growing more and more seduced.

'Sure, why not? But there's only one way to find out,' said Patch, snatching the bag from Hopper's paws and turning to face the back of the fairground. 'Come on.'

'Come on where?' cried Hopper, as Patch began bouncing off.

'To the boundary lands. Under the fence. We can't look here. We'll get caught,' returned Patch.

'Hey, wait, what are you doing with my lucky charms?' cried Bunnyflower, as he struggled to keep up with his brothers, who were all much bigger and faster than he was.

'We're guna eat them to see what'll happen,' said Patch. 'But don't ever tell Mum.'

'Why not?' panted Bunnyflower.

'Cos she'll get her ears in a knot.'

The Bunnies soon arrived at the fence which marked the end of the Festival, and notably there were no Snowflakes nor Reindeer here to police the area. With a great heave, they squeezed themselves underneath the fence and began bouncing off, skirting the unfamiliar territories of the Kingdom.

In the meantime, a much celebrated member of the Kingdom had just entered the park to attend his general patrol for the evening.

'Hello there, Blitzen,' said the Snowflakes as he went in. There was no need for Blitzen to be checked since he was the head Reindeer and part of the Kingdom's security system. He had just seen Santa and Rudolph, and had promised to catch up with them at the slalom race as soon as he had taken a stroll around the fair. He was then approached by an old acquaintance of his.

'Good evening, Blitzen,' came a small voice from down below.

'Why, good evening, Sergeant. How are you?' smiled Blitzen warmly. It was Sergeant Squirrelseed of Cinnamon Forest. Sergeant Squirrelseed was the highest ranking official in the forest, and was second in command only to the Reindeer and the Snowflakes. He was responsible for upholding order amongst the Woodland Creatures, and every now and again he was honoured with the privilege of delivering a message to the next world - otherwise known to us as Earth.

'A good turn out this year,' said the Sergeant proudly.

'Yes, absolutely,' returned Blitzen.

'Well, I must be off. I promised my wife, Trixitail, that I'd help her out at the Cinnamon Stand. Cheerio, Blitzen.'

'Yes, goodbye Sergeant,' replied Blitzen.

Blitzen then walked in, past the food stands and the giant ice cream bowl, into the fairground. He had only been there several minutes, when out of nowhere, a little purple Bunny, sparkling with purple dust, shot into the air and flew over his head, swirled around for a few moments and then landed, rather inconveniently for *him*, at Blitzen's hooves.

Blitzen looked down sternly, though somewhat confused as to how this situation had arisen. Indeed, while certain flying spells were permitted in the Kingdom, they were severely restricted to its senior members. The Bunnies certainly weren't allowed to use them. And things became even more confusing when suddenly three more Bunnies, all a bright sparkling purple, shot through the air and landed next to the first one.

The Bunnies were quite dazed and were initially oblivious to Blitzen's presence.

'Whoa, I *really* didn't expect *that* to happen. Are you guys ok?' asked Patch, as his eyes now adjusted to his surroundings. 'Hopper, Topsy, Bunnyflower. Hopper, Topsy, Bunnyflow- huh!!!! Bounce!!!' yelled Patch as he suddenly saw Blitzen standing over them, looking most Christmacross indeed.

Panicked, the Bunnies attempted to scatter, but Blitzen was too quick for them and trapped all four of them under his hoof by their tails.

'I don't think so, Christmacubs. I think you've got some explaining to do, don't you, mmm? Stand to attention!' he commanded, releasing their tails and placing himself in front of them.

Patch was still clutching the purse, which was shimmering in waves like a fibre optic tree, and was desperately looking for a way out of the situation. Judging by the reaction it had given them, he knew they should never have got their paws on it.

'Well then. What's all this about, hmm?' asked Blitzen, pointing to the purse with his hoof.

All four Bunnies' noses simultaneously began to twitch as they looked from one to the other and then to the floor.

'Well?' pressed Blitzen, a little more intimidating this time.

'Uhhhhh,' they all chimed together in a desperate search for an explanation.

'We were uh, selling sweets for our mother from the sh sh shop,' stammered Patch, looking at the others and frantically nodding.

'Yes Sirrr, that's what we were doin',' cried Hopper who, living up to his name, was hopping up and down on the spot.

Carrot Top just looked from one purple brother to the other and then back to Blitzen again, nodding and smiling and scratching his head, while Bunnyflower was too afraid to look anywhere other than at the ground, his nose twitching uncontrollably.

'Really,' said Blitzen fatly, with disbelief. 'So your mother gave you *this* bag full of sweets then?'

'Yes Sir.'

'That's right.'

'She sure did.'

'I see. And what sweets are in this bag?'

The Bunnies began to twitch their purple noses in unison and looked back and forth for an answer in each other's faces.

'Elf Pops,' blurted out Hopper at last, nodding his head at his brothers to give them the green light.

'Yeah, Elf Pops,' chimed the others.

'Purple Elf Pops,' burst out Carrot Top, out of sheer fear more than anything else. Patch was now desperately scratching his tail with his foot, whilst still clutching onto the purse for dear life.

'Purple Elf Pops,' said Blitzen, leaning in towards them and craning his head into the purse which was still closed at this point.

'Why, I've never seen purple Elf Pops before. I'd love to buy some. I'm intrigued,' said Blitzen cheerily.

'Oh well, there's none left now,' remarked Hopper, quickly positioning himself in between Patch, who was holding the purse, and Blitzen, who was edging towards it.

'None left. Really?'

'Mmmmhmmm, none at all.'

'Well, in that case you'd better go back to your mother's stall for more supplies. I'll escort you,' smiled Blitzen.

The four Bunnies looked distraughtly at each other when, with that, Blitzen snatched the purse out of Patch's paws.

'Oh no,' cried Patch, jumping behind his brothers for safety. The Bunnies once again tried to make a dash for it, but were in such a hurry that they all tumbled over one another.

'Just a minute, cubs, I – good Christmas. What are *these?*' asked Blitzen, as he looked at the purple stars, completely flummoxed. 'Why, and they seem to have some kind of energy around them.'

The Bunnies looked around desperately for somewhere to bounce to. How *were* they going to get out of this one?

'Well?' continued Blitzen, who now tapped his hoof loudly on the ground.

'We – we – we don't know,' stammered Hopper.

'You don't know,' repeated Blitzen, sounding unconvinced.

'Uh-uh. We thought they were sweets. So we all bit into one and then shot through the air,' admitted Carrot Top, his cheeks turning bright red and clashing with his hair, which still remained orange, in spite of his purple transformation.

'Is that so?' asked Blitzen, looking down at Hopper inquisitively.

The purple Bunny nodded.

'And where in The Kingdom of Christmas did you get them?' continued Blitzen, still flummoxed by the stars. 'I mean, I certainly have never seen these before.'

Again there was an awkward silence until Patch spoke up.

'Bunnyflower found them in Cinnamon Forest earlier. He thought they were lucky charms.'

Bunnflower's eyes were now full of tears and he would have liked nothing better than to go home to his mother.

'In Cinnamon Forest! Where exactly?' asked Blitzen, now sounding perplexed.

'Near the clearing on the east side,' whimpered the little Bunny. 'I'm sorry, Mr Blitzen, Sir.'

'Are we in as much trouble now?' asked Patch, who had hoped that their telling the truth might exempt them from any further punishment that might be dished out.

'You're still in trouble, young Christmacub. A great deal of it, for you should have reported the purse to someone as soon as you found it. Why, for all you know, it could have contained an irreversible magic spell capable of turning you into a toad or a lizard.'

The four Bunnies hung their heads in silence. They hadn't thought of *that.*

'Right then. Follow me cubs,' ordered Blitzen sternly. 'I'll sort this out, but first I'm going to ensure that you get back to your mother.'

The four Bunnies groaned as Blitzen did just that. Mrs Bunnie did have quite a fright when she saw that her sons had all turned purple, and assured Blitzen that she would mete out harsh punishments suitable for the young rascals. Blitzen nodded his head and went off to find the only person who would be able to help him with such a matter – Snooks.

5 - The Festival of Christmas Mountain - Part Two

Snooks was an elder Snowflake and the supreme magic authority in the Kingdom. His exceptional flair for spells, at a young age, led him to the prestigious role of Protector of Magic. As a result, he did not reside with the other Snowflakes at The Forest of Magic Lanterns, but lived instead above his Shop of Christmas Wonders in Mistletown, where he brewed the Kingdom's Reindeer dust and various other charms and spells. He was a well-liked and incredibly trustworthy figure, hence no one in the Kingdom was better situated to answer Blitzen's question. Fortunately, he also hosted a magic show at his Pavilion of Mystery and Wonder at the Festival every year, so he would not be difficult to find.

As Blitzen approached Snooks' golden tent, he could see a few sparkling lights flickering above it. A large crowd was spilling outside, and a strange green smoke snaked its way from within. Blitzen excused himself past a crowd of Elves and Woodland Creatures to get to the entrance. As he made his way inside, the light dropped to a dim glow from a few flickering candles that were floating around in mid-air. There were large, silk cushions on the floor, occupied by various folk of the realm, as they waited for the show to start. Snooks stooped at the front, wearing a kindly expression on his face, as his scholarly hunch jutted out behind him, placing his wings at a rather odd angle. His white cloak sparkled with silver stars and butterflies that drifted across it in a most magical, yet distracting manner. He always reminded Blitzen of a beetle, or perhaps a rambling ladybird; even now his bug-like eyes bulged out from behind his spectacles as he greeted the audience.

'Good evening, everyone,' he said in his rosy yet befuddled voice. 'And oh!, have we got a show for you tonight. Uh, when you're ready, Edgar,' he called into the back of the tent.

As the flap opened, a malign looking Elf stepped out, wearing a long blue robe covered in silver crescent moons. He had long, black hair, streaked with pieces of grey, which trailed the floor when he walked, and his nose was large and covered with warts. This was Snooks' assistant, and Blitzen's face immediately crinkled as he approached the stage. Blitzen had never quite taken to Edgar. There was something about the way in which his beady, little eyes shifted in and out of focus, and his face assumed a perpetual disapproving frown, that Blitzen did not quite trust. Even now, as Edgar approached the trusty Snooks and held out a bowl of floating green smoke towards him, he sent shivers down the Reindeer's spine.

'Thank you, Edgar,' smiled Snooks. 'Now then, for my first act I will need a volunteer.'

A few keen paws presented themselves, but after a few minutes of pushing and shoving, a little Hedgehog by the name of Herbert Prickles was selected to enter the stage area. Herbert had been comically squeezed into a little green Elfin Wonders jumper, and now looked up with gazing eyes at the hunched-over old sorcerer.

'Hello there, Herbert, don't be shy,' chuckled Snooks, as he leaned even further over to look at the Hedgehog.

Snooks then dipped his crumpled fingers into the bowl and began weaving the air, causing it to ripple and turn to smoke. As he did so, Herbert began to rise off the floor. The crowd was fascinated and sighed in astonishment as Snooks continued to turn the air, first from ripples, to smoke, to a mass of colour, to a Christmas wreath. The wreath was perfect - green and red with boughs of holly intricately laced into it, and small, red, velvet bows at select points. It looked almost tangible, yet it was still merely air. Snooks delicately and skilfully pulled the wreath towards him and placed the timid little Hedgehog in the middle of it. Miraculously, instead of falling straight through it, the Hedgehog floated and began to turn daintily like a bauble on a Christmas tree. A sigh, infused with tremors, swept through the crowd, and the atmosphere was so intense, it could have cracked like ice. The wreath slowly began to change into the shape of a red Christmas bow that wrought itself around the Hedgehog's neck. Still, Herbert continued to float. Then Snooks snapped his crooked fingers, the ribbon disappeared, and the little Hedgehog began falling to the floor, until Snooks put out his left hand for Herbert to land on. The Hedgehog shook his head as he became aware of his surroundings, and the crowd cheered for more. Snooks chuckled and hurried the little Hedgehog along. Herbert gratefully scurried back to his parents in the crowd.

'Thank you, Herbert, thank you, everybody,' he said, as his wrinkled mouth stretched into a smile. 'And now for the real crowd pleaser.'

Edgar, who had all this time been standing stealthily in the shadows, now opened his cloak to reveal a multitude of pockets, each containing different potions and spells. Blitzen raised his eyebrows slightly as the Elf took out a purple potion and emptied it into the bowl. A flash of light was seen, followed by a cloud of pink smoke. Edgar dismissed the crowd's sighs with a condescending flick of his head as he mechanically, and somewhat disdainfully, presented the bowl to Snooks.

'Smile a little, Edgar, it's not that bad,' encouraged Snooks, as he once again kneaded his hands into the smoke and began swirling the air with his fingers.

The first image that appeared out of the swirl was a plate of scented, mouth watering Wish Biscuits. The plate swirled into the crowd, wafting delicious scents, and sparkling a multitude of colours. It caused a sensation as the crowd attempted to grab it, but each time their fingers fell through it, as they would fall through a shadow. The dish circled back towards Snooks like an obedient flying saucer, and changed shape as the colours drained away, until in its place now appeared the silhouette of Santa on his Reindeer-driven sleigh against the backdrop of the moon. But as you looked harder, the Reindeer slowly began to change shape until they took the form of robins fluttering in the mist. The robins circled for a while, and then one flew right out into the audience and landed on a Snowflake's shoulder, just in front of Blitzen.

From where the head Reindeer stood, it looked astoundingly real, and he had the urge to reach out and touch it. He stuck out his hoof, but the robin flew back towards Edgar, where it landed on his head and turned into a crow. Snooks, meanwhile, looked slightly alarmed and at a loss to explain what had caused this metamorphosis. He beckoned the bird back to him, and as it left Edgar's head, it changed back into a robin and flew back towards the sorcerer. The image then exploded like a tiny firework, out of which floated a beautiful Snowbelle, who danced gracefully along the air, creating sparkling ribbons as she moved her arms. She then curtseyed like a graceful ballerina and dissolved into the air. The crowd clapped with glee as Snooks bowed the little amount that his hunch would allow him and wiped a few beads of sweat from his forehead.

'Thank you, thank you, Christmas folk,' he said, as he let out a sigh of relief. 'And now for the disappearing show,' he added, producing a gold cloth from thin air. A loud chattering and cheering then erupted as several of the Snowflakes started pushing forward and volunteering themselves. As Blitzen looked again at the stage, he saw that Edgar had gone - vanished like one of Snooks' spectacles - without even the slightest sign or trace. Blitzen shook his head as he thought of the repulsive little creature. Realising he was not going to have any joy from Snooks that evening, Blitzen resolved to pay him a visit tomorrow at his shop in Gingerbread Lane. Perhaps he could even put a few questions to that little Elf of his. But for now he placed the mysterious stars inside his satchel and waded his way through the crowd before emerging from Snooks' tent.

Outside there was still much excitement, as Blitzen could see crowds of folk now making their way over to the mountain.

'Good Christmas,' he said to himself, as his eyes struggled to adjust to the change in light. 'It's already nine o'clock. It must be time for the slalom race.'

He too, a great fan of the race and a closet fan of the Elfin Wonders - although he liked on the surface to remain impartial - made his way to the mountain. As he reached the western side of the mountain, he could see that the Queen and her children had already arrived and that the slalom slope had been set up as usual with its traditional candy cane-styled ski poles. In front of the mountain were two large seating stands, one completely awash with a sea of green, and the other, with a sparkling white. Unfortunately, for the Elves, only a few of their supporters had made it into the Festival with their banners, in stark contrast to the Snowflakes. Separating the two stands of supporters was none other than Rudolph himself, holding a microphone in his hoof and surrounded by a swarm of Papa Ratzi.

'Good evening, Christmasdudes, and welcome to Christmas Mountain for our annual Christmas slalom race.'

There was a cheer from the crowd, and missiles were exchanged from one stand to the other, as the supporters expressed their rivalry.

'Ok, ok, party critters, calm down,' said Rudolph, as the cameras flashed and dazzled in his face. 'Now, put your hands, hooves and paws together for the Elfin Wonders and The Magic Lantern Marvels,' he cried, as the two teams came running, or flying past, in the Snowflakes case. They were met with both cheers and boos from the crowd as the excitement escalated to a whole new level.

'And skiing for the Wonders this year we have Grunch, Boris, Pretzel, Botch and Dora,' announced Rudolph, as the Wonders waved at the crowd. The Elfin Wonders looked physically inferior to the Marvels, to say the least. They were short, dumpy and very unathletic in build, and looked as if they would have great difficulty standing on skis, let alone participating in a slalom race. The green supporters nevertheless jumped up and down ecstatically, waving everything but their banners. The Snowflake supporters were less enthused by the team and more concerned with humiliating them. A few cookies came flying through the air towards the team and almost hit Rudolph on the commentator stand.

'Whoa, watch it, Christmasdudes. New sunglasses!' he exclaimed, as he dodged the biscuits.

The Wonders now climbed onto the ski lift and were carried through the air to the top of the Mountain.

'And neeeexxxt up we have the Maaaaaagic Laaaaaantern Maaaaaaarvels', shouted Rudolph ecstatically. 'Yeah. Wooohooo, give it up, everyone, for Hansen, Tristan, Lindsay, Loretta and Luella,' whistled Rudolph, clapping his hoofs against the microphone.

The Marvels looked much more athletic in build than the Elves. They were tall, slim and fit, and looked as if they had been tailor-made for the part. Their wings glistened under the fireflies, as they flew past their fans, giving them an impressive aura. The crowd roared so loudly that it echoed around Christmas Mountain, creating a thrilling sensation for anyone near. Banners were waved and chants were sung.

'Hansen, Hansen, Hansen, Hansen,' chanted a crowd of Badgers from Cinnamon Forest, as their hero paraded before them. The cameras flashed like fireworks to capture pictures of the Snowflake Team. Hansen looked like a Greek God, his teeth glinting and reflecting from the white of the snow while the Papa Ratzi photographed him. A few Elf Pops came showering down upon his head in protest from the Wonders' supporters, but he merely returned the favour by throwing them straight back. Still the cheers continued at fever pitch as the Marvels victoriously mounted the ski lift and ascended the mountain.

'And there go our Christmatastic teams for this year's annual slalom race,' continued Rudolph. 'The first team to have all their players reach the bottom, is the winner. And if you look really carefully, you can see them lining up at the top of the mountain.'

At the top of Christmas Mountain tension was high, and the Elves had huddled together for a final recapitulation of their plan.

'Now remember,' urged Grunch. 'If they start to play dirty and use their magic tricks on us, you trip them up with your ski pole. Got it? If they wanna play dirty, we'll give 'em dirty.'

The Elves then placed their stubby little hands together and raised them.

'Go the Wonders,' shouted Dora in a warrior's voice.

The Snowflakes, meanwhile, were practising their ski moves and were stretching their muscles for the race. They seemed less interested in running through their tactics. They were calm and confident and kept looking at their reflection in each other's protector ski glasses to check that they looked good. Prancer stood at the top of the slope in between the two competing lanes, holding a pink, sparkling flag in each hoof.

'Ok, guys. You ready?' he asked.

The teams lined up ready for the start.

'Alright, everyone. No magic. No flying. No funny business. Keep it clean. That's the rules.'

He placed the flags in front of the team leaders, Hansen and Grunch, respectively.

'Are you ready, Elf?' taunted Hansen through the side of his mouth.

'You bet, Flakey,' replied Grunch impatiently.

'Three, two, one. Go!' shouted Prancer, as he lifted the flags.

The race had started. Grunch was darting down the mountain, and to his immense pleasure, he was in front of Hansen. He continued to breeze down the slope and swung around the corner just as the first candy cane coloured slalom pole came into sight. He braced himself, bent his knees and pushed sideways with his pole to take the corner, when suddenly a succession of yellow sparks flashed over from the Snowflakes' track and hit Grunch, causing him to fall down in the middle of the track.

'Darn you, Snowflakes,' yelled Grunch, waving his fist at Hansen, who was sniggering to himself as he suavely eased himself out of the first bend.

'Oh no, it looks like the Wonders are one Elf down,' announced Rudolph from down below.

Next up it was Boris and Tristan.

Boris was so angry that Hansen had caused Grunch to fall, he was determined to complete the race. As he leaned in for the corner, he bent his knees and jumped over Grunch, who was now blocking the pathway and struggling to heave himself back up. Boris was through the first slalom and was now just in front of his opponent, Tristan. He continued to slide down the mountain in time for the next bend. He looked to his left to check that no colourful sparks were floating his way and, when he was sure of this, he prepared himself for the next turn. But just as he went to put pressure on his ski poles, he looked down with horror to see that they weren't there.

'My poles, my poles,' he fumbled, beginning to panic and lose his balance. 'Where are my poles?' He looked over to Tristan, who was just easing himself nicely around the bend, scoring another 100 points for his team, before half turning his head and poking his tongue out at Boris. One quick click of this crafty Flake's fingers and Boris' poles had been erased from existence.

'You! Why you...' Crash!! It was too late. Without another word, Boris crashed headlong into the slalom pole and consequently fell back onto the snow as a large red lump popped up simultaneously on his head.

'Oh no, and the Wonders have another Elf down. Looks like it's bad news for the Wonders, unless they can rectify this,' cried Rudolph into the microphone.

But it was momentarily payback time for the Snowflakes as their dirty dealings had enraged the Wonders' teammates. Next down the mountain was Pretzel, and he was certainly capable of being as crooked as his name suggested. He was racing Lindsay, a suave but effeminate looking Snowflake who was new to the team, and Pretzel was certainly going to make the most of this. As the flag was raised, he slid off down the mountain, buying himself a few seconds at the start of the race. He turned the first corner and swung his head around to see Lindsay still behind him out of the corner of his eye. The next bend was hidden from the view of the supporters, and being slightly ahead, Pretzel poised himself behind a large snow-covered rock that divided the two lanes. He crouched down and stuck out his pole just as Lindsay turned the corner. 'Smash!' the Snowflake was down, and Pretzel was back on the slope, tearing down the mountain and crossing the finish line, picking up 100 points for the Wonders and leaving them only 100 points behind. The next race was run in a similar fashion. Botch, who was determined not to live up to his name, managed to create a small avalanche on the Snowflakes' track, as his pole caught a snow spot too sharply on his way around the bend, leaving Loretta in second place. The teams were now equal, and Hansen was writhing with fury from his position on the ground. Insults were being exchanged between the fans, and the teams themselves looked like they were ready to come to blows. But now it was time for the last race between Dora and Luella.

Dora - who had extra ammunition after clashing with Hansen that morning - stood poised with sheer anger and determination at the top of the mountain, waiting for Prancer's clearance to begin the descent. Her opponent, Luella, could not have been more different. Tall, beautiful and feminine, she looked as if she had already won the race. She looked dismissively out of the corner of her eye and flung her head in the air.

'Ok, girls. Last lap. Three, two, one. Go!' shouted Prancer for the final time. Dora was off, her eyes glaring with determination. She pushed as hard and as fast as she could with her ski poles and took the first corner before Luella with perfect alacrity. Luella looked annoyed, but refrained from hurting the little Elf just yet. Still, Dora pushed her way faster down the mountain, taking the next bend once again before Luella did. The atmosphere down below was now frantic, and the Wonders' supporters began shouting and cheering and jumping up and down as Dora took the lead. Hats were thrown in the air in the place of banners, and screams and chants of *'Come on Dora'* ricocheted around the mountain. She was in the lead, and Luella was growing greener and more and more frustrated. She was now too far behind to catch Dora with a sly magic trick 'upon the hip', 3 and she would have to come up with something pretty good if she was going to win this. The Snowflakes were drawing level, and they could not suffer the indignity of losing to a team of Elves. They had always remained completely unrivalled and undefeated, and they had to keep up the winning tradition. As the contestants took the last bend they were slightly obscured from the crowd for a moment. Dora seemed completely unstoppable and beavered away with her poles as though she was carving her way through stone. Luella looked slyly to her right. It was now or never. She clicked her finger - so that she was now reduced to a mere firefly - and flew as fast as she could around the bend, before clicking her finger

---

3 *The Merchant of Venice*, William Shakespeare, Act 1, scene 3, line 42.

again and returning to normal size just in time to cross the finish line. But to her horror, Dora was already there waiting for her. How could she have beaten her? An Elf? And she had flown the last lap. It was not possible for an Elf to out-ski a Snowflake, especially when the Snowflake was flying!!!

'Cheat!' yelled Luella, flinging her ski poles to the floor and flying over to Dora and the rest of the Wonders Team. 'Christmas cheat!' she yelled, approaching Dora's face.

'What's the problem, Luella?' asked Prancer, who had now flown down from the top of the Mountain.

'She couldn't possibly have won,' declared Luella, enraged at the outcome of this. She *must* have cheated. She *must* have.'

'I'm sorry, Luella, but it's a clear win for the Wonders. Dora crossed the finish line three seconds before you.'

The Wonders were now crowding behind Prancer, and a few of the Marvels began to make their way over too, to see what all the commotion was about. The supporters were evidently confused, since a final score was yet to be announced, and they too began to voice their opinions out loud.

'Look, Prancer, clearly there has been some kind of mistake,' said Hansen smoothly, as he placed his arm around Prancer's shoulder.

'No mistake, Hansen,' replied Prancer firmly. 'You were drawing 2 all, and Dora crossed the finish line first.'

Comet, who now arrived on the scene, and had also been refereeing the game, seconded Prancer's opinion.

'But it's wrong, all of it. She must have cheated. There's no way she could have beaten me. I flew,' stomped Luella, before she quickly placed her hand over her mouth at the realisation of her admission.

'Sorry, Luella. But she won Christmas fair and square. And you know, flying's not allowed,' admonished Prancer.

The Snowflakes bowed their heads. They had been caught out, and thanks to Luella, this led to a public embarrassment. Prancer then held up a green flag signifying an Elfin Wonders Victory. A roar erupted from the Green stand, with sheer glee at this win.

'Alrighty, Christmasdudes, we have our winners. Please give a humungous round of applause for the Elfin Wondeeeeers. Yeah, woooo,' cheered Rudolph with much excitement. The team was thrilled with its victory, and after a prolonged sulk, the Snowflakes mustered up the dignity to shake hands with the Wonders, even though they were deeply humiliated. Trophies were presented and handfuls of Wish Biscuits were given to everyone, along with mugs of Cinnamon Punch. Celebrations went on late into the night as a firework display was followed by games and merriment and more fun at the fair.

As the evening drew to a close, the folk of the realm felt proud to be a part of this Kingdom. But as the purple stars continued to glisten mysteriously in Blitzen's satchel, concern now took hold of the head Reindeer as he tried to fathom this strange riddle.

6 - Blitzen's Discovery

The excitement from the night before certainly filtered through into the next day, and with Christmas Eve getting ever closer, the Kingdom really was in the grip of merriment.

The Elves were utterly ecstatic about their victory and went about every task that day with divided attention. Winterland Village was awash with green. Green fireflies lit up every one of their windows, green mats were put out on the doorsteps, green banners were draped across windows and hung down from rooftops, and some had even gone so far as to paint their front doors a sparkling green. Green silly string stuck to the snow from last night's celebrations, and every Elf wore their Elfin Wonders gear proudly. Mrs Bunnie had sent every Elfin family a batch of special Elf-shaped Wish Biscuits to mark the occasion, along with a box of Cinnamon Doughnuts to Blitzen containing a paw-written apology from Patch, Hopper, Carrot Top and Bunnyflower. The stars were still safely stowed in Blitzen's satchel, and as he read the note, he resolved to see Snooks later that day. He would then take his findings to the Queen at the castle, where a meeting at The Great Court of Christmas had been arranged. Normally the Queen held the annual meeting on December 5th, but given this most 'peculiar' incident, she had decided to bring it forward.

It was gone five o'clock before Blitzen was able to leave Reindeer Station One, for December was the Reindeer's busiest month. Fortunately, Rudolph had remembered to turn up for duty, so at least their work load was relieved slightly. Blitzen wrapped his scarf around him and set out onto the High Street.

The town was a lot busier than it had been the day before. Many of the animals from Cinnamon Forest had come up there to start their Christmas shopping, and Mr Bunnie's Bookie Bonanza was heaving with Elves, all collecting their unexpected winnings from last night. In fact, everywhere was so busy that Blitzen had great difficulty in getting through.

Wonderful Victory blurted the billboard outside The X-mas Times Print Shop.

Could this be the start of a new era for the Elves???
Also inside,
Purple Craze: The Bunnies who bit off more than they could

chew.

What exactly are these Suspicious Stars that were found in a purse in Cinnamon Forest?

Blitzen grunted at this story. Through the check-paned, snow-flurried window he could see the Rats ruthlessly scratching out their stories. He pulled his scarf up higher and hastened quickly past the print shop, trying to lose himself in the crowd. He did not want to be seen by the press, for he did not want to give an interview about the purple stars. After all, it would only hinder the investigation.

After a few more minutes of weaving in and out of the hustle and bustle, he soon passed Santa's Workshop and The Hollybush Tavern and found himself at the crossroad at the end of the High Street, from where he could reach Gingerbread Lane. This was where Snooks' shop was situated. Gingerbread Lane was a dilapidated part of Mistletown. It weaved off at a tangent from the High Street and trickled downhill, all the way to the edge of the Kingdom, where it met the Eastern Border. From here the Mountains of the North seemed alarmingly close, although in reality they were a good half a day's walk away. The shop had once stood at the centre of Mistletown, but its exterior was felt to be too distracting, and anytime a potion went wrong the whole town would fill with smoke – colourful smoke of course – but still smoke, so Snooks had moved his shop to the more secluded district of Gingerbread Lane. In a sense, it actually suited him better – after all, it provided the perfect eccentric setting for the eccentric, hunched-over, old shopkeeper. Blitzen, however, disliked its new positioning. Not that he distrusted the shopkeeper – that wasn't it. He had always found Snooks to be nothing more than affable and trustworthy. But he felt it to be too close to the boundary of the Kingdom. Too close to the Icicle River. And too close to the Mountains of the North. It was almost too easy for the Mountains to target it. Alright, it was common knowledge that the Queen had placed a powerful spell on the Guardian, locking him inside, but supposing he *still* found a way to steal their magic. Supposing he found a way to use the Kingdom's own magic against them. Supposing that little Elf, Edgar, could be tempted to.......... But Blitzen was getting ahead of himself. And besides, Snooks had assured him that there was absolutely nothing to worry about. If ever there was an attack, who better to defend the Kingdom than a sorcerer. In a sense, the shop was ideally situated. So the Chief Reindeer now shook his head and made his way down Gingerbread Lane, crinkling his nose in distaste at the state of disrepair it had fallen into. It featured a few crumbling, neglected houses which hunched over the road as though they were leaning in to whisper secrets to one another. A seedy, murky old tavern, known as The Snowman's Shadow, loitered in one of the corners, and some abandoned warehouses lurched like big, pathetic eyesores at the end. The stars sparkled quite strongly in his satchel now and contrasted greatly with the black snow and the dirty windows.

Then, as he continued a little further down the street, he arrived at The Shop of Christmas Wonders, with its famous illusory exterior. As Blitzen initially looked at it, he saw that it resembled a magic genie's lamp that spewed an enchanting green smoke out from its spout. The gold lamp glinted so brightly that it almost looked real. But then suddenly the illusion changed, so that the shop now took the form of a crooked old witch's castle, black and eerie, from which phantom ghosts now emerged and flew up into the air above Gingerbread Lane, hollering unsoundly cries. Blitzen grunted slightly at this, and as he did so, the castle changed again to a hollow pirate's cave, glistening with rubies and emeralds, and emitting a raw, chilling air. The air made him shiver, and rushed against his ears like the sound of the sea inside a shell. The emeralds inside it now grew and grew until they burst like a firework to form a multicoloured, and somewhat over excitable hot air balloon. Indeed, the balloon looked as if it were ready to fly away immediately, and Blitzen did wonder momentarily if he should jump aboard quickly before the shop disappeared forever. But the illusion finally settled down to form a delectable gingerbread house bursting with delicious smells. The head Reindeer turned the pink chocolate doorknob, and without further ado, he entered the shop.

'Snooks,' he called out, peering into the gloom as a shop bell, which Blitzen had not observed on his way in, now rang somewhere above him, announcing his presence.

He could hear a great deal of noise coming from the Reindeer dust maker in the back room, so made his way towards the counter in order to make himself heard.

The shop was almost entirely dark, apart from a dimly lit lamp which stood on the front desk and cast large shadows on the ceiling as anything approached it. Blitzen coughed a little as an unusual concoction of dust, smoke and strange scented incense tickled his throat. Little clouds of pink and blue and green smoke swirled through the air mysteriously, and there were stacks and stacks of dusty old books piled all the way up to the ceiling, on which there were many sets of stairs built upside down and quite literally leading into darkness. Chimes shimmered faintly as Blitzen brushed past them, and an eclectic array of spells - spells that made you shrink, spells that made you grow, spells that turned you pink, spells that made you talk incredibly fast, potions to make you grow Rabbit's ears, potions to turn your nose red (Rudolph's particular favourite) - paved the way to Snooks' counter, and stared eerily from their bottles. Blitzen's eyes began to hurt as the electric colour of the potions pierced the darkness so vividly.

'Snooks?' called Blitzen again, coughing loudly and squinting, as he was struggling to see through all the murk.

He had now reached the counter, and an enlarged shadow of himself with rather distorted antlers arose on the wall in front of him as he caught the light of the lamp.

'Snooks,' he began again, with the din still clattering away as a parade of mysterious shapes now began dancing on the counter in front of him.

Then he heard the patter of footsteps on the ceiling above, and suddenly saw Edgar the Elf appear, walking upside down. His steps grew louder and louder as the Elf got closer and closer, until the stairs eventually turned themselves the right way up and lowered the strange creature onto the stool behind the counter. Blitzen was quite taken aback, but recollected himself as he sized up the malign little creature. The Elf said nothing, but continued to look disdainfully at the customer as his black hair hung somewhere below him like a tattered curtain. The shapes had now stopped dancing and fell lifeless to the counter as the air seemed to turn cold.

'Edgar,' said Blitzen, narrowing his eyes in distrust. 'Is Snooks here? I have an important matter to discuss with him.'

The Goblin-like figure held Blitzen's stare coldly, and without turning around, he shouted out in a narrow, frayed voice, 'Snooks, we have a customer.'

As he spoke these words, Blitzen shivered involuntarily, but decided that he would make the most of his time alone with Edgar.

'Do you mix all the potions for the magic shows?' asked the Reindeer, observing how the lamp cast a large shadow of the Elf on the wall behind, rendering him like a fiendish Dwarf.

'Yes,' replied the Elf stiffly. 'But you must remember, Blitzen, that magic sometimes has a mind of its own. Snooks,' he called again causing the lamp to flicker.

'Just a minute, Edgar,' came the befuddled, yet somewhat reassuring voice of the shopkeeper from somewhere out the back.

The Elf continued to look at Blitzen, who was growing more and more irritated by the creature's rudeness.

'You don't happen to know anything about these purple stars, do you?' began Blitzen, now leaning towards the Elf in an intimidating manner.

But before the Elf could respond, a tremendous crash was heard in the back room, followed by a POP, and the entire shop suddenly filled with steam.

Blitzen coughed loudly, and when the clouds cleared, he could see the hunched-over old shopkeeper emerging from the back room with his hair sticking out and his glasses covered in soot.

'Why, hello Blitzen, what brings you here?' he asked, as silver butterflies danced playfully across his cloak.

The Elf now climbed down from the stool and walked over to the edge of the counter where he took out a cloth and began polishing it. Although the counter was quite high, Edgar's nose and eyes were still able to reach over the top of it, and Blitzen was painfully aware of this as he reached into his satchel for the purple stars.

'Well, something very serious, as a matter of fact,' he stated, turning his attention back to the shopkeeper, and noticing how the shapes on the counter now began to dance again before drifting off to the nether regions of the shop.

'Well, Blitzen, what is it?' asked Snooks, as he wiped the soot from his spectacles.

'It's these,' declared Blitzen. 'The Bunnies found them in Cinnamon Forest yesterday. I've never seen the likes of them before, and I was wondering if you could take a look.'

'Oh yes, I heard something about that,' recalled Snooks, taking the bag from Blitzen's hoof. 'Purple stars, wasn't it - at least that's what The X-mas Times stated.'

'Yes, that's right,' confirmed Blitzen, as he leaned over the counter.

The Elf was still dusting the counter, and shot a sly glance across at the bag, as Snooks emptied its contents onto the counter. As they had done the night before, the stars sparkled in a bewitching manner and lit up a small pocket of the shop.

'Good Christmas, what are these?' asked Snooks, as he now took out a small magnifying glass and held it up to one of the stars.

'Well, I was hoping you might be able to tell me,' ventured Blitzen, feeling his hopes to be slightly dashed.

'Well, dear me, Blitzen, I'm afraid I um, I'm afraid I've never seen these before. But my, my, they look very pretty, don't they? No wonder the Bunnies liked them. Good Christmas, and they seem to have an energy all of their own. Why, I feel half a Snowflake stronger. What did you say happened to the Bunnies?'

'They shot up into the sky and turned purple,' recalled Blitzen, thoughtfully.

'Hmm,' said Snooks, inspecting one of the stars closely. 'I wonder.'

He then knocked the star gently against the side of the table as though he were cracking an egg. It took only two gentle knocks for the star to crack, and as it did so, out poured a very fine, yet very eerie purple dust which sparkled like electric needles and burnt a hole in the counter. Blitzen was mesmerised and he leaned over to get a better look.

'Well, confound my Christmas crackers, Blitzen. No wonder the young Bunnies shot across the air. This stuff's highly dangerous.'

The butterflies and flakes of snow now disappeared from Snooks' cloak, and in their place fell jagged bits of silver ice, which Blitzen had seen happen before when the shopkeeper was worried about something.

'Is it black magic?' asked Blitzen, confronting his worst fears.

'Yes I'm afraid so, Blitzen, and it's much worse than your average batch too,' stated the shopkeeper, whose eyes had now grown wide and fearful. 'It's purple dust from Alendria.'

'From *Alendria* – you mean the Fairy world,' uttered Blitzen, dumbstruck, and realising that this was not good news. 'But why was it left in a purse inside Cinnamon Forest?'

'Well, I'm afraid I don't have an answer to that,' answered the shopkeeper sadly, 'but if you ask my opinion, it probably wasn't just left there in a state of carelessness. This stuff's precious. Notoriously hard to come by. My guess is that someone dropped it accidentally and now wants it back.'

'Hmm,' mused Blitzen, as the shopkeeper's cloak once again caught his eye. The pieces of ice had now melted, and Blitzen suddenly started at the sound of the shop bell ringing and the front door closing rather sharply behind him.

'What was that?' asked Blitzen, turning around to see that Edgar the Elf had now gone, without even a word of farewell, and apart from he and Snooks, the shop was otherwise empty.

'Oh that'll be Edgar leaving for the day,' said Snooks rather carelessly. 'He always goes about now.'

'What, without even saying goodbye?' asked Blitzen, feeling that there really were no limits to Edgar's rudeness.

'Yes, he is a strange little one, I'm afraid. Doesn't say much when he's here either,' remarked the shopkeeper, shaking his head. 'But back to the matter at hand, Blitzen. Whoever left this dust in Cinnamon Forest concealed it well. And it's not surprising either, because this stuff's illegal – I mean, it *is* a form of black magic. And see here,' added the shopkeeper, holding out the shell of the cracked star and pointing to where a green smoke now danced menacingly along its crevices.

Blitzen nodded, and as he did, his eyes began to itch.

'Well, there is something more in here,' continued the shopkeeper. 'This smoke is not produced by purple dust. It's something else.'

'Something else?' asked Blitzen, as he raised his eyebrows. 'Well, what else could it be?'

'I'm not altogether sure. I'll have to consult my Magic Dictionary,' said the shopkeeper, somewhat distracted as he continued to marvel at the unusual smoke. 'But look, Blitzen, leave this with me,' he added, picking up the remainder of the purple stars and popping them back into the purple purse. 'I'll have a proper look at them in the back room and scour through some books. I will see you at the castle in an hour and I'll bring my findings with me. I'm sure the Queen will want to know all about this too.'

'Very well, Snooks. I'll mention the whole thing to Santa, now. Goodbye.'

'Yes, goodbye, Blitzen,' returned Snooks, as he accompanied the Reindeer towards the front door.

Snooks placed a **CLOSED** sign in the shop window, and as Blitzen emerged, the exterior - which currently looked like a pirate ship - now disappeared and the shop turned into a crooked, wooden house with a thatched roof that hunched over the road like the shopkeeper himself. The two windows upstairs closed their shutters and the shop began to rise up and down, breathing in and out and releasing a succession of snores through its letter box. Blitzen turned as he left the eccentric shop and made his way back up Gingerbread Lane. The lane was now dark and deserted, apart from a dim and ruddy glow coming from inside The Snowman's Shadow. Day was now fading into night, and as Blitzen emerged from the lane he found himself back on the High Street of Mistletown, which was also very quiet. His head was completely knotted with the events of the past few days. What in the name of Christmas could those stars be for? They had never had purple dust in the Kingdom before. And that little Elf had snuck out so quietly. Blitzen hadn't even heard him go. He would quite like to know how he did it.

Then, as the head Reindeer glanced across to where the edge of Mistletown met the eastern side of Cinnamon Forest, a strange spectacle caught his eye. Blitzen had to blink to adjust his focus in the dusk, but as he did so, he now saw Edgar the Elf - that abominably rude little creature from Snooks' shop - walking stealthily, yet deliberately, towards Cinnamon Forest, and looking slyly from side to side as he did so.

'What in the name of Christmas does he want in Cinnamon Forest at this hour?' asked Blitzen, now wondering whether, in fact, Edgar was the culprit behind the purple stars. The head Reindeer galloped quickly towards the Elf in order to catch him up, but as he did so, a very strange thing happened. Edgar the Elf now disappeared into thin air, and Blitzen stopped dead in utter astonishment.

'What the devil?' he asked, swinging himself around full circle and pawing the air to check that he was not mistaken. The forest was still a few feet away, and not a soul could be seen in any direction. It was not possible for Edgar to have just disappeared near the edge of the forest - unless he had used some sort of charm or potion to do so, and if that were the case, Blitzen would never be able to find him. He looked around again, alarmed. Mistletown was empty, Cinnamon Forest looked still, and night was fast consuming the day. Even if the Elf had reappeared in the forest, he wouldn't know where to look for him. It was vast and dense and only dimly lit by fireflies at this hour. The Reindeer shook his head as behind him, in Mistletown, the Gingerbread Clock chimed half past six. The Court of Christmas commenced in just one hour. The Chief Reindeer took hold of himself, and after one last glance around him, he showered himself in gold Reindeer dust and flew towards Christmas Cottage to entreat the help of Mrs Claus.

Blitzen arrived at Christmas Cottage in under five minutes, and it provided such a stark contrast with Gingerbread Lane, that it warmed his heart just thinking about it. From the outside it looked like a gingerbread house. The pillars either side of the door were painted red and white purposefully to resemble candy canes, and the doorknob was shaped and stamped exactly like a mince pie. Through the window the hearth was emitting a joyous and inviting glow, and the house was oozing with delicious baking smells from Mrs Claus' cooking. Blitzen rapped twice on the door and was briskly admitted by Mrs Claus, who gave him a fat Christmas hug and insisted he take the best seat opposite Santa by the hearth, while she brought out some Christmas Punch and chocolate star cakes. Santa was already tucking into a plate full of goodies and gave a great big scoffing 'ggoooggg eeevvveeemmmiiinnng mmmwwwiiitttzzznnn,' as Blitzen entered. Little crumbs of Santa's food were sprayed across the room like flakes of snow, as Santa attempted to greet his most trusted Reindeer. After a laborious effort, Santa finally swallowed his food and had a clear mouth to speak.

'Well, well, Blitzen. What a pleasant surprise. And what brings you here? Mrs Claus' cooking, is it? It's a little early for The Court of Christmas yet,' chuckled Santa, whisking his head towards the kitchen in anticipation of a second course. 'Any more on the way, dear?' he ventured cheekily.

'You've just had a plate full of mince pies,' snapped Mrs Claus from the kitchen. 'You can wait a while before your next meal.'

Santa looked a little glum struck for a moment, but soon regained his cheery smile as he turned to face Blitzen. With that, Blitzen ceremoniously had a basket full of chocolate star cakes and a jug full of Christmas Punch thrust in front of him, all of which made Santa look at him even more. Blitzen flushed with embarrassment and lowered the basket onto the floor as he cleared his throat.

'Santa,' ventured Blitzen, in an effort to release him from his trance.

'Yes, Blitzen?' enquired Santa, whose eyes were firmly on the chocolate star cakes.

'I'm afraid there's something we need to discuss. It's very important.'

'Important,' said Santa, still blinking, and wondering what sort of food that was.

'Yes, Santa. I need your help,' returned Blitzen.

'Oh,' said Santa, still quite apparently lost in the distance.

'Santa,' cried Mrs Claus, as she banged her rolling pin on the table in front of him. 'What has gotten into you? Blitzen is trying his hardest to have a conversation with you and you're off in chocolate land with crispy cream doughnuts and snap butter cakes.'

'Crispy cream doughnuts and snap butter.......Now see here Mrs Claus,' he began, shaking his head again, and finally beginning to enter the conversation.

'Don't you *see here* me!'

'Well I was uh, uh....'

'Yes, that's right, you was uh, uh, daydreaming about F-O-O-D. If you don't watch yourself, I'll be putting you on a diet.'

'A diet.' She had spoken the unspeakable. Santa rubbed his eyes and shook his head for the tenth time now, before looking up and staring directly at Blitzen in a most sincere effort not to be distracted.

'Yes, Blitzen. I do apologise. As you were saying.'

'Not at all,' answered Blitzen, clearing his throat again. 'Well, I went to see Snooks this afternoon about the purple stars.'

'Oh yes, the ones the Bunnies found in Cinnamon Forest,' added Santa, now sounding intrigued. 'It's been the talk of the workshop all day. And the Queen is *most* concerned about it.'

'Yes, well they're actually purple dust from Alendria, concealed to look like magic stars. There's another mystery ingredient inside, which Snooks is looking into at this very moment.'

'Good Christmas,' exclaimed Santa, his eyes growing wide with shock. 'Did he say what they were for?'

'Well, he's not altogether sure, Santa,' replied Blitzen, 'but the strangest thing just happened to me concerning Edgar the Elf.'

Mrs Claus, who had caught a whiff of the conversation from the kitchen, now burst into the sitting room to share her opinion on the subject. She too distrusted Edgar the Elf and needed little invitation to let this be known.

'I knew it. I knew it. I always knew there was something wrong with that one,' she cried, brandishing her rolling pin in the air like a warrior. 'What's the little Goblin gone and done then, Blitzen?' she asked, quite ready to hang the little Elf on account of him merely being quite strange.

'Now now, Mrs Claus, calm down. You're talking about Snooks' assistant,' warned Santa, not quite as ready to write off the culprit as his wife was.

'Yes, he's Snooks' assistant,' she scoffed. 'We all know that. He nagged him for the job until poor old Snooks didn't have a choice. Why won't he work with all the other Elves at the workshop, eh? He asked for that job so that he could get close to things he shouldn't be,' declared Mrs Claus firmly, with a nod of the head.

'Mrs Claus, please,' sighed Santa. 'Blitzen hasn't even said anything yet.'

'Well, I'm sure he'll tell us plenty. Go on, pudding,' entreated Mrs Claus, as she perched herself on the sofa next to Santa and looked expectantly at the head Reindeer.

'Well, the thing is,' began Blitzen, clearing his throat, 'I can't be quite sure of what I saw, so I'll need your help to verify it. You see, as I was leaving Snooks' shop just now, I saw, or at least I thought I saw, Edgar walking towards the east side of Cinnamon Forest.'

'And what did the little stealth want in there at *this* time of night?' barked Mrs Claus, still waving her rolling pin around.

'My thoughts precisely,' agreed Blitzen. 'So I ran after him, but as I approached him, he disappeared.'

'*Disappeared?*' repeated Santa, now blinking incredibly fast. 'But where did he go?'

'Well, that's it. I just don't know. But I suppose he went into the forest,' mused Blitzen, his mind still in knots.

'Ooh, he's a sly one. He's tricking you alright, and he's using black magic to do it, I'll bet my Christmas puddings on it,' remarked Mrs Claus, getting up and entering the kitchen. 'But it's alright, Blitzen. We'll use the Mixing Bowl to find him. Wherever he is in the Kingdom, whether he's hiding behind magic or not, it'll find him. Gather round now and let's have a look.'

Blitzen and Santa now followed Mrs Claus into the kitchen, where she took out a large china bowl with a red berry trim.

This was the Magic Mixing Bowl, which revealed certain truths about Christmas past, present, and future that would otherwise remain unknown. It could also find creatures hiding behind disappearing spells or help to solve certain Christmas conundrums. As Mrs Claus put the Bowl onto the counter, she took out a few potions from the cupboards and then reached into her pocket for a full bag of Reindeer dust.

'There now,' she said, emptying some of the potions into the Bowl and stirring it with a red and white striped wooden spoon before sprinkling in a smattering of pink Reindeer dust.

'I'd like to see him hide from this,' she added, firmly.

The Reindeer dust danced magically across the cake mixture like a trail of tiny fireflies, before soaking into it and creating a succession of purple and pink clouds.

'What time is it, Santa?' asked Mrs Claus sharply. 'The Bowl is almost ready to start.'

'Oh my,' said Santa, who had been eyeing the mixture rather fondly, and had half a mind to dip his finger in it. 'It's uh quarter to seven.'

'Quarter to seven,' she repeated, just to make sure. 'Well, the little stealth could never have made it across Cinnamon Forest that quickly.

Show me Edgar the Elf,' she added, as she leaned over into the Bowl.

The Bowl flashed as the trio looked into the mixture, and a clock with the current time floated across it. A picture then emerged of Edgar the Elf, but to the group's surprise, he was not roaming the tracks of Cinnamon Forest, nor was he in fact anywhere near it. Instead, he was seated rather placidly inside The Snowman's Shadow on Gingerbread Lane, enjoying a mug of mulled wine and a cinnamon pretzel. The clock on the wall behind him showed that it was still quarter to seven, so they were obviously looking at him at this precise moment in time. Mrs Claus now scratched her head, and Blitzen was completely flummoxed.

'But it's not possible,' insisted Blitzen, staring at the Bowl in disbelief. 'I saw him just 15 minutes ago on the edge of Cinnamon Forest, about to enter it. Why, by the time he got to wherever he was going in the forest and then came back out again, he could never have made it to The Snowman's Shadow by quarter to seven. He is only an Elf, after all.'

'I *do* believe you, pudding,' declared Mrs Claus earnestly. 'But I'm afraid the Bowl has never been wrong about these things, and the times on the clocks match exactly.'

'Maybe he's faster than we think,' suggested Santa, thinking that if the Elf was capable of disappearing in the way that he did, then he was also capable of moving much more quickly than he'd originally thought.

'Yes, Santa's right,' agreed Blitzen thoughtfully. 'Perhaps we should be a bit more accurate, Mrs Claus, and ask the Bowl to show us Edgar at the exact moment he disappeared.'

'Why certainly, pudding. What time did you say you saw him again?'

'Half past six,' replied Blitzen thoughtfully. 'Actually, it was just a few seconds before half past six. I know, because as soon as he disappeared, the clock in Mistletown began to chime.'

'Well, there's no better proof than that,' ascertained Mrs Claus with a nod, as she threw in another pinch of Reindeer dust and began stirring the mixture again. 'We'll see if we can catch the little tyke out this way! Show me Edgar the Elf at just before half past six this evening,' she said into the Bowl.

A clock appeared in the mixture again, and its hands began to move backwards to just before half past six that evening, when Blitzen had been tricked by the Elf. The clock then melted away to reveal Edgar the Elf, once again seated in The Snowman's Shadow, this time ordering from the menu as if he had just arrived and pointing to a pretzel and a mug of mulled wine. The clock in the tavern was again in tandem with the time required, since its minute hand now moved to half past six and a miniature snowman popped out, showering the floor with drops of snow.

Blitzen again was flummoxed and began to grow slightly irritated.

'It just doesn't make sense,' he vexed, shaking his antlers. 'I mean, how can he be in two places at once? All the clocks in the Kingdom are set to the exact same time, right down to the last second. Not a single one of them is slow because they are all controlled by magic. This is the exact time that I saw him by Cinnamon Forest, so it's not possible that he was in the Snowman's Shadow at that point in time. I mean, he can't be in two places at once, and as far as I know, there is no magic potion that can make him do that. I don't mean to be rude, Mrs Claus, but are you sure that the Bowl is working properly?'

'I think so, pudding. I can't understand how it could be wrong. It's a magical device, after all, but I'll try it with someone else, just in case. Someone whose whereabouts we know.'

Here she sprinkled another pinch of Reindeer dust into the Bowl and stirred the mixture.

'Show me Santa Claus at this exact moment in time,' she said into the cloudy paste. There was a flash in the Bowl and the picture now changed to show Santa seated in the kitchen of Christmas Cottage, sitting next to Blitzen. It was like looking in a mirror.

'Well, it must be working,' remarked both Santa and the Bowl simultaneously, as the real Santa leaned in to look at himself. 'I mean, I am exactly where the Bowl shows me to be.'

'Yes, you're right,' agreed Mrs Claus, stirring the mixture again. 'I'll just try it with one other pudding though, just to be sure. Now, who do I know who is really predictable?'

Blitzen was about to venture the most predictable creature in the entire Kingdom, when Mrs Claus just managed to beat him to it.

'Show me Rudolph, the red-nosed Reindeer,' she ordered, as the Bowl flashed pink and a picture of the celebrity appeared, preening himself in front of his ornate dressing table, with antler wax and nose polish.

'My, don't you look handsome, Christmasdude,' said Rudolph, as he puckered up his lips and added a bit more nose polish to his already shiny nose. 'You're guna look Christmatastic at the castle tonight, Rudi baby.'

Blitzen sighed and shook his head, partly at the ridiculousness of Rudolph's behaviour, and partly because the Bowl seemed to be working perfectly fine.

'Everything seems in order,' commented Blitzen, wondering what in The Kingdom of Christmas he was going to do now.

'Yes, it does, I'm afraid,' agreed Mrs Claus, now looking worried. 'But don't panic, pudding. There's one more thing we can do. After all, it's the only place we haven't looked yet,' she said, getting yet another potion out from the cupboard and emptying it into the Bowl before throwing in an extra large helping of pink Reindeer dust this time. 'If the little stealth can hide from this, I'll eat my Christmas pudding,' she added, as she slopped the mixture around quite vigorously.

'Now then, Magic Mixing Bowl. I want you to draw on your deepest powers. Show me the edge of Cinnamon Forest at just before half past six this evening, and look through all the magic spells you can, that are being used there.'

A clock appeared in the mixture, and the hands went back, as before, to just seconds before the minute hand struck half past six. The picture then changed to show the edge of Cinnamon Forest, sparkling with fireflies, and Blitzen the head Reindeer charging intently and most deliberately towards it. Yet there was no sign of Edgar the Elf. In fact, there was no sign of anyone, and as Blitzen began pawing the air, the gingerbread clock in Mistletown could be heard inside the Bowl chiming half past six. Absolutely nothing happened to indicate that any spell had taken place whatsoever. The picture then turned blank, leaving Blitzen the most confused he had been all evening.

'Well, I'm completely gobsmacked, puddings,' exclaimed Mrs Claus, as she stared at the empty picture. 'The little Goblin must be using such a strong spell that even the Mixing Bowl can't see through it. And that is just completely unheard of.'

'But this is ridiculous,' cried Blitzen, shaking his head. 'The Bowl is making me out to be an out and out liar.'

'No, pudding. That little Goblin is doing that,' contradicted Mrs Claus firmly. 'No one's disputing what you have seen. It was quite clear you could see something when we were looking at you in the Bowl. You wouldn't paw the air for nothing.'

'I would sincerely hope not,' worried Blitzen, who until this moment had always felt completely in charge of his own sanity. 'But tell me, Mrs Claus, can he control the image in the Bowl?'

'No one can do that,' declared Mrs Claus, shaking her head. 'Such a deed is beyond even the Queen's power.'

'Well, there's obviously something strange going on here, and if he is behind those stars, then he's got to be stopped at once, whatever they are for,' resolved Blitzen, banging his hoof on the counter.

'Yes, but I'm afraid, Blitzen, if he is tricking us, then there's nothing we can do about it for the Christmas present,' added Santa earnestly. 'The Mixing Bowl is not giving us any answers, and we don't have much time to go out looking for him. The Court of Christmas starts soon.'

'Yes, that's what I'm worried about,' mused Blitzen gravely.

'Well look, Edgar is Snooks' assistant, and as such he is expected to be at the Court,' began Santa. 'Perhaps we can put a few questions to him there.'

'I most *certainly* will do that,' said Blitzen, nodding firmly as he thought about the malign creature. 'Whatever he's up to, he's not going to get away with it.'

'Of course, of course,' agreed Santa, a bit more enthusiastically.

Blitzen nodded blankly, when there was a knock at the door of Christmas Cottage, which, given the events of the evening, succeeded in quite startling the company.

'Well now, who could that be?' said Mrs Claus, walking over to the front door and using a tea towel to handle it as though she was opening an oven.

'Hey, Mrs Claus, is Santa there? We've come to take him to the castle. I know we're a little early. Blitzen's not in there with you, is he?' came a cheerful voice from outside.

'Oh, Dasher, pudding,' cried Mrs Claus in delight. 'Thank Christmas it's you. We've had some strange goings on here tonight. Burnt puddings all over the place. Yes, yes, they're both here. Come in, come in,' she added, drawing back the door to reveal Dancer also standing by his side.

'We would do Mrs Claus, but we're kind of all linked up,' replied Dasher, nodding his head behind him to where the rest of the Reindeer formed a train and were all tied up to Santa's sleigh on the driveway.

'Evening, Mrs Claus. Evening, Glenda,' they all called one by one into Christmas Cottage.

'Oh, good evening, puddings. My, my, how Christmaclumsy of me. I should have known you would be. Alright then. I'll call them out. Santa! Blitzen! The sleigh's here,' she cried, turning towards the sitting room.

'Ho ho ho. It's that late already, eh? Alright then,' said Santa, moving towards the front door, closely followed by Blitzen. 'Hello, boys. Nice night for it, isn't it?'

'Hi, Boss,' chirped the Reindeer, as they all trotted forward so that the sleigh moved up the driveway, in line with the front door.

'Hey, Chief. Did Snooks shed any light on those stars?' asked Comet, as he nibbled rather swiftly through yet another portion of carrot sticks.

'Yes, as a matter of fact he did,' said Blitzen taking his position next to Donner. 'They contain purple dust from Alendria.'

'From *Alendria*?' piped up Cupid. 'That's a little unexpected.'

'Yes, it is,' agreed Blitzen. 'And he's bringing more information with him to the Court tonight. But if you ask me, that stealthy little Elf, Edgar, has got something to do with it.'

'What, Snooks' assistant?' asked Prancer, shuddering. 'Ooh, he gives me the Christmas creeps.'

'Oh now, now, we don't know it's him for certain,' remarked Santa, as he fussed about with the cushions on the sleigh. 'And we don't want to write off a potentially innocent little Elf without Christmacause. Now then, let me see, we've got 1,2,3,4,5,6,7 and Blitzen, 8 - but where the Christmas cakes is......?'

'Hey, Christmasdudes, wait for me,' came a familiar voice from inside a mass of colour that was now advancing towards the driveway at a rather hefty pace.

'Jeez, it's Rudolph,' exclaimed Vixen cynically, as the mass of colour now expanded into a shiny red nose and a pair of polished antlers, generously trimmed with fluorescent pink tinsel and a pair of electric blue baubles.

'Phew!' breathed Rudolph, as he reached the top of Christmas Hill, with his tongue hanging out like a dog. 'Sorry I'm late, Christmasdudes. I had to trim myself up a bit for the castle. Ya like it?' he asked, casting himself into a pose as he flashed his decorated antlers.

'Aw fer Christmas sakes, Rudolph. You look like a Christmas tree,' snapped Donner from the back of the train.

'Thanks, Kebabs,' beamed Rudolph, clearly happy with this remark. 'Hey, Mrs Claus. Like the new do?'

'Wonderful, pudding,' replied Mrs Claus, as she stood on the doorstep smiling.

'Hey, Santa. Hey, Blitzy. How's it going?' chirped Rudolph merrily. 'Hey, Santa, can you hook me up?' he then added as he stood in prize position at the front, smiling merrily at the other Reindeer.

'Certainly, Rudolph,' said Santa, attaching the reigns to him so that he was now tied to the rest of the pack.

Santa then produced a large bag of Reindeer dust and began sprinkling its contents over the train before climbing into his sleigh and taking hold of the reigns. In his seat he suddenly felt the thrill of Christmas seize him. The purple stars seemed insignificant now. Whatever their intended purpose, they could not ruin Christmas, and whatever Edgar's role in this, he *would not* get away with it.

'Alright then, boys, it's off to the castle. Here we go,' shouted Santa, as he pulled back on the reigns.

'Alright, Christmasdudes. Let's do this,' cheered Rudolph, as he backed up slightly to gain some runway.

Then with a great heave, they were off climbing high into the air, with the Reindeer dust twinkling magically beneath them.

'Goodbye, puddings. Take care,' cried Mrs Claus, waving at them with her handkerchief from below.

The sleigh then disappeared behind the clouds and pushed on into the north towards the magical, spellbinding Enchantment of Christmas Castle.

8-The Court of Christmas

As the sleigh flew over the Kingdom, Santa paused momentarily to admire its beauty. The Elves' houses had been lit up for the winter's evening, and from above they looked like little gleaming jewels decorating an iced snow cone. Their green Elfin Wonders banners blew vibrantly in the breeze, while to the left, Villa Noël continued to blaze boisterously with its lavish, luminous lights. Just south of the village, Santa could distinguish Cinnamon Forest, glistening with fireflies and emitting a mystical aura, as though it were full of whispers and secrets that were yet to be disclosed. The fireflies pierced the cold night air and twinkled in Santa's eyes until the forest suddenly went out of view and the sleigh entered a cold, dense area of cloud. Then, as the sleigh broke through it, the castle was in sight. Sparkling in the winter evening, it looked more splendid than ever. Its concentric ivory towers spiralled high into the air and were crowned with crimson roofs and holly vines. Around the outside of the towers thousands of tiny fireflies flew, lighting up the dwelling in the most magical manner. The castle grounds were bordered on either side by two large forests - the one to the left served as the Queen's private garden, the one on the right was The Forest of Magic Lanterns. The moat that skirted around the castle was frozen, as usual, and this evening featured an array of Snowbelles gracefully skating along it. It seemed as if it was going to be quite a busy meeting, for there was a vast string of other carriages outside the castle already. Sergeant Squirrelseed's Nutshell Carriage was there, oozing out the scent of cinnamon, as were a considerable number of butternut shell coaches, which was the method of transport used by the Snowflakes whenever there was an official meeting.

As the sleigh landed near the formal entrance, the Papa Ratzi were in full flow, and camera flashes punctuated every step that the guests took up the causeway. Rudolph's face already formed a pose at the sight of the media, and he unhooked himself from the sleigh so that he could check his appearance in the frozen moat.

'There he goes,' observed Vixen, shaking his head. 'Hey, Rudolph, you sure you don't wanna stay outside with us? You can look at yourself all night then.'

A laugh erupted from the other Reindeer who were still busy disengaging themselves from the sleigh. Rudolph was so busy admiring himself, however, that he barely heard Vixen.

'What's that now?' he asked, taking one eye off the moat.

'Oh, come now, Rudolph. You look fine,' assured Santa, stealing him away from the moat and pushing him towards the causeway. 'Alright, boys. The Snowflakes are at the doors and around the gardens, so I want you positioned around the moat and towards the rear of the castle. If you see even the slightest thing out of place, sound the Christmas alarm.'

'Yes, Boss,' the Reindeer nodded, and immediately set off to do their duty.

'Ready, Blitzen, Rudolph?'

'Oh yeah, I'm ready,' grinned Rudolph, as he looked at the parade of bright lights before him.

A quick glance in the moat was enough to assure Santa that he looked presentable, and with a nod of his head, he turned and strode off up the causeway in between the two Reindeer. The Papa Ratzi went wild when they saw the newest arrivals. Rudolph immediately grabbed their attention, but they were always keen to picture Santa Claus and Blitzen.

'Santa, how do you feel about the standard of toy production this year?' snapped a Rat named Pervis, who was a rising assistant at The X-mas Times.

'Oh, wonderful. The Elves have produced some very exciting gifts for the children,' smiled Santa, as he continued to climb towards the castle entrance.

'Rudolph, will you be sporting any of the new winter wear for The X-mas Times Style Page?'

'Well, it wouldn't be Christmas if I didn't,' chirped Rudolph, who flashed his trademark gnashers for the cameras to feast on. He would have liked to have stayed longer, but he was physically restrained by Blitzen, who kept one hoof on his back and continued to push him up the causeway.

'Hey, Blitzen, are the Reindeer ready for the approaching season?' shouted another.

'The Reindeer are always ready,' replied Blitzen bluntly, without looking up.

'Hey, Blitzen, Blitzen….'

'Good evening, Santa, Blitzen, Rudolph,' said the Snowflake guard on the door, whose authoritative voice came as a welcome relief from the din of the press behind.

'Good evening,' they replied, looking up at the huge, golden arch in front of them and feeling rather miniscule. The Snowflake guard stood aside to let them pass, and with excitement whirling in their stomachs, they entered The Enchantment of Christmas Castle.

Of course, the castle inside was as splendid as the season which had inspired it. The walls were a tasteful mix of alabaster and gold and were generously decked with boughs of holly, ivy and mistletoe, while the carpet was a rich, winter crimson that sparkled elegantly under the glimmering light of the chandeliers. A grand and beautiful stairway unfolded in the hallway, inviting guests to climb upwards towards the great Court of Christmas. It really was wonderfully spellbinding and seductive.

From the galleries upstairs came the silvery sound of instruments playing carols, and one could detect a chitter chatter coming from the Court, which was evidently not in session yet. More importantly however, the waft of mince pies came floating along the air and tickled Santa's nostrils until his nose twitched.

'Ho ho ho. Can't have a meeting without those,' he chuckled, as his stomach suddenly hastened his climb towards the Court.

Several Snowflake guards lined the stairway and bowed majestically as the trio ascended.

'Merry Christmas,' smiled the Snowflakes, always ready and willing to show respect to Santa and the Reindeer.

'Merry Christmas, guys,' chirped Rudolph excitedly. 'Hey, Blitzy, I can see myself in a place like this. What do you think?' he asked, as he admired the splendid decor.

'You're not royal, Rudolph,' sighed Blitzen.

'Hey, what do you mean?' asked Rudolph, perplexed.

Fortunately Blitzen did not have to answer, for they had just arrived at the entrance to the Court, which quickly succeeded in diverting Rudolph's attention elsewhere.

'Hey, look, there's the Snowflakes!' blurted out Rudolph, who, no sooner had he spoken these words, was inside the room and busy sporting and mingling loudly with them.

Blitzen and Santa were about to enter the Court too, when their entrance was suddenly blocked by a small male Elf clad in green stockings, a bright red tunic and green, curled-up shoes with bells on the toes that tinkled when he moved.

'Good evening, both. Care for some mince pies and mulled wine?' he asked, flashing them a gleaming smile and thrusting a tray of goodies in front of them that even the strongest willed creature couldn't resist.

'Ooh, don't mind if I do,' smiled Santa, greedily taking a handful of pies and a large glass of wine and setting to work on them straight away.

Blitzen bowed and accepted a mince pie, which he nibbled on thoughtfully as he entered the Court.

The Court itself was much more formal in appearance than the rest of the palace, though still richly decorated with the trappings of the season. A throne of solid gold with a red velvet cushion stood grandly at the centre of the room. To the left was a parade of arch-shaped windows that looked out onto the Queen's gardens below, whilst to the right was an enormous medieval fire bedecked with acorns and Christmas stockings. The room was full, although noticeably the Queen and her children had not yet arrived. The company was mainly composed of Snowflakes, a few representatives of the Elves and the Forest Creatures, in addition to Santa and the Reindeer. Snooks too had yet to arrive, much to Blitzen's dismay, but one particular figure did stand out to him as he made his way across the room, and on seeing him, the blood in his veins immediately began to boil. Edgar lingered eerily at the back of the Court, standing on the fringes of the shadows like a chilling phantom. He did not mingle with the other guests but looked upon them in such a disdainful manner that it made Blitzen's nerves simmer. He immediately made his way over to the Elf to confront him about his journey earlier, but as he did so, the Elf suddenly disappeared again as though the shadows had entirely swallowed him up. Blitzen stopped dead in the middle of the Court and blinked hard.

'What in The Kingdom of Christmas is going on here?' he asked himself, as he scoured the room, looking amongst the crowd and in every corner. Edgar was nowhere to be seen. He had simply vanished again, just as he had done by the forest earlier. Blitzen was now convinced that he was using black magic in order to trick him, and he chewed so angrily on his mince pie that he was quite taken aback when a tiny little voice at his feet suddenly addressed him.

'Hello, Blitzen. How are you?'

On hearing this, Blitzen jumped up in mid-air and dropped the remainder of his mince pie on the floor.

'Good Christmas. Are you alright?' came the little voice again, now seeming quite alarmed.

'Christmas crackers,' exclaimed Blitzen, shaking his head and rolling his eyes back into focus so that he now saw the little Squirrel who had spoken to him. 'Goodness me, Sergeant Squirrelseed. I do apologise. My mind was elsewhere,' he added, still haunted by Edgar's stealthy behaviour.

'Oh, not to worry,' replied the Squirrel. 'I hear there was an incident at the Festival last night with Mrs Bunnie's cubs.'

Blitzen nodded in assent, but as he glanced upwards, he saw Edgar had reappeared again and was now standing in the opposite corner of the Court on the edge of the shadows, his black hair trailing behind him like a ghastly snake. The Reindeer was utterly baffled and stared in disbelief as his jaw dropped to the floor.

'I'm sorry, Blitzen. Is everything alright?' enquired the little Squirrel, now growing concerned. 'It's just that you do seem to be rather distracted.'

'I do apologise, Sergeant Squirrelseed,' said Blitzen, now shaking his head and looking down at the Squirrel. 'Tell me, do you see Edgar the Elf standing over there in that corner?'

Squirrelseed turned around to where Blitzen's hoof was pointing, but as he did so, the wily Elf once again disappeared into the shadows like some kind of Christmas ghost.

'I'm sorry, Blitzen, but I'm afraid I don't see him,' replied the Squirrel, as he only saw the shadow cast by the minstrel gallery above and a tiny flicker in the air.

'Oh, confound it all. I *know* that he is tricking me,' muttered Blitzen, shaking his head and now growing more and more frustrated.

'Well, he's definitely a strange one. And not to be trusted,' agreed the Squirrel, as he thought about the malign, little creature. 'I, myself, have never been able to take to him.'

'Nor I, Sergeant. But I'm afraid there's more. You see....' He was just about to relate to Sergeant Squirrelseed the curious incident with Edgar near Cinnamon Forest earlier, when his thoughts were suddenly cut short by the sound of trumpets.

'Her Royal Highness, Queen Krystiana, and her two children, Prince Michael and Princess Sarah,' announced the Elf who had greeted them at the door. The Court became silent and stood to attention as the beautiful Queen appeared, followed by her children and a group of Snowflake guards, who now lined themselves at the Courtroom door and closed it. Everyone in the room bowed or curtseyed as the Queen glided towards her throne, filling the room with an even brighter glow as she did so. Michael and Sarah also bowed, and Michael scoured the room for Blitzen, motioning that he would come and see him as soon as the trivialities were over. The Queen produced the Altra from her sleeve and released it from her grasp so that it floated above her throne and stopped dead in mid-air. She looked kindly upon everyone and smiled. Then she spoke in a soft, silvery voice: 'Greetings, folk of the realm, and welcome to The Enchantment of Christmas Castle. As you know, our meeting has been moved forward this year, but before we begin the evening's discussions, I would firstly like all of you to raise your glasses to celebrate this time of year. To Christmas.'

'To Christmas' repeated the Hall.

The Altra shimmered slightly as these words were spoken and emitted a faint pink glow as, inside it, thousands of tiny flakes of snow began to fall.

'And to our most magical and wonderful Kingdom,' added the Queen, raising her glass a second time.

'To the Kingdom,' cheered the folk.

Suddenly, the Courtroom door shook violently and was promptly thrown open as an incredibly flushed Snooks burst in, looking most anxious indeed.

'Your Majesty,' he gasped, out of breath, as he wiped the condensation from his glasses. 'Your Majesty, I am so sorry I'm late. I am afraid I have some rather terrible news.'

'What is it, Snooks?' faltered the Queen, now sounding alarmed.

Blitzen scanned the room quickly and saw that Edgar had now reappeared out of the shadows and stood as still as a stony gargoyle.

'It is very serious, Your Majesty. Please,' he panted, 'bolt the doors! I am afraid we have a traitor in the Kingdom, and he is standing in this very room.'

Michael and Sarah looked at each other in astonishment as a murmur ran through the Court, and the Snowflake guards, on Snooks' command, hurriedly bolted the doors and stood in front of them.

'Who is it?' asked the Queen, looking around desperately.

Snooks hobbled across the room to the centre of the Court, still stooped over, ready to unveil the culprit. But then, a very strange thing happened. A purple smoke drifted up from his feet, and to the Court's absolute horror, Snooks now stood up straight as his glasses disintegrated and the butterflies disappeared from his cloak, leaving in their place a deadly snow spider that began to weave a sinister web on the garment.

'Why, it is *I*, Your Majesty,' he said in a sinister voice, very unlike the lilt of the little shopkeeper. '*I* am the traitor in your Kingdom. And I have been working for the Mountains these past ten years.'

The Court recoiled in horror as Snooks stood there, sizing them up like a deadly bird of prey. He looked much younger as his white hair had now turned to a very light blonde that was greased back to his head, drawing attention to his long, roman nose.

'Well I, I cannot believe this,' breathed the Queen, utterly flabbergasted. 'But why?'

'It's quite simple, Your Majesty. Your morals restrict my genius,' replied the lofty Snowflake, as his cloak grew more indigo by the second.

'But what about Edgar?' growled Blitzen, as he stared at the fiendish Elf, who had not moved even the slightest inch since the sorcerer had unveiled himself.

'Ah yes, Edgar,' returned Snooks, as his face now relaxed into a smug grin. 'Do you mean *this* Edgar, or *this* Edgar?' he asked, pulling back his cloak to reveal the real Edgar, now gagged and bound, whilst causing the one which had haunted Blitzen in the Courtroom and by Cinnamon Forest to rise off the floor and turn in mid-air like a hog on a spit.

Blitzen's stomach knotted, as it dawned on him what had happened. The ever-vanishing Edgar had been an illusion!

'You made an illusion of Edgar to try and trick me!' blurted Blitzen, now glowering with the real Edgar.

'Brilliant, isn't it!' sneered Snooks, snapping his fingers and thus causing the illusion to disappear. Snooks' cloak had turned a deep indigo and rose up over his large wings, bestowing him with a demonic aura. The real Edgar was writhing and moaning behind his restraints, and Snooks now un-gagged him, enabling him to speak.

'You set me up to try and frame me,' he snapped, as beads of sweat now dripped down his wart-covered nose. 'You set me up, and you're guna pay for this, you devil, you.'

'Oh, there, there now, Edgar,' said Snooks, re-gagging him and looking upon him with feigned pity. 'Don't be too disheartened. It was almost too easy, what with your gruff manner and your astonishing lack of social skills. The folk of the Kingdom already disliked you, hence they were ready to believe anything about you. It's a terrible state of affairs really, given that this is The Kingdom of Christmas.'

'That's enough of that, Snooks,' interrupted the Queen angrily. 'Now explain yourself. How could you do such a thing to an innocent little Elf?'

'Why, with great ease, Your Majesty, naturally. At my magic show I created dark illusions around him in order to jade the audience's reaction. And given his rigid routine of going to The Snowman's Shadow after work every day, I knew I could create an illusion of him and not get caught. He left my shop every day at exactly six o'clock without saying goodbye, and he stayed at The Snowman's Shadow for precisely 45 minutes after. I could place an illusion of him anywhere I wanted between these times and there would have been no danger of him running into himself.'

'So the Mixing Bowl wasn't lying. He really *was* in The Snowman's Shadow earlier?' asked Blitzen.

'Yes, Blitzen. That is correct. It was merely an illusion you saw by the forest. And as Edgar left The Snowman's Shadow at 6.45, I then captured him and brought him here with me.'

'But how could you *control* him? It's not possible,' continued Blitzen, whose mind was tangled in knots.

'It was quite simple, Blitzen, or are you forgetting that I am a Snowflake and can change size whenever I want,' he boasted, now snapping his finger and shrinking down to the size of a firefly. 'Earlier, I flew out through the lock in my shop and positioned myself behind the trees of Cinnamon Forest to create the illusion. And in the Courtroom just now, I flew up to the minstrel gallery.'

'But I don't understand. If you created an illusion of him near Cinnamon Forest, then why did the Bowl not *show* this? And why did it not show *you* inside Cinnamon Forest?'

'The purpose of the Mixing Bowl, Blitzen, is to find creatures who are hiding behind magical spells. Its chief objective is to see *through* magic. As Edgar was an illusion, then the Bowl would have looked straight through the magic that created him and showed you what was underneath – nothing. Or no one as the case may be,' explained Snooks, as he now returned back to normal size.

'And you?' questioned Blitzen, feeling a prized fool for not seeing through any of this.

'Quite simply, Blitzen - the Bowl could not see me because I was deep in the forest, hidden from its line of vision behind the trees and dense foliage. But don't look too crestfallen,' sneered the sorcerer smugly. 'No one could have possibly foiled this plan. It is too clever. The illusion was designed purely to make you look one way and not the other. Such is the art of the mighty conjuror. For indeed, while you all suspected Edgar, no one suspected me. And I am afraid, Blitzen, that while you were busy focusing on Edgar, wasting time at Christmas Cottage, I had free reign to carry out the final stages of my plan.'

The entire Courtroom continued to stare in astonishment at the sorcerer, as he now reached into his cape and produced the object that had been the cause of much contention over the past day.

'Recognise this?' he asked, holding it out before the Court and swishing it tantalisingly.

'Why it's the purple purse,' gasped Michael, as he ran forwards.

'Yes, that's correct Michael,' laughed Snooks heinously. 'It is the purse that has had the entire Kingdom in a stir. The very same purse that Bunnyflower picked up yesterday, and the purse which just hours ago Blitzen returned to me (quite unwittingly of course) at my shop when it was full of magic purple stars containing purple dust from Alendria.

'Purple dust from Alendria,' repeated the Queen, raising her eyes suspiciously and feeling a vague trembling of fear in her stomach at the mention of this. 'But that is one of the most powerful magic substances of all worlds.'

'It is,' cackled Snooks, cruelly. 'And no doubt you are wondering why I had it. Well, let me tell you then, Your Majesty. Let me tell you all about the whole ingenious little history,' stated Snooks, as he now turned to face the Court.

'I have been acquiring purple dust from Alendria for many years and concealing it within little stars. Of course, I could not keep it at the shop for fear of getting caught, so I found, instead, a little hideout in Cinnamon Forest where I could hide them, separating them into little purses to make their transportation to the Mountains easier.'

'Why, you evil little snake,' growled Blitzen, who now writhed furiously behind the flames.

'Well, I suppose you would say that. But do let me finish before you go making such accusations,' interjected Snooks, as a bolt of lightning shot down his cloak.

'You see, this charming little treasure from Alendria has hidden properties, and when used correctly and consistently over a long period of time, it conspires to break that hateful spell that you, Krystiana, once placed on the Mountains, locking the Guardian inside.'

'What!' winced the Queen, now pale and distraught, as anger boiled within Michael's veins.

'Oh yes,' continued Snooks, rubbing his hands together impatiently. 'Of course, we needed more than just one batch. It took many years to unstitch your magic dungeon. Unfortunately for you, Blitzen, this little purse here was the final batch, and thanks to you returning it to me it is now empty,' he added, emptying the purse upside down.

'How *could* you?' cried the Queen.

'Oh, believe me, I could,' stated Snooks, in a lowered voice. 'Your end is nigh, Krystiana.'

'But wait. What about the mystery ingredient?' ventured Blitzen urgently. 'The green smoke found inside the stars?'

At this, Snooks paused menacingly. 'Ah yes, the mystery ingredient,' he added, now wallowing whole heartedly in his own malice. 'It was quite ingenious, actually, that little ingredient. It was only ever added to the last purse-full. That's why retrieving it was so important. It hasn't even been fully tested yet. It is meant to transport a creature from one place to another. From, let us say, a mountain to a castle, and can only be done by the strike of a tinder box. I am sure you understand me, Blitzen,'

Snooks now turned to face the Courtroom, theatrically.

'And now, pathetic creatures of Christmas, after all these bitter and hate-drenched years. After all the deceits and the heartaches. Here he is. The Guardian of the Mountains.'

With these words, Snooks pulled out a silver tinder box and struck it with a match, causing a gust of wind to race through the Courtroom, thus extinguishing the green flames.

The room went cold and icy, as a wave of deathly air swept across the floor and ran up the windows, shaking the curtains and the lights, which flickered and dimmed. Then the double doors were flung back once again, only this time in came a huge black mass that sent the Queen and her subjects into a violent state of panic.

'Oh no,' she breathed in fear, as she tried to move from her throne to protect the Altra. But the situation was unfolding too quickly, and the Guardian moved in, closer, while the Court stood motionless and completely frozen in fear. Then the Guardian held out his Staff and drew the Altra towards it. A scream came from Santa and the Queen as Blitzen, Rudolph and the Snowflakes rushed forward to try and grab it. But they could not reach it in time. The Altra was drawn in and stuck tightly onto the head of the Staff, causing a fierce crack of lightning and a tumultuous roar of thunder. The room turned to ice. The Queen suddenly began to fall weak, as a yellow smoke encircled the globe.

'This is the end of your rule, Krystiana,' said the Guardian, in a voice which dripped pure malice. 'This is the end of Christmas.'

He then held out his mighty new weapon and pointed it towards the Queen and Santa. A curious green light flashed across the room, and the two victims were sucked inside the glass of the Altra, trapped like two prisoners in this darkening dungeon.

'No,' yelled Blitzen, as he began to charge forward, before being knocked down by the Staff.

'Get them,' roared the Guardian fiercely, as he struck the floor to punctuate his command.

Out of the shadows, to the Court's horror, a thousand Snow Wolves materialised from every corner, closing in on them. Rudolph's eyes rolled in his head, Squirrelseed's tail began to shake, and the Snowflakes looked from one to the other, wondering what they could do. But they were given little time. The Wolves sprang forward viciously, gnawing at the creatures, and throwing them against the frozen walls, their eyes glowing a fierce, luminous yellow as they did so.

Snooks drew a magic potion and began attacking the Snowflakes, while Edgar was taken captive along with all the other Elves present.

'Oh my goodness, what do we do?' cried Sarah, as she and Michael witnessed their Kingdom crumbling around them.

'I don't know,' cried Michael, quickly snatching a piece of ivory paper and a sharp fountain pen from a clerk's desk. 'But look! There's Blitzen over there. Here - Blitzen,' he continued, as he grabbed his sister by the arm and advanced forwards fearlessly. 'Blitzen, what are we supposed to do now?'

'Oh children, thank Christmas! - I was just relating to Sergeant Squirrelseed,' said Blitzen, as the children spotted the timid little Squirrel seated on board the Reindeer's saddle, clutching onto his collar for dear life. 'There's a *Magic Scroll* at Cosy Cottage. We have to consult it immediately! We have no time to waste.'

'Which way do we go?' asked Sarah, who really did feel that they would need the assistance of a Christmas miracle to get out of here.

Blitzen was about to reply when a Snow Wolf charged towards him and began biting at his ankles. Blitzen thrust himself forward forcefully, managing to push the Snow Wolf back with his antlers, before heading for an empty space near the castle windows and beckoning the children to follow. Battles were being fought all around, and screams were heard racing up to the ceiling as Christmas Blood was spilt.

'I do apologise, children, now listen. I think our best option is to fly directly through the castle windows. I know it's risky, but we can't go down the stairway, and the minstrel gallery is blocked. Now, my Reindeer dust is in this satchel here. Do you think you can manage it?'

'Yes, of course,' nodded Michael, as he kept one eye on the battle around him.

'Ok then, quickly. Jump on board!'

'Wait, where's Rudolph?' cried Squirrelseed, as the children joined him on the saddle. The quartet looked around. Rudolph was at the opposite corner of the room, backed into the wall by a pack of venomous Wolves, whose claws sunk deeply into the frozen floor with every step they took. Their eyes lit up the surrounding walls like the burning fires of Hell.

'Guys, guys, come on,' whimpered Rudolph. 'We can work this out. You don't need to be so angry. Why don't you form a Christmas Rock band or sumthin?'

The Snow Wolves continued to gain on him, when Blitzen charged straight at them and began hurling them to the wall. Rudolph sank down in the corner, covering his eyes with his hooves. The three Wolves had momentarily scattered as Blitzen shook his antlers.

'Come on, Rudolph, quickly, let's get out of here,' yelled Blitzen, pulling him by his antlers. Michael quickly sprinkled the two with gold Reindeer dust as they headed towards the window.

'Hey, Blitzy, where are we going?' asked Rudolph, who suddenly realised that he was being pulled straight towards sheer glass.

'Through the window. It's our only way,' declared Blitzen ruthlessly.

'Oh, I'm not sure about this, Blitzy,' screamed Rudolph, shutting his eyes as they broke through the glass windows and out into the icy air.

'Stop them,' growled the Guardian from behind. A bolt of lightning shot from his Staff and hit Rudolph, who lost consciousness and suddenly began to fall.

'Oh no, Blitzen, look. Rudolph,' cried Squirrelseed in horror.

'Hang on tight,' commanded Blitzen, who swooped down, dodging more lightning bolts that shot from the Staff. He flew just underneath Rudolph, who landed with great force right on his back, almost squashing Squirrelseed. He then immediately began to climb higher, moving over to the east as he did so. 'Is he alright?' asked Blitzen, trying to navigate his way through the air.

'He's unconscious, but he should be alright,' answered Michael, patting him on the back and feeling that this was going to be a bit of a squash.

'Oh, good Christmas – look. Look down there,' cried Squirrelseed suddenly, as his eyes had now been averted to the frozen moat and the surrounding grounds of the castle. The Snow Wolves were *everywhere*, and to his horror they had rounded up the Reindeer and chained them together like convicts.

'Blitzen, the Reindeer!!!'

Blitzen looked down to see the Snow Wolves rounding up his greatest friends and marching them into the castle dungeons.

'No. This cannot be,' he thundered.

'Look out!' shrieked Squirrelseed, as a large net came flying past them, narrowly missing them and falling back to the ground again.

'It's the Wolves. Quickly. They're trying to capture us too. We have to climb higher.' Blitzen then waded through the clouds and climbed higher and higher, before turning south towards Cinnamon Forest.

9-The Scroll at Cosy Cottage

Blitzen, the children and Sergeant Squirrelseed were still heading as fast as they could in the direction of Cinnamon Forest. Squirrelseed was clutching onto Blitzen's collar tightly and tried his very best not to look down for his fear of heights, while Rudolph was still unconscious and slumped rather precariously over the head Reindeer's back. The children, meanwhile, took in their surroundings in disbelief, and Michael now wasted no time in penning a letter to his father.

Dear Father,
He scribbled in a hurry.

The Kingdom has been attacked, the Staff joined to the Altra, and our mother and Santa trapped inside. Do not return to the Kingdom at Christmas present. You know how dangerous it can be for humans under dark rule. Get to a secure hiding place as soon as possible. The Guardian may have recruits in the Northern Regions, particularly in somewhere like The Town of Flickering Candles. We will contact you when it is safe to return.
Yours Truly,
Prince Michael and Princess Sarah

He then pierced his fingertip with the point of the pen and emptied a drop of his blood onto the letter, before jabbing the pen into Sarah. This was *The Secret Seal of Christmas* — a signature in blood to show that the subject of which you spoke was of the utmost and absolute truth and gravity.

'Ouch, Michael. That hurt,' cried the little Princess, who was caught quite unawares.

'I'm sorry, pigtails. It's for the letter. Here, put the drop next to mine.'

Sarah scowled slightly, but obeyed, and the drops dried quickly on the ivory sheet as Michael folded the paper in half.

'There now, all we have to do is find a place where the North Wind passes so that it can pick it up,' said Michael anxiously. 'Keep your wits about you and be on the lookout.'

Sarah nodded, as Blitzen chatted independently to Sergeant Squirrelseed, missing the children's conversation.

They were now directly above Cinnamon Forest. It was, at Christmas present, calm and undisturbed by the Christmas chaos that was seizing the rest of the Kingdom. As they found a clearing, they began to alight slowly and carefully, looking in all directions to ensure they weren't being followed. They landed firmly and safely on the ground.

'Looks like they haven't arrived here yet,' whispered Squirrelseed with enormous relief.

'Thank Christmas,' sighed Sarah, who really felt that her adrenaline had been all but used up for the winter.

'Listen,' whispered Blitzen, suddenly stopping dead. 'Can you hear a rustling?'

Michael looked around alertly, and Squirrelseed's face assumed such a tremendous look of fear that it was almost comical.

'There, look out!' bellowed Blitzen, as he jerked sharply to avoid an object that came hurtling through the air from the trees above.

Squirrelseed, who was not as brave as Blitzen, had jumped for cover under Blitzen's legs, and was hiding his eyes with his paws while his knees shook uncontrollably. 'Oh, it's over, it's over,' he whelped like a little puppy. 'My life as a Squirrel is over.'

'What *are* you talking about?' asked a confused and slightly irritated female voice.

'Trixitail?' murmured the timid little Squirrel, peering between his fingers.

'Yes, who did you think it was?' she demanded, jealously. 'And what's the matter with *him*?' she asked, raising her eyebrows and pointing towards Rudolph, who was still slumped over Blitzen. 'Had too much to drink at the Court, did he?'

'Oh uh, well uh, where to begin, uh, the Snow Wolves, you see, no, no, uh, the Guardian uh,'

'The Guardian,' she squealed with a look of horror.

'Good Christmas, where?' yelped Squirrelseed again in a little panic.

'You just said his name.'

'Oh yes, well he's here.'

'In the forest?'

'Oh, well uh.......'

'No, not in the Forest. Not yet,' added Blitzen, intruding, as his little friend was evidently in a bit of a fumble. 'Look, Trixitail, this may all come as a bit of a shock, but you'll have to listen and try to stay as calm as possible, for we don't have much time.'

'Oh,' she said, evidently stunned. 'Of course, Blitzen, do go on.' The little Squirrel fluttered her eyelashes at Blitzen as she waited for him to continue.

'The Guardian has broken free from the Mountains and has taken control of the Altra.

'Huh! Oh no!' she squealed in devastation, as tears filled her eyes.

'Yes, he's taken Santa and our mother prisoner, and he's shackled all the Elves and Reindeer, the little dirt bag,' added Prince Michael, joining in.

'Santa? The Queen? Oh no,' squeaked Trixitail again in an inconsolable voice.

'Yes, and I'm afraid that it was all with the help of our Protector of Magic, Snooks,' explained Blitzen, now sounding incredibly ruffled.

'Don't call him Snooks, Blitzen. Call him *Snivel Puss Sly Eyes*!' ordered Michael indignantly. 'He doesn't deserve to have a proper name anymore.'

'Well, he certainly doesn't if he betrayed us,' agreed Trixitail, in between gushes of tears. 'Oh dear, dear, dear, what a Christmaterrible mess to be in.'

'There, there, Trixi,' consoled Squirrelseed, wrapping his tail around her shoulders. 'It'll be alright. We just need to get to *The Scroll.*'

'Yes we do,' Blitzen confirmed. 'It's the only thing that can help us now.'

'Why yes, of course,' said Trixitail, suddenly pulling herself together. '*The Magic Scroll of Christmas.*'

'That's right,' nodded Blitzen. 'We need to get to Cosy Cottage at once. As you can see, Rudolph's out cold. He was hit on the head during the attack. Could you go around the forest and tell everyone to get to the hideout under the Oak Tree as soon as possible? The Snow Wolves will certainly be coming for us.'

'Oh, of course, right away. I'll come with you as far as Cosy Cottage. This way, follow me!'

She began scurrying through the trees and did not stop until she reached the entrance to a little clearing which was encircled with holly and ivy and was shaped like a Christmas wreath.

She hopped through, calling back, 'Mind the thorns on the way in.'

Soon they were all inside the clearing and were standing amidst the prettiest little village you have ever seen. The snow lay on the ground like big fluffy clouds of cotton wool and sat fatly on the rooftops of the houses. In front of them stood an enormous oak tree, lit up with fireflies that sparkled in the winter evening. To the right of the tree stood a little white and black beamed cottage with a thatched roof peppered with snow. Outside the house lay baskets full of holly and a little perch by the front door for the robins to stand on. This was Cosy Cottage, and it was so snug and homely that it almost made one forget about the terrible war just beyond the forest. Just to the left of the Oak Tree, a frozen stream was traversed by a small wicker bridge that led to Cinnamon

Village. This was *very* small - tiny as a matter of fact - with its little wooden houses forming a semi-circle above the stream. A huge Christmas tree stood at the centre of the crescent, upon which the Woodland Creatures had pinned their Christmas wishes.

'I'll leave you here and come back to the cottage when I'm done,' said Trixitail, turning towards the stream.

Blitzen now carried Rudolph up to Cosy Cottage. Michael tapped on the window and the door was promptly opened to reveal a most confused-looking Mrs Bunnie.

'Why, Prince Michael, Princess Sarah. What are you doing here, dearies? Aren't you supposed to be at the castle?' she asked, before noticing Blitzen and the Sergeant standing behind them, carrying Rudolph.

'Oh, Good Christmas, what's happened to Rudolph?'

'Well, it's a long story Mrs Bunnie. Do you mind if we come in?' asked Michael, peering behind her.

'Yes, I'm afraid we don't really have a lot of time,' said Blitzen, still flitting his eyes around the village to check that it was safe.

'Oh dear. Oh yes, yes of course. Come in and I'll get some bandages for Rudolph while you tell me all about it.'

The children went into the kitchen to help, while Squirrelseed hopped into the parlour, keen and eager to get to somewhere secure. As Blitzen approached the tiny door however, he conceived a great problem that he had not foreseen earlier – he and Rudolph weren't going to fit. They were simply too large! As he tried to heave himself through the doorframe, he sent the entire cottage into convulsion, causing the Christmas stockings to shake and sending two strings of candy canes that hung diagonally across the sitting room ceiling, into a tuneful rattle. Mrs Bunnie, who was currently reaching for some bandages from her kitchen drawer, suddenly looked up at the sound of the rattling to see Blitzen trying to extricate himself from the cottage doorframe and looking most ruffled indeed that he could not overcome this problem.

'Oh, darn it. I didn't think of that,' she said, opening a little snow-sprayed cupboard to reach for a bottle that looked as if it was filled with chocolate milkshake. 'The cottage was only built for Woodland Creatures. Here now, drink half of this,' she added, holding the bottle up to Blitzen. 'And we'll have to make sure that Rudolph gets some too.'

Mrs Bunnie forced open Rudolph's mouth and emptied the potion down his throat before letting his jaws slam shut again. There was a quick burst of light, accompanied by a POP, and with that, Blitzen and Rudolph were reduced to the size of canine dogs. Blitzen looked at himself in bewilderment for a few seconds. He did not seem best pleased with his less masculine form, nor would Rudolph be when he woke up – although that would be worth the wait! But he quickly forgot about it as they bundled Rudolph onto a little Christmas pudding-shaped seat in the sitting room. The room actually featured a number of these little pudding-styled seats, which were all placed in a semi-circle around the fire and commanded a wonderful view of the candle-lit Christmas tree to its right. A soft, red carpet and green, scalloped curtains certainly gave justification to cosiness, while the baskets of muffins, which were scattered generously throughout the room, including at the centre of the seating area, made one feel quite hungry.

Blitzen had little time to notice such niceties at Christmas present however, since he had to relate the Christmatastrophy that had occurred at the castle that evening. Mrs Bunnie listened with stoic acceptance as she continued bathing the lump on Rudolph's head, which was fast becoming the same colour as his nose.

'Well, I just can't believe it,' she sighed, blinking back a glistening tear. 'Snooks! Our very own Protector of Magic.'

'Actually, it's *Snivel Puss Sly Eyes* now, Mrs B,' said Michael, interrupting. 'We're not calling him *Snooks* anymore.'

'Of course not, dearie,' agreed Mrs Bunnie with resolve. 'But whatever he is, I'm shocked. I never would have marked him down as a traitor.'

'Nor I, Mrs Bunnie. I mean, I actually approached him for help,' confessed Blitzen. 'I feel like a prized fool for allowing him to trick me the way he did.'

'Oh there, there, Blitzen, that crafty snake has tricked us all,' sighed Mrs Bunnie. 'I suppose all we can do now is hope and pray that the *Magic Scroll* can find a solution for us.'

'Yes, indeed,' said Blitzen, a little more optimistically, before turning to Sergeant Squirrelseed. 'How's it looking outside, Sergeant? Still safe in the forest?'

'Oh,' gulped Sergeant Squirrelseed, who didn't really want to get up from his little pudding. 'I'll have a look right away.'

The Squirrel tottered over to a small window next to the front door, the sill of which was decorated with acorns and was lit up warmly with a cinnamon-scented candle.

'Well, I can't make out much from here,' he said, rubbing the condensation off the glass. 'It's very dark outside. But it seems as if there's a large queue to get inside the Oak Tree. And what looks like a..... oh dear. What is *that?*' added the little Squirrel, quivering as his ears picked up an unusual noise coming from outside.

Blitzen and Mrs Bunnie now pricked up their ears too, to hear that there really was quite a commotion without, and it seemed to be heading directly for the cottage. It grew louder and louder and got more and more boisterous, until it could finally be discerned as a chorus of three little voices of about the same age, echoed by another little voice, much younger than the first three.

'War, war,' came the first three, followed by a round of giggling and excitement. 'Warrr, warrr,' followed the fourth voice, accompanied by what sounded like an apache dance.

'Oh, Christmas cakes!' exclaimed Mrs Bunnie, folding her paws and rolling her eyes. 'Unfortunately, Sergeant Squirrelseed, I know exactly what that noise is, and I'm going to deal with it right away.'

Mrs Bunnie opened the door to reveal Patch, Hopper, Carrot Top and Bunnyflower, now returned to their normal colourings, all dancing around in a circle, like Red Indians, and patting their mouths with their paws. 'War, war,' they chanted. 'Isn't this exciting?' cried Patch.

'Yawooooooooooo,' howled Hopper. 'It sure is.'

'Christmacubs!' shouted Mrs Bunnie, who had placed herself in the centre of the doorway and was standing with her paws on her hips, eyeing them all sternly. 'What's all this?' she demanded, looking at them one by one.

The Bunnies all stopped suddenly and looked up at their mother in surprise.

'Ummmmmmmm, hi Mum,' smiled Hopper gingerly.

'Hello, Christmas comrade,' giggled Bunnyflower, saluting his mother with his paw.

At this, the other three Bunnies fell about laughing and started clutching their tummies which had begun to ache with all the excitement. But Mrs Bunnie was not impressed.

'Now, that's enough!' she snapped. 'Bunnyflower, do you even know what war is?' she asked, leaning down to look at her youngest son, whose eyes were even wider than they had been when he had initially discovered the stars.

'It's like playing cowboys and Indians,' replied Bunnyflower with childish enthusiasm.

'Oh really, and what are you going to do when an arrow hits you?' demanded Mrs Bunnie, looking very impatient.

'Go woowooowooowooowoooo,' howled the youngest Bunny, jumping around like a Jack-in-the-box.

'Indeed. Is this what you teach your younger brother?' snapped Mrs Bunnie, turning towards the other three.

'No. Course not. Bunnyflower wants to go to war. It's nothing to do with us,' said Hopper, shaking his head.

'Oh, yes it is,' scolded Mrs Bunnie, grabbing him by the ear. 'When he sees his brothers' excitement, he wants to join in too. Not one of you is going to fight, do you hear? Not one of you. And where is your father? I thought he was out bouncing with you!'

'He was,' said Hopper, shuffling free. 'But then Trixitail told us what happened at the castle, so he's gone to help the other animals move into the Oak Tree.'

'Yeah, he told us to come home and get a few things,' piped up Patch. 'He said he'll meet us down there. I think he's having a hard time calming some of the villagers though. They're really scared.'

'Aw, what big Christmas wusses,' sniggered Hopper.

'Yeah, who would be scared of a war?' giggled Carrot Top.

'Cubs! I said that's enough,' snapped Mrs Bunnie. 'Wars aren't exciting things. They're dreadful, dreadful affairs! Now, I'll not hear another word about you fighting in one, do you hear? Get inside, all of you,' she scolded.

This was met with a great many moans and groans as the four young Bunnies slumped inside, feeling that they had been denied a great privilege. However, no sooner were they inside the cottage, than they wanted to dart straight back out again, and if it wasn't for their mother blocking the doorway behind them, they would have done so.

'What is it *now*?' she asked, exasperated at their childishness.

'Oh uh, well uh,' they mumbled.

'Good evening, cubs,' smiled Blitzen, guessing straight away what the problem was.

'Oh, but we didn't do anything else wrong,' insisted Patch, vehemently protesting his innocence after last night's affair.

'No one said that you did,' said Blitzen calmly, yet obviously amused.

'Yeah, we said sorry about the purple stars. We only ate one – Cubs' Christmas Honour! And we've been really, really good all day,' cried Carrot Top, nodding.

'Cubs, cubs, calm down, there's nothing to worry about,' Squirrelseed assured them. 'Blitzen's not here for you. He has a much bigger Christmas cake to bake tonight.'

'But what happened to *him*?' asked Bunnyflower, pointing to Rudolph.

'He was hit on the head,' said Blitzen.

'Didn't you used to be bigger?' asked Hopper, looking a bit confused.

'Yes,' replied Blitzen, clearing his throat. 'This is just a temporary spell, enabling me to fit inside your house.'

'A *shrinking* spell. Christmatastic!' yelled Patch, his eyes growing enormous.

'Don't go getting any ideas, young Christmacub,' said Mrs Bunnie sternly.

'No fun,' moaned Patch kicking one of the Christmas puddings in a

Christmasulk.

'Hey, hey, we'll have none of that, thank you.'

Patch now sat on a chocolate log in the corner - which incidentally had a large chunk missing from one end where Carrot Top had gotten overly hungry – and held his head in both paws, pulling a face. The other three took up residence in front of the fireplace, and began pushing their Christmas stockings back and forth in frustration.

'Everyone else is making their way into the hideout, Mrs Bunnie,' said Squirrelseed. 'We may not have a lot of time. Do you think you should prepare yourself and the Christmacubs?'

'Yes of course.'

With that, there was another knock at the door. It was Trixitail.

'Oh hello, Mrs Bunnie. Hello, everyone. I've just come back from the village. Most of the animals are inside the hideout now. Mr Bunnie is already down there trying to keep everyone calm. He was most helpful in rounding everyone up. We had a right to-do with Mr Prickles, mind you. Silly Hedgehog. I told him the Kingdom was under attack, but he was more concerned about his Hedgehog Funds. He wanted to go into Mistletown to collect them. I told him that was ridiculous. He would be killed.'

'What did he do?' asked Squirrelseed, looking more and more aghast.

'Oh, well, between us, Mrs Prickles and I managed to talk him round. He's muttering *all* sorts of things to himself now. 'My Funds, my Funds!' he was crying. He didn't notice his two little Pricklings falling headfirst into the hideout. Mrs Prickles gave him a bump on the head, but he just thought it was about his Hedgehog Funds. I think he's a little worried too because most of the animals in Cinnamon Forest have Christmas coins in the funds.'

'Yes, but only he'd be greedy enough to worry about it at a time like this,' said Mrs Bunnie with a tut.

'Yes, what an absolute idiot,' remarked Michael, rolling his eyes. 'What about the other royal subjects? Have they made it down the Oak Tree safely?'

'Yes, everyone's safely inside. The Badgers tried to take half of their house down with them, bless me. I told them that it was all furnished and there was no need to worry. That does remind me however, is there anything we need to take down there with us, Squilsy dear?' she asked, turning to Sergeant Squirrelseed.

'Just some nut supplies, I should think. We've got weapons in the hideout. And a store of magic potions, including Reindeer dust. It's all in the emergency chest,' replied Squirrelseed, quite comforted by this.

'What's the plan, then?' asked Trixitail.

'Well, the hideout is underground, and it's nice and secure, so I suppose we'll all just hide there until the war is over,' suggested Squirrelseed optimistically.

'Oh, wonderful. Then we'll all be together,' said Trixitail warmly.

'Well, yes. But then there's the Kingdom to save,' continued Michael bravely. 'We haven't yet consulted *The Scroll*, and I'm Christma-crackered if I'm not doing *my* part to help.'

The whole cottage now turned their eyes towards Mrs Bunnie. It was time.

'Very well. Hopper, Carrot Top, put out the lights and draw the curtains. Patch, Bunnyflower, bolt the doors and close all the shutters upstairs. No one else must hear what I am about to tell you.'

She moved into the kitchen as the lights, one by one, went out. The cottage was now very dark, so she lit a solitary Christmas candle which drew everyone in closer - everyone except Rudolph, who was still out cold.

She then removed a dusty old cookbook from the bookshelf, and stretched as far as her paw would reach. 'Oh, dash it all, I've pushed it so far back for my cubs not to reach it that now I can't reach it myself. Wait, wait. Aha, got it!' With that, she brandished a very old, dusty, brown scroll in the air and laid it on the kitchen table. Patch had just returned from upstairs and now joined the others around the circular table.

'Did you see anything suspicious outside, my love?' asked his mother in a low, secretive voice.

'Nope,' answered Patch, shaking his head. 'Everyone must be inside the Oak Tree, cos Cinnamon Village is really quiet. The fireflies have left the trees and the cottages are all shut up. I could see some weird lights being shot up in the sky near the castle, though.'

'Snow bombs, more than likely,' spat Blitzen in disgust. 'The Guardian's speciality, no doubt.'

Silence fell upon the room which looked pale and ghostly in the light of the flickering candle. Mrs Bunnie took this moment to remove the red binding from *The Scroll*. As she untied it, *The Scroll* lit up with a blinding white light and began to float in mid-air. It glistened along the edges, and gold letters slowly appeared that looked as if they had been written in Reindeer dust.

'What's it say?' asked Bunnyflower, who just about managed to raise his jaw off the floor to be able to ask this question.

'It says, *The Magic Scroll of Christmas*,' breathed Squirrelseed, completely spellbound. As he read this, *The Scroll* landed on the table and glistened with silver spirals of light.

'What is it?' asked Patch, unable to detach his eyes from the magical document.

'It's an oracle,' answered Squirrelseed in his dapper little voice. 'The only oracle in the entire Kingdom.'

'What's an *or-ub-le*?' asked Bunnyflower, knitting his eyebrows together, and joined in confusion by his brothers, who were looking more and more perplexed by the minute.

'Oh, well uh. It's like a.... well I suppose you would say it's sort of a.... a......,' struggled Squirrelseed, as the four Bunnies' eyes grew wider and their heads wrapped in knots.

Squirrelseed quickly looked at Mrs Bunnie for help, while everyone else was too focused on *The Scroll* to be able to answer Bunnyflower's question.

'An oracle, my love, is something you consult in times of trouble. It allows us to speak to a higher power. To the great governing powers who created and protect this Kingdom as best they can,' Mrs Bunnie informed them, looking from her youngest son to everyone else who was sitting around the table. The company were now looking at Mrs Bunnie as though she were the great gatekeeper of the Kingdom's knowledge.

'So it's like a Christma-caller to the higher powers,' said Hopper, who drew on the only thing he could relate to.

'Almost,' nodded Mrs Bunnie, 'except an oracle will write to you, not speak.'

'But what's it doing here, in Cinnamon Forest?' asked Patch, blinking rapidly. 'Shouldn't it be kept somewhere more important?'

'Well,' said Mrs Bunnie in a mysterious voice. 'It was felt it would be safer here, in a little cottage in Cinnamon Forest, than it would be at the heart of the Kingdom in The Enchantment of Christmas Castle. And so it is. If *The Scroll* had been kept at the castle, then it would have been destroyed this very night, and the Kingdom would have been lost to us forever. As it stands, we now have a chance of saving the Kingdom and the fate of Christmas in this world and on Earth.'

'But Mum, I don't get it. Why do we have to ask some stupid *Scroll* what to do?' asked Patch, tapping his foot on the floor in frustration. 'Can't we just draw up our own plan of attack and go after the Guardian?'

'Oh no, no, no, my love. The Guardian is too powerful now that he has the Staff and Altra,' exclaimed Mrs Bunnie, shaking her head. 'The two must be separated, and it would take a magic gift in order to do it. You see, this is a magical world with hidden codes and rules, and at a time like this it is imperative we understand these. Now gather around and I will consult *The Magic Scroll of Christmas*.'

She then placed both paws on the document and picked it up.

'Oh, Mighty Powers of Christmas. Oh, Protectors of this magical land. Please hear me now,' she said with her eyes closed. 'Our magical Kingdom has been attacked. The Queen and Santa have been kidnapped, and the Altra has been joined to the Staff of Evil. Tell us what we can do to save the Kingdom. Tell us what we must do in order to save Christmas.'

The document gleamed fiercely momentarily, then shimmered with fountains of different colours of light that eventually drained away to reveal a message written in gold dust that reflected in each and every one of the creature's faces. Mrs Bunnie now cleared her throat slightly before she began to read.

This enchanted Kingdom, The Kingdom of Christmas, is bound to the magical Altra. Whoever controls the Altra, controls the entire Kingdom. Now that it has been joined to the Staff of Evil, it must be released if Christmas is to be saved. There is a marble tablet at Mistletoe Falls – a tablet which contains a sacred reading. If this reading is spoken by 'the chosen creatures', its words can release the Altra. This done, the Queen and Santa shall be free and the Kingdom shall be delivered from evil.

'The chosen creatures,' repeated Michael, as the words now disappeared from The Scroll like grains of sand. 'What does it mean by that? Who are the chosen creatures? Do you think that could be us because we're the children of Christmas?'

'I don't know,' murmured Sarah, turning slightly pallid at the thought. 'But look, it hasn't quite finished yet.'

The group now turned their eyes to The Scroll, where a fresh set of writing now appeared.

'The chosen creatures' are creatures with exceptional souls – souls which contain a continuously moving thread of silver, otherwise known as The Essence of Christmas. It is this thread, and this thread alone, that can empower the words on the tablet. So delicate is this thread, that should any spell or curse of evil afflict the bearer, it will snap in half like a sprig of holly, and cease to work its magic.
There are only two creatures left who possess The Essence of Christmas. Creatures who are standing in this very room.

A sparkling silver arrow now appeared on the paper and began spinning round and round, pointing to each and every one of the creatures in turn, until it began to slow down. Slower and slower it went, until finally it split in half and pointed to the only two creatures who could save the Kingdom – Michael and Sarah. The company all gazed for a moment until the document printed the children's names and a myriad of stars came showering over them.

'Oh, good Christmas, it *is* us,' uttered Sarah, trembling slightly, as the stars lit her up like a magic angel.

'Yes, look, and there's more,' said Michael, whose chance to prove himself a hero had finally come.

Fear not, children of Christmas, for you shall not go alone. You must take the Sergeant and the two Reindeer with you for protection.

A parcel will be delivered to you at Christmas Street Station within the hour. This parcel contains the key to unlock the entrance to Mistletoe Falls. Inside you will find the tablet. You must not remove the tablet, but copy its words down, and then read them in unison before the Staff and Altra.

This way and this way only can you save the fate of Christmas.

Now place your left hand on The Scroll and repeat these words:

I do solemnly accept this mighty Quest and will do my utmost to rescue the fate of Christmas.

Sarah and Michael both quivered nervously before drawing a deep breath.

'I do solemnly accept this mighty Quest and will do my utmost to rescue the fate of Christmas.'

This spoken, a gold shower of light fell upon the children and wrought its way around them as though binding them to its words.

Good Luck, children, and a word of advice before you go.

Do not contact your father via the North Wind. It is too dangerous to do so in times of Darkness. We, the Keepers of the Scroll, shall contact him using a more 'secure' means of delivery. He shall be ordered to a hideout nearby, where he is to stay until the Quest has succeeded.

Good Luck, and may the Star of Christmas guide you.

With that, the words disappeared, and *The Scroll* then rolled itself up and sealed itself shut before landing with a thud on the kitchen table. The creatures now stared in silence for a few minutes as their eyes adjusted to the change in light.

'A more 'secure' means of delivery,' said Michael, knitting his eyebrows together and looking most dissatisfied with this piece of information. 'What the devil does it mean by that? Why can't it be more specific?'

'Michael, if *The Scroll* has spoken, you must trust and accept it,' urged Blitzen, with authority. 'At least this way it has less chance of being intercepted.'

'And how do you know? They haven't even stated what method of delivery they're going to use. Open the document again! I want to ask it to be more specific.'

'Look, Michael, we can't open *The Scroll* again. Once it's sealed shut, that's it. If it promised to inform your father for you, then it will. Leave it in their hands. There is a bounty of secret methods of delivery at their disposal. Have some faith, will you? Now I really think we ought to make a move for Christmas Street Station. We don't want the Snow Wolves to get there first.'

Michael huffed for a moment, wrapping his hands around the letter that was placed in his pocket, with a reluctance to let it go. He wasn't happy about this, but he would think it over before he made up his mind.

'Alright then, I suppose we'd better be on our way. Rally yourselves. I take it I'm in charge,' announced the Prince of Christmas, finally removing his hand from his pocket.

'And what makes you think that?' demanded Blitzen, raising his eyebrows slightly and squaring up to the young boy.

'Well, I'm the Prince of Christmas. I'm automatically in charge, am I not?'

'No, Michael - you are 10 years old and ill-equipped to head such a dangerous Quest, in spite of your impressive achievements to date. No, I shall head this Quest. At least, with my years of experience, we're less likely to fall into any blunders.'

Michael turned quite red for a moment. He really wasn't getting his way at all tonight. But after a few protests from the others, he soon sucked in his bottom lip.

'Alright then, fine. But I want you to know that I'm not particularly happy about this. And there are one or two ground rules which I insist upon if this is to be the case.'

'And what are they?' asked Blitzen, raising his eyes somewhat impatiently at the boy.

'One - if I disagree with you, then I'm not obeying you, and there's nothing you can say or do to try and make me.'

'And two?' asked Blitzen, looking slightly amused now at this childish outburst.

'And two, if you get on my nerves, I'll call you *Stiff Ears*,' added Michael in a rather spoilt tone.

'Charming. Now then, shall we make a move for Christmas Street Station?' suggested Blitzen authoritatively.

'Oh yes, good Christmas, you'd better get going,' exclaimed Mrs Bunnie. '*The Scroll* said the parcel would be there in ten minutes. It'll take you almost as long as that to get there.'

'But what about Rudolph?' asked Sarah, looking over at the celebrity, who had no chance of coming around anytime soon. 'He's still out cold. Can we wake him up?'

'Actually, I have a suggestion to make that I'm sure *The Scroll* can overlook,' said Blitzen. 'I suggest that we fetch the parcel from Christmas Street Station *now* and then return to the Oak Tree for the night. It's dark outside, and it'll be far better if we start the Quest in the morning after a good night's sleep. Do you agree?'

'Yes, alright. That sounds fair,' said Michael, who liked the idea of a whole night's sleep to prepare himself. 'Red Nose can join us in the morning.'

'Very well, then,' said Blitzen, opening the curtain slightly and peering through. Outside it was silent - deathly almost. No light, no creatures, just a thick dense night of fear and uncertainty. He took a step out, followed by Squirrelseed and the two children, before shaking his antlers and returning to normal size. The door to Cosy Cottage had now shut.

'Jump aboard, everyone, and hold on tight. It can get quite bumpy near the floating tracks.'

He then dipped his hoof into the little brown bag that Mrs Bunnie had given him and showered himself with the gold Reindeer dust. He took off and was soaring through the air high above Cinnamon Forest, higher still through the clouds, as he headed northeast, in the direction of Christmas Street Station.

10-The Parcel at Christmas Street Station

When the Quest arrived at the station in the clouds, it was deserted, and stacks of luggage lay abandoned on the platform. News of the annex had evidently reached there and the neighbouring lands, although the floating lampposts were still lit, as were the sconces inside the station waiting rooms. The tracks themselves also provided light, since they were made of Aurora Borealis, and danced magically along the clouds.

'If it wasn't for the suitcases, you'd never know there was a war on, would you?' remarked Sergeant Squirrelseed, as Blitzen landed on the floating platform, and the Christmacreatures alighted.

'No, not really,' agreed Michael, noticing how the heavy clouds obscured much of the Kingdom. 'Although the Christmas clock looks different,' he added, pointing to the archway above the entrance to the main waiting room. The clock, which normally wore a smile on its face, now had its eyes shut tight and its lips cast into a frown. Snow also fell from underneath the station shelter, which only happened when there was a Christmacrisis.

'Hey look, why is that blocked off up there?' asked Sarah, pointing to a large wooden gate directly ahead to the north with the words **NO PASSAGE** written in cruel ice.

'Oh, that's the old train track that used to run through the Mountains of the North. It was open long before you were born,' said Blitzen, looking up. 'We had to shut it when the Guardian was locked inside there and open a new one.'

'Goodness,' exclaimed Sarah, peering through the fog beyond the barrier so that she could just make out the jagged, harsh formation of the Northern Mountains. 'It's incredibly eerie. I don't think I'd have ridden the train through there even before the Guardian inhabited the Mountains.'

'Yes, well that's because you're a big wuss, Sarah. Now do you think any of these parcels are for us?' added Michael, scanning the luggage.

'I don't think so, Michael. *The Scroll* said that yours would arrive by train,' Blitzen assured him. 'If it's gone to this much trouble of getting you a key to help with the Quest, it's not going to just abandon it any old where on the station.'

'I suppose you're right,' said Michael, catching his reflection in the window. He didn't *look* like much of a hero at Christmas present. He would need to buck up at bit if he was going to win this.

Sergeant Squirrelseed, meanwhile, was perched on the candy cane-shaped signals, and pricked his ears keenly in the cold air.

'What are you doing, Sergeant?' asked Sarah, who was beginning to shiver. Indeed, they were a good 200ft high above the Kingdom, and the air was definitely colder there than it was down below.

'I'm listening,' said the Sergeant, placing his paw to his lips. 'I can hear howls coming from the direction of Mistletown. The Snow Wolves must have already reached there.'

'I think we'd better wait inside until the train comes. We don't want the Snow Wolves to know we're here.'

Blitzen and the children now entered a small, sconce - lit room that stood beneath the clock tower, while Squirrelseed dusted away their footprints with his tail. This was the station master's room (which incidentally belonged to Mr Badger from Cinnamon Forest) and it was certainly very cosy. It was warm and homely with large, scalloped, red curtains and a red velvet clothed table at the centre, on which stood an untouched pot of tea and a plate of cupcakes. Several long mirrors were placed amidst the wall panels, making the room look larger, and a grand open fireplace stood next to a Christmas tree decorated with stockings and boughs of holly.

'Check in all the stockings,' ordered Blitzen, scouring the room. 'If any Christmascreature has tried to contact us, they may have left something inside.'

As the children checked the stockings, one by one, they found nothing of great importance – some sweets, some cinnamon cigars, a button, - until suddenly Sarah found a note placed inside an icicle in the lining of the last one.

'Look, Blitzen, I've found something,' she said, handing it to the Reindeer. Blitzen's hooves proved too cumbersome for him to merely pull out the letter, so he had to smash the icicle against the table before being able to release it.

'Good Christmas, it's from Clarinda, from the Gates of the Air,' exclaimed Blitzen with surprise.

'Really? What's it say?' asked Michael, who had quite forgotten about the plight of the Snowflakes in all of this.

Call of Christmas Distress, began Blitzen.

Our Kingdom has been attacked. The Forest of Magic Lanterns has been locked inside an eerie mist, with the Snowflakes trapped inside. I, Clarinda, am outside the Forest and I am at a loss what to do.

'Hey look, there's more,' said Michael, pointing to the back of the letter. 'See how the paper's gone blotchy? That means she's used magic ink. There must be some kind of hidden message on it too.'

'Why, good Christmas, you're right,' cried Blitzen, turning the paper over and sprinkling it with a smattering of gold Reindeer dust.

The children now gathered around, intrigued to see what the rest of it said.

Dear Blitzen,

The Scroll sent word to me about the Quest. I will get the Snowflakes to assist you as soon as they are free. I am currently travelling to Whispering Island to find a potion that will release them. Good luck!

'She knows,' exclaimed Sarah, feeling somewhat more confident about this.

'Yes,' said Blitzen. 'But this letter must now go onto the fire. We don't want to leave any trace of it.'

The children agreed, as Sarah examined the notice board.

'Hey, look at this,' she added, as a dusty old newspaper article caught her eye. 'I've found something else too.'

Local Snowflake goes in search of The Testament of the Snowflakes.

'Good Christmas - I think I've heard about this. Lysander, wasn't it? Did he ever find it?'

'I don't know, I'm afraid, Sarah. He left some 30 years ago and has never come back. If you ask me though, he probably perished on his way across the Icy Plains.'

Both children stared for a moment as they pondered the implications, but their thoughts were suddenly cut short as Sergeant Squirrelseed came tottering up to them.

'The train's coming,' he announced with a faint smile.

Blitzen and the children immediately jumped up and walked out onto the platform to be greeted by an enormous cloud of sparkling smoke. It caused them to cough and splutter, but as the cloud retreated, it revealed a large steam train with a string of red and gold carriages all trimmed up with festive holly. **The Christmas Express** was written in silver writing on the side, yet there was no driver aboard, nor were there any passengers seated in the carriages.

'If it wasn't so frilly-looking it would be like a phantom ghost train,' observed Michael, looking at it with a fixed stare.

'I say, look at the window of the first carriage!' exclaimed Squirrelseed, pointing over with an unsteady arm.

Michael looked up to see the carriage window wind itself down, as out of it floated a sizable green parcel tied with a red bow and addressed to Prince Michael and Princess Sarah. It floated directly up to them, at which point Sarah picked it up and the cloud of smoke swiftly rose again, taking the train with it.

'Careful with it, Sarah. You don't want to drop it off the floating station,' warned Michael, as they hurried back inside the Captain's cabin.

'Yes, thank you, munchkin, I would never have thought of that until you pointed it out to me,' retorted Sarah indignantly.

Once inside, Sarah eagerly pulled off the bow, as though she were unwrapping a Christmas present, to reveal an envelope inside bearing a note.

To Prince Michael and Princess Sarah.

Thank you for accepting the Quest to Save Christmas. The key to access Mistletoe Falls can be found inside. To release it, please answer this selection of riddles.

'Riddles. What riddles?' asked Michael, as Sarah turned the paper over and looked everywhere inside the box, which seemed otherwise empty.

'Good Christmas, look, there's more writing appearing on the letter,' said Squirrelseed, as a new set of words appeared.

The children looked down to see a single line now appear before them in a sparkling silver dust.

The sky at night would not be bright
If I did not bless it with my light.

'Why, that's got to be the Star of Christmas, hasn't it?' ventured Michael, appealing to his sister for help.

'Perhaps,' said Sarah, unconvinced. 'Or maybe it could be the *moon*?'

As soon as she had spoken these words, the bottom of the box peeled back slightly to reveal something glistening inside.

'My goodness. What is it?' asked Sarah, trying to stick her hand inside, only to find that the gap was too small.

'I don't know, but look, here's another riddle',

I fall from every living thing,
Sometimes a touch of magic I bring.
One form you could not reach Earth without,
Another, be able to fly about.

'What is that? Reindeer dust?' asked Michael, but there was no movement inside the box.

'Try just 'dust',' said Blitzen, helping them out.

'Alright, dust,' answered Sarah, and once again the cardboard retreated revealing even more of the glistening object beneath.

'Ok, last one,' cried Sarah, who had now grown hot and flustered with all the excitement.

The greatest and most exciting night,
Whispering these words has the power to excite.
It brings every child in the universe delight,
It's the one you must save with all your might.

'Why, that's got to be Christmas Eve.'

No sooner had Sarah spoken these words than the entire base of the box shrivelled up to reveal a small, silver key with an instruction attached to it.

Place the key on the spot marked X and the way to the falls
will open before you.

'Is that going to be difficult to find?' asked Michael, who couldn't see why an ordinary keyhole wouldn't suffice.

'No – the key will probably lead us to it,' said Blitzen, observing how it sparkled along the handle and edges as though it were a gift from Heaven itself. 'But you must make sure you keep it safe. Don't lose it, whatever you do.'

'Yes, alright,' said Sarah, now wrapping it in a handkerchief and putting it in the front pocket of her red coat.

'So that's it then? We can go now?' asked Michael, looking around and wondering if there was more.

The Quest went to make a move, when suddenly Sarah turned towards the fireplace, noticing that the flames were dancing in a way she had *not* seen them doing earlier on.

'Wha wha what's going on?' she asked, as the fireplace began to shake.

Squirrelseed rushed over to the window, when suddenly the sconces went out and the fire extinguished itself, leaving the room in complete darkness.

'Oh no,' exclaimed the Sergeant, stiffening in fear. 'There's only one creature who has the ability to do that.'

'Who?' demanded Sarah, as her eyes glittered in the dark.

'The Snow Wolves,' returned Squirrelseed, as his tail began to quiver.

The company looked panicked as they could now hear growling in the distance, tearing up the night air.

'Oh my goodness, we've got to get out of here,' shrieked Sarah, now clutching the key. 'We've got to get out of here right away.'

'We can't get out of here, Sarah, we don't have time,' barked Blitzen, noticing how the yellow glow was fast approaching the Captain's office.

'Well then, we hide,' commanded Michael, scouring the room in darkness. 'It's not cowardly under the circumstances. They catch us now, we'll *never* get to Mistletoe Falls. Everybody find a hideout and get to it.'

Everyone immediately obeyed - the children dived under the table, Squirrelseed hid inside a stocking, while Blitzen clambered up the chimney and managed to hold himself in place by latching his antlers between two bricks.

A Snow Wolf stood directly outside the Captain's office, and they had no way of knowing if he was acting alone or had company. There was little time to speculate, however, as he was soon inside the room, his eyes lighting up the darkness like the burning fires of Hell.

His claws sunk into the floorboards with every inch he took. Squirrelseed clutched his legs tightly and shut his eyes, fearing that the Snow Wolf might see him wobbling inside the stocking. The Snow Wolf did not seem to notice however, and was more interested in smashing up the mantelpiece and knocking the Christmas tree over. He then turned his attention to the table and pulled at the table cloth, before releasing it from his claws, leaving a small gap between the cloth and the floor. Now for the first time the children saw him, and Sarah clutched tightly at the magic key in fear. He looked more fierce than any of the Snow Wolves they had seen at the castle. More savage and cruel. His white fur was scratched and soaked with blood, and his claws were like deadly talons. Yet it was the strange, luminous glow that shone from his eyes that she found most distracting. They lit up the room in a way that could almost induce hypnosis. She hoped there weren't more on the way. If so, they were well and truly done for.

The mirror directly behind the Snow Wolf did not help matters either, since it seemed to magnify the glow, rendering it more intense. Still he continued to tear up the room, slashing cushions and shaking the Christmas tree in the hope that some unwitting Christmascreature might fall out.

Then he did something remarkably strange. He took a frozen candle out from his satchel and placed it on a sideboard next to the fireplace, before looking around. Convinced that he still had missed something, he then shut the door tightly, and as he did so, a thick ice formed along the edges.

Sounds from the outside now disappeared, and Michael and Sarah stayed under the table for a moment, their hearts pounding.

'What's he doing?' whispered Sarah, as the room seemed to take on an uncanny stillness. 'Why did he leave that candle there?'

'I don't know,' returned Michael, trembling slightly. 'But it feels as if the outside world has disappeared.'

Michael now slowly emerged from beneath the table, closely followed by Sarah, to find that, to his surprise, a whole range of other oddities had been caused by the placement of the frozen candle. The hands on the clock had stopped firmly at a quarter to 9, and the window had entirely frozen up so that nothing could be seen from it. The mirror too, although gashed into distortion, revealed no reflection of the children, nor of any living thing inside the room. It was as if they did not exist.

'What's happening to us?' asked Michael, walking up to the mirror to see no trace of his existence at all, but only the solid objects all around him. 'Where am I? Why am I not appearing in the mirror?'

'We've been frozen in time,' came the voice of Sergeant Squirrelseed, as he suddenly emerged from his Christmas stocking, and similarly observed the state of affairs that Prince Michael had.

'What are you talking about, Double S? How can we have been frozen in time? We're still moving about with complete freedom,' contended Michael, moving his arms around on purpose so as to prove his point.

'It's the curse of the frozen candle,' exclaimed Squirrelseed, walking up to the table and pointing it out. 'It's an ancient method of northern torture. Once a frozen candle is placed inside a room and the door is shut, that entire room is frozen in time. The clocks stop, time ceases to move, yet the creatures inside continue to move about, creating the illusion that they are still free.'

'But that doesn't make any sense. I *am* free. I continue to exist,' argued Michael, who was utterly determined to try and force a reflection of himself from the mirror.

'Well – not really you don't, because you have been taken *out* of time. Any actions you do whilst trapped in this frozen bubble have no consequence. Here, let me show you. Try and open that door, for example.'

Michael walked over to the door and pulled on the handle, only to find that he was immediately shot back across the room to the point where he started from.

'See what I mean? Now try and pick up that cup and saucer.'

Michael tried again, only to find that the cup and saucer flew out of his hands and landed back on the table in the exact same spot.

'What - so I've got the illusion of freedom even though in reality I'm in complete and utter stalemate!'

'I'm afraid so,' Sergeant Squirrelseed confirmed, with a quiver in his voice. 'It used to drive ancient prisoners insane. It was far more effective than if they were physically frozen, for it's the illusion that ultimately destroys them.'

'But how are we supposed to get out?' asked Sarah, thinking that if everything they did in the room was being simultaneously undone, then they really were doomed to be trapped forever.

'The room must be opened by a creature from the outside. As soon as that happens, the frozen candle crumbles, and time and the normal state of existence return. Only then, and then only will you be put back into time.'

'But how the devil would....?'

The next thing Michael stopped talking as the door burst open and the hardy figure of Blitzen appeared.

The candle, just as Squirrelseed had said, simultaneously shattered, the children's reflections returned to the mirror, and the hands of the clock began to move again, only this time they jumped forward 5 minutes to catch up with the state of time in the rest of the Kingdom. It was now 10 minutes to 9. They had lost a full five minutes of their lives.

'Did you break it?' asked Michael, who was so concerned with having his own free will back that he didn't think to ask Blitzen where he had come from.

'Yes - everything's returned to normal,' said Blitzen, walking into the room. 'Here, try something just to check.'

Michael didn't like to embrace his destructive side, but he picked up the cup and saucer and hurled them at the wall, just the same. The action was completed, and they smashed into tiny shards, causing Michael to smile and sigh heavily.

'Oh, thank Christmas for that! I thought I was going to lose my mind then for a minute. I hope to God that I never encounter a situation like *that* again. How the devil did you manage to get out of the room in the first place anyway, Blitzen?' asked Michael, clutching his chest slightly at the state of panic he had just experienced.

'Well, when the Snow Wolf came in, I hid inside the chimney, and as he started tearing up the room, I climbed up onto the roof and out of it altogether, with the intention of surprising him from behind. Of course, by the time I got down here, he had already left, and from the window I could see you were all frozen in a freeze frame.'

'Wait – so from the outside we looked like we were frozen?' asked Sarah, looking perplexed.

'Yes – like absolute statues. It was really quite alarming.'

'But where did the Snow Wolf go?' asked Squirrelseed, now fearing he could return again.

'It seems as if he's gone to get back-up. We've got to get out of here, quickly. Sarah, do you still have the key?'

'Yes – here,' answered Sarah, partially revealing it from her coat pocket, before concealing it again.

'Excellent. Well then, let's go. The sooner we get to the hideout, the better.'

The company agreed, and after a quick safety check of the platform by Squirrelseed, they left the Captain's cabin - Sarah first, Blitzen second and Michael following behind. As the Prince was about to shut the door, a sharp gust flew over the fireplace and caused him to stop. The North Wind! He hesitated. If his father didn't get word of the attack in time, there's no telling what might happen to him. Who's to say that the Guardian's followers weren't already on their way to arrest him and place him inside a frozen candle? He didn't think his father should have to endure that. He quickly removed the letter he had written earlier from his pocket and showered it with pink and gold Reindeer dust.

'You must deliver this safely to my father,' he whispered, standing beneath the fireplace and holding it up to the gust. 'You must deliver it quickly and you must not let me down.' The letter stayed in his hand only for a second and then, with a mighty swoosh, it was gone, attached to the clutches of the wind, and carried high into the sky. Michael ran out of the cabin in time to see it disappear from view, before catching up with the others.

They were flying towards the hideout - and they didn't have much time. For across the clouds in the distance, the Snow Wolves were coming back, and there were many more of them this time.

11-The Frozen Castle

Meanwhile, far across the Kingdom, The Enchantment of Christmas Castle now stood utterly ravaged by evil, with every last vision of 'fairy tale' clawed into the enveloping nightmare of gothic horror. The towers were frozen, the windows were cracked, and as a result, torrents of snow blew in through the slits, leaving an ever increasing blanket of snow on the castle floor. The Court itself was completely transformed. The once elegant gold and crimson cushioned throne was now a cold stone slab engraved with frost. The fireplace was bare, the clock had turned cold, and the multifarious boughs of holly, ivy and mistletoe that had generously decked the hall were now black, shrivelled and frozen inside pipes of ice. The Guardian sat amidst this frozen wasteland, cradling his newly won weapon, when the door was swiftly opened and his sorcerer walked in.

'Good evening, Heinous. How nice to see you settled,' bowed the sorcerer, as he slithered across the icy floor. 'You sent for me, did you not?'

The Guardian's eyes flickered momentarily with the palest of yellows, as he now hid the Staff and Altra beneath his cloak.

'Yes, I did, Snooks - about half an hour ago. I wish to know how you are progressing with your anti-Christmas potions?' he asked, now tapping his shrivelled and talon-like fingers together.

'Oh, they are coming along exceedingly well, Your Heinous. I have one here I can demonstrate for you, if you wish. It is called a *frozen kiss*,' said the sorcerer, as his demonic wings rose high above him, still concealed beneath his indigo cloak.

The Guardian lowered his head in silence, and without further ado, the sorcerer drew back his cloak to reveal a little Elf he had acquired earlier from the castle prisons. The Elf looked petrified as Snooks now began to swirl the air around him with his fingers, producing one of his famous illusions. The victim looked on confused as the illusion gradually took the shape of a Wish Biscuit - a red and green holly-shaped Wish Biscuit – that drifted straight up to his nose. It smelled delicious and looked uncannily real, so unable to overcome his temptation, the little Elf reached out and grabbed it. But as he did so, the biscuit now melted, and a lace of frost wrapt its way around him before erasing him from existence. Snooks then pulled back his cloak in a bat-like fashion and bowed before his audience, while his own resident snow spider crawled menacingly across his shoulders.

'You see, Heinous, it is not yet finished,' he began. 'But when it is, it will be most deadly. 'No creature of Christmas will be able to withstand it.'

'Excellent,' breathed the Guardian, in an unsettling tone of monotony. 'And the prisoners?'

'All are either inside the castle dungeons or in the Mountains, Heinous,' bowed Snooks.

He was about to demonstrate another anti-Christmas potion when the Courtroom door was suddenly flung back and in burst a Snow Wolf by the name of Snow Claw.

'Heinous,' he panted, swiftly crossing the threshold and sinking his claws into the ice, like deadly talons. 'Heinous, I have some urgent news from Christmas Street Station - I have got Snow Blood and his team on the silver medallion. He says he must talk to you at once.'

The Guardian looked up, as his eyes flashed sharply. 'Well, get on with it then - did I hire you to be inefficient?' he bit acerbically, as the indigo sorcerer folded his arms with interest.

The Snow Wolf bowed and quickly removed a medallion from around his neck, at which point a beam of light shot up into the air and produced an image of Snow Blood standing in the Captain's office, where he had only moments ago activated a frozen candle.

'Heinous,' he said through a slightly distorted reception. 'Heinous, I have some terrible news, but I may be able to rectify it if you give me chance.'

'News? What news?' seethed the Guardian, sitting upright and crushing a piece of the frozen throne beneath his claw-like fingers. 'Have you found the Queen's children and the missing Reindeer?'

'Yes, Heinous - I just had them. I locked them in this very room using a frozen candle, but somehow they managed to escape.'

'They what!' roared the Guardian, as his fury rose up to the ceiling of the Courtroom and clawed and gashed at every nook and cranny in the castle.

'I am sorry, Heinous - I will track them down right away. It is virtually unheard of for prisoners to break out of the frozen candle,' continued the Snow Wolf, now looking quite tame and abashed before the wrath of the Guardian.

'Maybe you should place Snow Blood inside a frozen candle, Heinous, as punishment for his gross disservice and miscalculation,' bit Snooks, as he slithered towards the Guardian. 'In other Kingdoms such an act would not be tolerated - his head would be mounted on the battlements.'

'Snooks, please. I can rectify this,' pleaded the Snow Wolf, as the backdrop of the Captain's cabin shimmered eerily behind him. 'I believe I know the reason they were here. You see, I believe they are part of a

Quest to save Christmas, and they were at Christmas Street Station for the sole purpose of collecting something.'

The words pricked across the Courtroom as the Guardian's eyes flashed a cruel yellow.

'How exactly do you *know* this, Snow Blood? Since when have you been endowed with magic powers?' demanded the Guardian, his voice laden with impatience.

'I haven't, Heinous. I merely found *this*,' he said, holding up the box that the key had arrived in, along with the list of riddles and instructions.

To Prince Michael and Princess Sarah, breathed the Guardian aloud.

Thank you for accepting the Quest to Save Christmas. The key to access Mistletoe Falls lies inside. To release it, please answer this selection of riddles.

'What else do you know, Snow Blood?' continued the Guardian, as intrigue now replaced his rage. 'What else do you know about this precious little Quest?'

'Nothing more about the Quest, Heinous, at darkness present - I have only just discovered this note. I will do whatever you desire in order to hinder their progress.'

The Guardian said nothing, but turned to Snooks for more answers.

'What do you know about Mistletoe Falls, Snooks? What secrets could this key be unlocking? I know nothing about Mistletoe Falls.'

'A great deal, I am afraid, Heinous; I have been trying to crack its protective charms for many years now. I am quite confident however, now that this Quest has been set in motion, that the information should be more easily attainable.'

'Excellent. Well, get to it at once. I want you to find out everything you can about this Quest. I did not spend 11 years locked up in the Mountains only to be overthrown on the first night,' declared the Guardian, his words spoken with hot breath.

'Of course, Heinous. I go at once,' hastened Snooks, swishing his indigo cloak behind him and turning on his heel to leave.

'You, Snow Blood,' continued the Guardian. 'Search for anything else you can find. I want you back here within the hour, in which time Snow Claw here will have assembled a team of his finest followers.'

'Yes, Heinous,' answered Snow Blood, bowing before his master.

With that, the image disappeared, and Snow Claw promptly picked up the medallion and placed it around his neck.

*　　　　*　　　　*　　　　*

Meanwhile, down in the castle prisons, the Reindeer and a handful of Elves and Snowflakes sat in a state of dismay as they remained locked behind a set of iron bars.

'They can't keep us locked in here like this,' complained Comet, as he shook the frost from his antlers. 'We're the creatures of Christmas. They've got to let us out sooner or later.'

'Don't worry, Comet. Blitzen's going to come for us. You know he got away,' said the Snowbelle, Luella, whose wings were rapidly losing their sparkle.

'Sssshhhh. Listen. Can you hear that?' asked Dora, the maid, suddenly, as a sorrowful lament drifted like an eerie lullaby along the night air.

'Hear what?' asked the other Reindeer, startled. *They* had heard merely the wind.

'Sshhh. Listen. Listen! There it is again.'

'*Help me. Help me,*' came a hollow voice, sounding otherworldly and yet so near. '*Save me. Please save me.*'

'Good Christmas. Where's it coming from?'

'Why, somewhere up above us! Somewhere behind the castle wall,' observed Cupid, as he placed his ears against the cold walls.

'*Help me. Please help me,*' came the mantra again. '*Save me. Please save me.*'

'What are we going to do?' asked Comet, looking afraid. 'Do you think it's a trap?'

'I don't know – it sounds sincere enough,' added Dora. 'But whatever we do, we should wait until the Snow Wolf leaves for his meeting. He'll be back soon. We'll sort something out when he's asleep.'

12-A Night Underneath the Oak Tree

Back in Cinnamon Forest, thoughts and feelings were running wild. However, at least for the time being the children and the Woodland Creatures were safe. The hideout underneath the Oak Tree was certainly very cosy, given that it was underground. The slide at the entrance led directly onto a fluffy mat in a spacious and homely sitting room that communicated with an open-plan kitchen. To the left of the kitchen stood a door which led to a long passageway, off which branched numerous bedrooms and storage cupboards. Of course, the underground hideout had no windows, so naturally a great deal of effort had been made to make it look as light and cheery as possible. The walls and the ceiling were made of dirt, but wooden planks had been placed along the floor, and a few wooden pillars and beams were built in to support it. Attached to these were generous boughs of holly and ivy, while in the right hand corner, next to the slide, stood a large Christmas tree that had been decorated with white, sparkling lights. Christmas pictures had been painted in various coloured chalks along the pillars and beams, and a few cushioned seats were placed in a circle at the centre of the lounge to form a communal seating area.

At this moment a tasty meal was being prepared by Mrs Bunnie and Mrs Prickles in the large kitchen. The hideout already had a generous supply of food in the storage hamper, but as everyone had managed to bring a little something down with them, the chefs were able to cook up a real feast. There were chocolate star cakes, jam sandwiches, iced doughnuts, crispy cream biscuits, Christmas cake, chocolate log, sugar bread, mince pies and cinnamon pies. The Christmacreatures all sat down excitedly at the table to tuck into this hearty spread.

When everyone had finished their main course, Mrs Bunnie got up.

'Right then. Time for the pièce de résistance,' she announced, scampering across to the kitchen counter and picking up a large tray full of biscuits and a warm, spicy jug of punch.

'What have we got, dear?' enquired her husband, Mr Bunnie, who actually looked more like a Hare than a Rabbit. He was long and thin, with tall, stiff ears and a sandy-coloured coat. A few long black whiskers sprouted outwards from his pastel pink nose, on top of which were perched a pair of small, round spectacles.

'We've got Wish Biscuits and Cinnamon Punch,' replied Mrs Bunnie, as she placed the treats down on the table.

'That ought to cheer us up nicely,' smiled Mr Bunnie, his whiskers twitching as he did so.

The smaller Bunnies looked down at the selection of Wish Biscuits in awe. There were so many of them, all of different shapes, colours and sizes, that they really did not know which ones to choose.

'Do you mind if we go first, Princess Sarah?' asked Patch, who had been growing increasingly more restless since his spell underground.

'Not at all,' answered Sarah, giving the Christmacub a pat. 'You need something to get you through this terrible war.'

Patch beamed before jumping onto the table and selecting a red, holly-shaped biscuit. 'I wish for a gingerbread house,' he announced, nibbling the biscuit voraciously. As his biscuit disappeared into his tummy, there was a strange sensation in the air. A cluster of sparkling clouds suddenly appeared and then dispelled to reveal an absolutely delectable gingerbread house, not much different in size to Patch himself. It had candy cane doors and windows, with chocolate buttons and sugared almonds on the roof, and whipped cream and icing trimming along the edges.

'Oh wow, that's amazing, Patch. Can I look inside?' asked Hopper, peering in through the sugary glass windows.

'Sure. But don't knock anything over,' ordered Patch, who was already squeezing himself down the chimney.

'Oh, if only we could all have a little gingerbread house,' thought Sarah, as she now looked at the plate of Wish Biscuits and held it tightly for a moment. 'Hmm let's see. I wish for something extra to help me on the Quest,' she said, biting into the biscuit.

There was a loud POOF, followed by a little cloud of pink smoke, and there suddenly appeared a palm-sized silver compact with a little red ribbon for a clutch.

'What is it?' asked Sarah, perplexed, as she turned it around in her hands.

'It's a compass, pigtails,' explained Michael, opening it up to reveal an arrow pointing NW by W and a picture of the Falls at the tip. 'I use them in adventuring classes all the time. You would, too, if you were as far ahead on the royal programme as I am,' he added cockily, pulling the plate towards him.

'Well, I suppose I'd better wish for something if *you* have. I wish for something grand and mighty, something befitting a hero.'

He bit down firmly into the biscuit, and as he did so, a cloud whirled like a tornado, out of which dropped a sheathed dagger that fell directly onto his lap.

'Wowww,' exclaimed Hopper, staring at the magnificent object cased in its green leather scabbard. 'It's one of the daggers of Christmas.'

'Unsheathe it. Unsheathe it!' ordered Carrot Top, getting very excited now and clapping his paws.

Michael was taken aback. He had never held a real weapon before -

all the ones he used in his adventuring classes were made out of wood - so he pulled the leather scabbard off hastily to reveal a spotless silver dagger that glittered poignantly in the light of the hideout. On the handle was embedded a clear jewel, which at times seemed to repel the light, and at others sparkled like electricity. The creatures crowded around the weapon in awe, as Michael's grip on the handle began to tighten.

'It's really quite something, isn't it,' he remarked in smug fascination. 'Sort of puts your little compass to shame.'

To this, Sarah merely poked out her tongue, and Mrs Bunnie picked up a plate of Wish Biscuits to keep the party moving.

'Alright then. Who's next?' she asked.

'Ooh, I'll go if I may,' squeaked Trixitail, reaching forward for a pink, heart-shaped biscuit.

'Hmm. I wish for, ooh, I wish for a beautiful fur muff to keep me warm in this difficult time,' she said, as she nibbled swiftly through her treat. As the biscuit disappeared, a shower of pink hearts fell gracefully around her and joined together to form a soft muff which landed in her lap.

'Oh, how wonderful,' she cried, as she slid her paws through it. 'Ooh, this will do nicely.'

'Oh, there's lovely,' smiled Mrs Bunnie. 'Now then, my turn. Oh dear, which one shall I pick?' she asked, as she eyed the eclectic assortment of biscuits. 'Aha,' she said, catching sight of the one she wanted. 'I think I'll choose this one.' Mrs Bunnie then reached for a small purple teapot and bit into it before closing her eyes tightly. 'I wish for a nice, new, cooking apron to wear inside the hideout,' she said.

A few twinkling stars appeared in the air, out of which dropped two little robins carrying, between their beaks, a red and white apron with the name *Mrs Bunnie* embroidered on the front. The birds then tied the apron around the recipient's waist before dissolving into a little shower of stardust.

'Oh, this is so magical,' enthused Sarah, clapping her hands together in sheer delight.

'Ooh my turn, my turn, my turn,' cried Bunnyflower, as he rushed forward to grab the biscuit tray.

'Now, just a minute, Son,' snapped Mr Bunnie, pulling his youngest Christmacub back by the tail. 'Wait your turn. I do believe that Rudolph was going to pick a biscuit.'

Rudolph, who was seated next to Mrs Bunnie, and was perched for his turn, gushed a little at these words.

'That's ok, Mr Bunnie. Let the little dude go next if he wants to.'

'Alright,' cried Bunnyflower, who broke free of his father's grip and dived straight back onto the table again.

'Bunnyflower, get off the tray,' scolded Hopper, poking his younger brother, who shuffled around on the table trying to choose a biscuit.

'Shut up, Hopper,' he cried, eyeing the biscuits one by one.

'Which one are you going to pick, Master Bunnyflower?' asked Sergeant Squirrelseed, who was eyeing the plate rather fondly himself.

'Ummmm.... this one,' announced Bunnyflower, as he snatched up an orange snowman and bounced back to his seat.

The little Bunny stuffed the entire biscuit into his mouth in one go, and began munching it furiously as he announced his wish: 'I wiff for a fower of Elf Mbopfs,' he said, spraying small bits of Wish Biscuit everywhere.

'You wish for a what?' asked his father, half mockingly.

Bunnyflower took a big gulp before repeating his wish again. 'I said I wish for a great big shower of Elf Pops,' he repeated gleefully.

There was a small rumble above his head, and Bunnyflower opened his mouth wide as a little cloud suddenly appeared. The cloud then exploded into hundreds of tiny green Elf Pops that fell, ten at a time, into the greedy little Bunny's mouth.

'Ha ha, look how fat his cheeks have grown,' chuckled Carrot Top, as Bunnyflower struggled to hold all the sweets in his mouth.

'Bunnyflower, only swallow a few at a time,' his mother reprimanded, as the rest of the group fell about laughing.

The Elf Pops then began to burst, one by one, and Bunnyflower leapt high into the air with every BANG, like a manic Jack-in-the-box.

'Ha ha. Well, that will teach you for being so greedy, Son,' chuckled his father, as Bunnyflower swallowed the last of his Elf pops and finally landed back on his seat.

'Oh dear, oh dear,' laughed Mrs Bunnie, wiping a tear from her eye. 'Well, that certainly has cheered us up nicely.'

Next up it was Rudolph, who really couldn't wait any longer, and picked up a gold and red cracker.

'You know, the crackers always give the best gifts,' stated Rudolph, snapping the cracker in half so that a crackle of lightning flickered in between the two halves of the biscuit.

'What are you doing?' asked Sarah, looking perplexed. 'I thought you had to bite into it first.'

'Oh, sure you do, with most of them,' explained Rudolph. 'But crackers are special. You see, if you break them in half first, like a real cracker, then you get two wishes. Here, watch this now.'

Rudolph then lifted the first piece of the cracker and popped it into his mouth.

'I wish for a Christmacocktail,' he said, gulping down his half a biscuit.

A small tornado whizzed around in the centre of the table and then took the shape of a cocktail glass containing a pink Dashing Daiquiri with a fiery sparkler on top.

'Oh wow, that's so cool,' exclaimed Carrot Top, as his eyes were struck by the little needles of fire that danced wildly on the sparkler.

'Is it alcoholic?' asked Michael, eyeing the colourful potion naughtily.

'Oh sure it is, Princey. I need sumthin to help me through this war.'

'Well, come on then, Red Nose, let me have some. It's very rude not to offer some to your Prince and co-Quester,' blurted Michael, reaching his hand out to grab the glass.

'Leave that cocktail alone, Prince Michael. You're enough of a handful as it is, without having intoxicating liquors inside you,' scolded Blitzen firmly, as he began to sweat with all the childminding he was having to do.

'Sorry, Blitzen,' smirked Michael, drawing his hand back across the table. 'You know, you are so very easy to wind up.'

Blitzen grunted at this, as Rudolph began making loud slurping noises with his straw.

'What are you guna wish for next, Rudolph?' asked Hopper, intrigued by the other half of the Wish Biscuit.

'Oh uh, well, ya know, I think I might wish for a mirror,' said Rudolph, as he tossed the remainder of his biscuit into the air and caught it in his mouth. A flash of light spread across the table and there, face down in front of him, lay a small looking glass with a shiny silver handle.

'Hey, look at that,' exclaimed Rudolph, picking it up and prodding his cheekbones. 'This war's not taking such a toll on me, after all.'

'Oh, for Christmas sakes, Rudolph,' uttered Blitzen, as he reached onto the tray for his own biscuit.

'Hey, which one have you got, Blitzy?' asked Rudolph, as he began slurping his cocktail.

'I'm picking a nice, sensible one, thank you,' replied Blitzen, as he reached for a green Christmas tree.

'Ooh, the mystical Christmas tree. What are you guna wish for - branches?' chuckled Rudolph, as he continued to slurp his daiquiri.

Blitzen turned his head away indignantly and took a firm bite of his biscuit.

'I wish for stronger antlers,' he announced in his deep, majestic voice.

A large beam shone down upon Blitzen from above, and his antlers grew at least an inch larger. They then sparkled magically as though they had just been showered with gold Reindeer dust.

'Oooo, very impressive,' remarked Sarah.

'Yeah, Blitzen. I might have to start calling you *Sparkles*,' ribbed Michael.

Mrs Bunnie smiled fondly, before pushing the tray of Wish Biscuits in front of Sergeant Squirrelseed.

'Your turn, Sergeant,' she said .

'Ooh, oh well uh, thank you, Mrs Bunnie,' he gushed. 'Now then, uh, let's see. Oh, there now,' he muttered, reaching for a red and brown robin and taking a bite. 'I wish for a cluster of nuts to keep me warm,' he said, as he nibbled his way swiftly through the biscuit.

There followed a loud crackling, as though someone were cooking popcorn, and on the table suddenly appeared a little red Christmas stocking, full to the brim with acorns and peanuts.

'Ooooo, Christma-scrumptious,' smiled Sergeant Squirrelseed, who tucked into his supply immediately.

Next was Mr Bunnie, who wished for an extra supply of firefly sticks, followed by Hopper, who wished for a bow and arrow, and lastly Carrot Top, who wished for an extra Wish Biscuit. The remainder of the creatures all wished for more food and punch, with the exception of Mr Prickles, who merely wished that his bank was safe.

By the time everyone had finished, the plate was empty.

'That's it now, I'm afraid,' announced Mrs Bunnie, as she emptied the last of the crumbs into the bin. 'No more Wish Biscuits.'

The little Bunnies, Hedgehogs and Badgers looked very glum at this thought.

'Mother, how long will we have to stay down here?' asked Herbert Prickles, in a rather dejected little voice.

'Until this horrible war is over, Pricklekins,' replied Mrs Prickles, leaning down over him to give him some Christma-comfort.

'But I don't like it down here. It's dark and horrible, and there's no sunlight,' complained his sister, Herbulia.

'When *will* the war be over?' piped up a little Badger with a white, stripy nose.

'Oh, not long, now, Sooty,' assured his mother, Mrs Badger. 'Not long at all.'

'So we're just guna have to sit here and wait,' groaned Patch, pulling a face and feeling slightly exasperated with his inactivity.

'Well......' Mrs Bunnie began to speak, when suddenly Mr Badger interrupted her.

'You know what, I don't think we *can* just sit here and wait while all that's happening up there,' he stated, straightening his waistcoat. 'I've been thinking about it all evening and I just cannot come to terms with the idea. It's morally wrong of us to hide down here and do nothing.

The Kingdom needs our help.'

The room went quiet, as all eyes were now turned on Mr Badger, and it befell Mrs Badger to contend with her husband.

'Mr Badger, dear, do calm down,' she urged, approaching her husband and placing her paw on his arm. 'We all know how you feel, but I'm afraid we really don't have a choice. If we go out there we're as good as dead.'

'Well, I'm sorry, Mrs Badger, but I find it quite impossible to remain calm when there's a war going on involving some of our dearest friends. Why, there's the Reindeer, the Snowflakes, the Elves – who knows what's happening to them at the hands of the Snow Wolves? Surely we can't leave them to that fate?'

A tremor went through the creatures, and Mrs Badger was now doubly cross with her husband for causing such an uproar.

'Mr Badger! Pull yourself together!' she snapped, as she placed her paws on her hips. 'Those Wolves will kill us as soon as look at us. Have you forgotten that they eat Woodland Creatures? You should be thankful that you've *got* a bed to sleep in tonight and that you're not up in the prisons with the rest of them.'

Mr Badger looked annoyed with his wife and stood up in protest. 'I'm sorry that you feel that way, Mrs Badger, but I for one cannot sit here and bury my head. If I was locked up in the castle or the Mountains, I'd hope that my fellow creatures would come and help me.'

'What exactly are you getting at then, Mr Badger?' asked Mr Prickles, as he looked up from his copy of The X-mas Times and lowered his pipe.

'I propose that we try and free them,' announced Mr Badger boldly, 'and that we fight those rotten enemies of ours while we're at it. If we stay down here then we're nothing more than a bunch of Christmas cowards.'

'Now just a minute, Mr Badger,' began Blitzen, stepping into the conversation. 'As honourable as such sentiments are, what exactly do you intend to do? Any mission launched in the Kingdom at Christmas present could prove highly dangerous.'

'Well, as I understand it, we cannot go on the Quest,' continued Mr Badger, looking at Blitzen and Mrs Bunnie for confirmation.

'That's correct,' affirmed Blitzen.

'*The Scroll* has already stated who it wants for the Quest. You can't just go tagging along as well, you might anger it,' added Mrs Bunnie in a serious tone.

'Yeah, but you know, technically, if you really wanted to go, you could always have my place, Christmasdude,' ventured Rudolph, scratching his hind leg. 'I mean, I'm not that into trekking and my hooves get really brittle when I have to walk over long distances and............'

'Rudolph, for Christmas sakes be quiet! You have no choice in the matter,' scolded Blitzen firmly. 'Now, I'm sorry, Mr Badger. As you were saying.'

'I have another plan which just might work,' suggested Mr Badger enthusiastically.

'What might that be, Mr Badger?' asked Mr Bunnie, now sounding intrigued.

'There's a small tunnel attached to the back of the hideout which is built underground and leads to the edge of Cinnamon Forest. I see no reason why we can't follow it and then tunnel the rest of the way to the castle ourselves. We've got paws, after all. We could break directly into the prison from below ground level and save the prisoners. We'll be able to infiltrate the whole site. *The Magic Scroll of Christmas* says that only the children can restore the Altra. It doesn't forbid us from trying to defeat the Guardian in other ways, and it certainly doesn't forbid us from trying to rescue the prisoners at the castle.'

'Well said, Mr Badger. I for one am in favour of that motion,' concurred Mr Bunnie, fully impressed with Mr Badger's speech.

'Is this the wisest idea, Mr Bunnie?' asked Mrs Bunnie, placing her paws on her hips and looking sternly at her husband.

'I really don't see we have a choice, Mrs Bunnie,' he replied. 'Mr Badger's right. If we stay here and hide under this Oak Tree, then we're nothing more than a bunch of Christmas cowards. We must go up there and fight for what's right, and for Christmas. What do you say, Blitzen?'

'I say that as long as our paths don't cross and you stay away from the Altra, well then it's a jolly good idea. Here, here!' cried Blitzen, thumping his hoof on the table.

A roar of approval then went through the room, and paws, hooves and hands were clapped in favour of this new proposal.

'We all wanna go too, Dad,' said the triplets and Bunnyflower, jumping forwards towards Mr Bunnie.

'Oh no, you can't,' objected Mrs Bunnie, now sounding quite cross. 'I've had this discussion with you before.'

'Oh come on, Mrs Bunnie, they're old enough. It'll do them good. Besides, we'll need all the help that we can get,' urged Mr Bunnie earnestly.

'Yeah, come on Mum, please let us go,' cried Patch. 'We'll be restless down here and we really wanna help save Christmas.'

'Yeah, Mum. We'll just get on your nerves if we're stuck down here all the time, anyway,' reasoned Hopper, as his tail started twitching.

'Well........' said Mrs Bunnie, looking at her triplets and considering the dreadful plight of the prisoners at the castle.

'Come on. Christmas pleeeeeeeaaaaaaassssssseeeeee,' they all chimed together.

'Alright,' she agreed finally. 'But you must stay with your father at all times. And only you three can go,' she said, pointing to the triplets. 'Bunnyflower, you have to stay here with me.'

'What? No. That's not fair. They're all going,' protested Bunnyflower, folding his arms and pulling a jib. 'Why can't I go?' he stomped.

'Because you're too young, Bunnyflower. You can't bounce fast enough to escape from the Snow Wolves. They'll eat you up for supper,' said his mother firmly.

'But it's not fair,' he cried. 'I wanna go!'

'No, Bunnyflower. I've said my piece,' insisted his mother with an air of finality.

The little Christmacub huffed and puffed, and was about to protest even further, when a few strong words from his father soon sent him running into Sarah's arms for comfort.

'Well, how are we going to work this out?' asked Mr Prickles, looking at the enthusiastic crowd.

There was soon a hefty discussion underway about who should stay with the younger members and who should go and fight. After much deliberation, it was decided that Mrs Bunnie and the other mothers should stay and look after the young cubs in the hideout, while everyone else was to tunnel to the castle and rescue the prisoners. Christmacubs over the age of ten were welcome to go, which meant that the little Prickles twins, Sooty the Badger and Bunnyflower were left behind. Bunnyflower was still most put out about this, and continued to bury his head deep into Sarah's pinafore dress, refusing to look at either his parents or his brothers. Mr Bunnie felt that it was just better to leave him be, and continued with his discussions. It was then decided that the Woodland Creatures would begin tunnelling the next morning when the children left for their Quest, and that a good night's sleep was in order so that they would be fresh and ready for whatever the next day threw at them.

Just as everyone was settling down for the night and getting ready for bed, Bunnyflower decided it was time to approach his brothers. He entered the little room they had been assigned and bounced up to Carrot Top, who was in the process of getting changed.

'Hey, Topsy. Could you smuggle me in tomorrow?' he asked, looking up at his older brother with big, wide eyes.

'Bunnyflower, you know I can't do that. Dad'll just go ballistic and send you back to Mum. And guess who'll probably have to take you?' he said rather grumpily.

'Who?' asked Bunnyflower.

'Me,' replied Carrot Top, jumping into a large Christmas stocking that hung on the wall.

'But........,' began Bunnyflower.

'No, Bunnyflower. I'm not doing it,' said Carrot Top, turning his back on his brother as his Christmas stocking began to sway back and forth.

Bunnyflower poked his tongue out at his brother, before turning to Patch and Hopper, who were busy practising their fighting skills for the next day. Patch was pretending to be the Snow Wolf, while Hopper was failing miserably in the art of self-defence.

'Take that, you big slobbery beast,' cried Hopper, as he beat his brother playfully around the head with his paws.

'Ouch, Ouch, be careful, Hopper you're hurting me,' groaned Patch, trying to block his brother's attack.

'I'm a Snow Wolf. I'm supposed to hurt you,' he growled.

'Patch, Hopper, will you let me come with you tomorrow?' asked Bunnyflower, hopefully.

'Get lost, Bunnyflower, we're practising for the big fight,' snapped Hopper, who was now holding Patch in a head lock.

'But I really wanna come with you. Christmas pleeeeeeaaaaasssssse,' pleaded Bunnyflower.

'OUUUCH. Let go, Hopper,' squealed Patch, as he tried to extricate himself from his brother's grip.

'Patch, Hopper. You're not listening to me,' shrieked Bunnyflower, as he stomped his foot on the floor.

'Look, Bunnyflower, just get lost, ok? Dad said you can't go,' said Hopper, as Patch suddenly tumbled from underneath his paws and landed on the floor with a bump.

'But I don't care what Dad says. I really wanna go, and I don't think it's fair that I'm not allowed to just because.....'

'Argh, Bunnyflower, quit yelling,' stomped Patch, as he sat on the floor, rubbing his head from the fall. 'Look, if Dad said you can't go, then tough Wish Biscuits. Just go and play with the other Christmas kiddies or sumthin.'

'Christmas meanies,' shouted Bunnyflower, before bouncing out and slamming the door loudly. He then took a right turn and wandered off by himself deep into the eerie tunnels of the hideout, trying desperately to think of a way in which he could be included in all the action.

Meanwhile, across the corridor, the children were anxious too. Michael continuously spun his dagger on the nightstand as he thought about the Quest. He *had* to prove himself a hero, and he could not let the Kingdom down.

'Michael,' ventured Sarah suddenly, as she broke the young Prince's trance. 'Don't you feel nervous about tomorrow? I mean, about going on the Quest? It's all happened so fast, I think I'm only now beginning to realise what we're up against.'

'You can't think about it too much, Sarah. Over-thinking will inevitably lead to nervousness. If you doubt yourself, then everyone else will too,' urged Michael, now re-sheathing the dagger and laying it flat on the table.

'But what if we *don't* succeed?' vexed Sarah, as grains of anxiety moved across her face. 'What if we *don't* defeat the Guardian and save Christmas? What is going to happen then?'

'Look, Sarah, we *will* succeed. You've got to be more of a tough-heart than that. We've got the Reindeer and Double S looking out for us, and when it comes to the Guardian, you've just got to think of *Hansel and Gretel.*'

'Think of *Hansel and Gretel?*' asked Sarah, stitching her eyebrows together and hurriedly recalling the events of the fairy tale they had performed just two nights ago. 'What has *that* got to do with anything?'

'Hansel and Gretel defeated the witch because they outsmarted her,' stated Michael, tucking himself in under the covers. '*Alone* they could never have escaped her, but *together* they were able to outsmart her. We've just got to remember *that* when we're at the castle, Sarah. There are *two* of *us* and *one* of *him*. If we put our brains together, we can't fail.'

'But how are we going to outsmart the *Guardian?*' asked Sarah, climbing into bed too and watching the last ember fade in the fireplace.

'I don't know, Sarah. But I'm sure we'll think of something when the time comes.'

With that, Michael blew out the candle, leaving the small room in utter darkness, and Sarah's eyes glittering like a timid ferret.

'I sincerely hope so, Michael. Good night,' said the little Princess, now burying her head beneath the covers in an effort to block out her external reality.

'Good night, munchkin,' came her brother's voice, before his thoughts trailed off into the murky realms of what lay ahead and he soon fell fast asleep.

It was a pity that neither child was awake to hear the handle of their bedroom door turn an hour later, as an uninvited visitor hid himself deep inside the lining of Sarah's coat pocket. Nor did they feel the North Wind breeze past and bequeath Michael a piece of red ribbon - the trusted signal that a letter had been sent successfully along the North Wind.

13-Back at the Prisons

Back at the castle prisons, the Snow Wolf had now been asleep for a full hour, and the creatures sat amidst the shafts of moonlight rationed out through the icy bars. The mantra came and went, failing to have any effect on the Snow Wolf, who continued to sleep right through it. Finally, however, in a sudden fit of snoring, he fell off the battered stool and woke himself up, deciding to take his leave of the cells directly for a full half hour break. The prisoners were finally free to explore the ghostly author of this lament.

'Has he gone?' whispered Donner, leaning forwards and holding a piece of glass out through the bars in the absence of a mirror. 'I thought he'd never leave us. I thought he was guna be here all night.'

'Yes, well, he will be, once he gets back from his stroll on the causeway, so the faster we move, the better,' said Dora, rallying the cell. 'Now, do we have any idea where the sound is coming from?'

'I think it's probably coming from the old chamber – you know – the Queen's chamber. But I'm guessing that the Guardian has transformed it a little,' suggested Luella, her wings glittering faintly.

'Yeah, that sounds about right. Uh hey, look at this,' remarked Comet, sitting up suddenly, as a piece of stone now fell away from the prison wall and landed most conspicuously in front of them. Luella bent down and picked it up, only to find that it had a note written on it.

Go to the left of the room. Push the central most stone in the wall.

'Good Christmas – who sent us *that*?' asked Dora, looking surprised, and wondering in the pit of her stomach if it wasn't in fact a trap sent to them by evil.

'No, it's not from evil. It's the castle,' added Luella, rather spookily, as she suddenly remembered that it had limited intrinsic powers. 'It wants to help us rescue the creature. It wants to help us solve the mystery.'

The prisoners looked around now with uncertainty, as Luella marched straight to where the stone had directed her and found the central most slab in the wall.

'This is it,' she announced, running her glistening fingers along it. 'Now what am I supposed to do?'

She needn't have asked the question, for no sooner had she touched it, than the entire wall now disappeared, and in its place stood a crudely carved archway, with a spiral staircase leading upwards.

The Guardian's Chamber read a sign on the wall, dimly lit in this mysterious setting that both invited and scared the creatures at the same time.

'It must lead right up into one of the towers,' suggested Luella, stepping inside and peering up the never-ending cylinder. 'I suppose he must be keeping this creature up there.'

'*Help me. Please help me,*' came the voice, as if it were answering her. '*Save me. He's trapped me.*'

'Are we all guna go?' asked Dancer, looking up sceptically. 'I mean, it's awfully narrow.'

'Yes, you're right,' agreed Dora, now stepping forwards. 'I think the Reindeer should stay behind. I've trodden these tracks before in my time. There's probably only room for us two,' she added, motioning to the Snowbelle.

Luella scowled for a moment. She wasn't enthralled about the idea of working with an Elf, but she supposed she could manage it for the good of Christmas.

'Alright then, Doris. If you insist. But I'll go first.'

'It's Dora, actually, and no you won't. I will. If the Snow Wolves come back, strike the bottom of the tower with a rock. The sound should carry all the way upstairs. '

The Reindeer nodded, and Dora and Luella began their climb up the hollow stairway to the Guardian's chamber, following the ghostly voice that called out to them. The climb seemed to take forever, and not all the sconces were lit, but eventually they came to an opening which brought them out into an open fireplace.

'Is this it? Is this the Guardian's chamber?' asked Luella, looking around at the room which was now dark and decrepit.

'Yes it is,' replied Dora a little nervously. 'It certainly hasn't escaped the curse of evil.'

Indeed, Dora was right. Flakes of ash lay scattered all over the frozen floor, and the windows were smashed and exposed. A large four-poster bed stood at the centre of the room, enshrouded with moth-eaten drapes, and a large spider's web had formed near the headboard. Not a single candle was lit - light came only from the patches of ice on the walls - and an abundance of trunks lay scattered in every corner.

'There's any number of places that this prisoner could be. And yet - not one in particular seems to suggest itself any more than the others,' said Luella, looking around in a snap of panic.

'*Help me. Please help me. I'm cold and I'm shivering.*'

'Good Christmas. It's coming from under the bed,' cried Dora, marching over to it directly and lifting up the valance.

To both the Elf and the Snowflake's astonishment however, they did not find that the owner of this voice was a timid child, nor did it come from any creature at all, but it came instead from a glass mirror which was printing the words, as they were being spoken, in cold, jagged frost.

'*Help me,*' came the voice, as it rose straight off the glass, and the words magically appeared simultaneously like etchings. '*You have to find me.*'

'I don't understand,' said Luella, pulling the mirror towards her slightly. 'Is it a trick? There's no creature here at all. Was it simply meant to lure us here?'

Dora looked worried for a moment, but then she noticed a pink jewel on the handle, lighting up like a receptor, a split second before the voice began crying.

'Why, it seems to be picking these thoughts up from somewhere. From someone. These thoughts and cries are the genuine pleas of a creature, but the creature himself is not here - or at least, he doesn't seem to be.'

Luella leaned into the mirror now and spoke to it in a clear voice.

'Are you a prisoner of the Guardian?' she asked, as the mirror rippled slightly. 'Have you been locked up?

'*Help me. Please find me,*' cried the mirror, as the jewel lit up.

'Whoever it is obviously can't hear us,' said Luella, now looking around. 'Can you at least tell where the jewel seems to be picking the message up from?'

'No – it hasn't left a trail of light. But look at this,' observed Dora, as the jewel now turned yellow and the tone of the voice became remarkably different.

> *'Anger and hate are destroying me.*
> *Let me out, set me free.*
> *To hurt, to burn, to harm you all.*
> *My fate is sealed, the world must fall.'*

'Good Christmas. Are they spoken by the same creature?' asked Luella, as her fingers curled slightly and her nerves quivered.

'I don't know. But if they are, can this creature be trusted?' asked Dora, as a shadow passed her face.

'*Help me. You have to help me. I am closer than you think. I may die of agony if you don't help me.*'

The voice was convincing, as the jewel turned pink again, and the two prisoners stared at one another, completely baffled.

'Let's see what we can find out about this creature first. Perhaps the Reindeer will be able to help us. We can look at it in the prisons before that brute of a Snow Wolf gets back.'

Luella nodded and placed the mirror under her arm before hastening through the fireplace and going back down stairs.

14-The Start of the Journey

As dawn approached, the hideout awoke to mixed feelings. Michael was up first and was delighted to find the piece of red ribbon on his bed. He decided to say nothing to his sister, but put it quietly in his coat pocket as he went to breakfast, failing to question its true origin. Rudolph, meanwhile, bumbled on and on about how celebrities weren't supposed to go on quests like this, and eagerly asked if any of the Woodland Creatures wanted to swap places with him. They had their own problems to worry about, however. Mrs Bunnie was particularly anxious and had prepared a generous stack of food for her sons, and an even bigger one for her husband.

'Goodness, dear, we'll barely be able to fit underground with all this baggage,' remarked Mr Bunnie, looking at the bulging handkerchief.

'You'll need it,' she said, kissing him and wedging and extra piece of cake inside the bundle, with half a mind to go back to the kitchen and fetch some more.

'What's in here altogether?' asked Patch, as he began fumbling around in his bundle. Out from the sack came chocolate cake, sugarloaf bread, a flask of cinnamon punch, cranberry sandwiches with Christmas stuffing, Christmas cookies, marshmallows, fruit, sausage rolls - the red and white handkerchief really did seem bottomless.

'Patch, put them back in, or you'll end up leaving something behind!' reprimanded his mother. The other Bunnies, who had also seized on Patch's cue and rummaged through their own packed lunches, simultaneously began putting their food back.

Mrs Bunnie wiped a tear from her eye as she looked at her three brave Christmacubs.

'Oh dear, I'm going to miss you all so much,' she sighed, rubbing her eyes with her paws. Both Mrs Badger and Mrs Prickles were in a similar emotional state, although at least they did not have to say goodbye to their Christmacubs. The Reindeer, the Squirrels and the children stood at the other end of the room to give the families some space.

'Good luck, Christmasdudes,' cried Rudolph.

'Thanks, Rudolph. And we'll remember the advice you gave us from when you fought the Snow Wolves at the castle,' promised Patch, earnestly.

'Just use your heads, cubs,' said Blitzen, feeling quite sure that any advice from Rudolph was the wrong advice, especially given that Rudolph hadn't even fought the Snow Wolves at the castle.

'Hey, where's Bunnyflower?' asked Hopper, suddenly noticing that his youngest brother was missing.

'I dunno,' shrugged Carrot Top. 'I haven't seen him since last night when he was whining about missing the Quest.'

'Yeah, but I thought he'd come and say goodbye,' grumbled Patch, looking disappointed.

'I'll go and get him. He's probably in his room, sulking,' ventured Mrs Bunnie, who wandered off in the direction of Bunnyflower's room. She soon returned without him however, shaking her head.

'He's hiding in his Christmas stocking,' she said. 'I'm not sure whether he's fast asleep or whether he's just ignoring me. Either way, he's not coming out.'

'Should we go and see him?' asked Hopper. 'I don't really wanna leave without saying goodbye.'

'Oh, I'm not sure, Hopper,' said Carrot Top. 'He was pretty mad that he couldn't come with us. He might take it the wrong way if we all parade into his room.'

'Topsy's right, Hopper. He needs some time to get over it,' added Patch.

'Yeah, I suppose you're right,' agreed Hopper, looking a little dismayed.

'It'll be fine, cubs. You can tell your brother all about your adventures when we get back. I'm sure he'll be proud of you. One day he'll understand why we wouldn't let him go,' said Mr Bunnie in a commanding tone.

The triplets nodded and looked up at their father for further direction.

'Right then, shall we make a move? The tunnel won't dig itself, you know.'

There was a gurgle of affirmation from the party and three Christmas cheers from the young Bunnies. The party was accompanied to the end of the corridor in the hideout, where they reached a panel built into the dirt wall. Mr Bunnie pulled the panel across to reveal a long, dark, winding tunnel.

'This is it,' he said. 'This is the start of our Christmadventure. The tunnel only stretches to the edge of the forest, so we'll have to start digging from there on.'

'Wow, that's Christmatastic,' bellowed Patch, jumping forward and sticking his head inside to have a better look.

'Not so fast, Patch,' scolded his father, picking him out of the way by his tail, and placing him at the back of the line. He then handed everyone in the group a firefly stick.

'You'll need these in there,' he said. 'Now, I'll go in first, my cubs will be directly behind me. Badger, Prickles - you're at the back. Any trouble at any time, use the Christmas alert. Are we ready?'

'Ready,' came a unanimous cry.

After a minor scuffle between the triplets, over who should go in first, the team climbed into the hole and headed off towards the castle. Then, as Mr Prickles disappeared from view, Mrs Badger slid the panel shut again.

'What if they get into trouble and need to turn back?' asked Sarah, with an air of concern.

'Oh, they know how to find it,' replied Mrs Prickles, with unwavering confidence. 'We can't leave it open, for if the Snow Wolves see the light, they'll be in here before you can say *Merry Christmas.*'

The children looked at each other for a moment before Mrs Prickles resumed, 'Now then, don't you think it's time that you lot were on your way too? Christmas clock's ticking, you know. The countdown to Christmas Eve has begun, and Christmas has got to be rescued, otherwise millions of children the world over won't get their presents. The Kingdom, well, the universe will be a.....'

'Yes, yes, Mrs Prickle-bush. I think we get the picture,' interrupted Michael, who didn't need to be reminded of how difficult the task was, and distracted himself by counting the ribbons in her spines.

'I'm just saying, Your Majesty, that if....'

'Oh, Mrs Prickles, pipe down will you. They're nervous enough as it is,' snapped Mrs Bunnie, rescuing the children from this thorny creature. 'Now then, I've prepared some food,' she said, producing a large bundle tied and decorated with a crisp bough of mistletoe. 'It's probably best if one of you carries it in your satchel,' she suggested, looking at Blitzen and Rudolph.

'Rudolph can take it,' said Blitzen sternly. 'I'll carry the children.'

'Ahem,' came a modest voice from down below.

'Yes, and you, Sergeant Squirrelseed. I will carry all three of you.'

'Oh dear. Do be careful, won't you?' said Trixitail, turning to her husband, with bulging fat tears in her eyes.

'Of course, dear, don't you worry about me,' he assured her, wrapping his bushy tail around her. I've got the Reindeer with me, and the children. It'll be fine. You just worry about Mrs Bunnie and the Christmacubs and leave the rest to us,' he continued in an unconvincing tone of bravery.

'Right then. To the trap door,' ordered Blitzen, leading everyone back down the corridor from which they had just come. This time, however, instead of going to the very end of the corridor, Blitzen turned right into a little room, which at Christmas present was being used for storage. At the top of the room a little crack in the ceiling showed that another trap door was present, yet well concealed, and led to the forest above.

'Up there is where we are headed,' indicated Blitzen. 'Sergeant Squirrelseed, you're the smallest, so you go first. I need you to peer out at the top to check that the Christmas coast is clear.'

'Right you are,' said Squirrelseed, clambering up onto Blitzen's antlers and pushing the trap door open slowly. Evidently, the trap door had not been opened for some time, for as it was inched up, a torrent of snow came tumbling down into the hideout.

'Oh darn it,' complained Squirrelseed, sneezing and shaking the snow off himself. He pushed the door a little further open so that he had just enough room to squeeze the upper part of his body through. Outside, the forest looked bright and still, and the snow had actually eased up so that visibility was sharp and clear.

'All's well,' said Squirrelseed, giving a thumbs up below. Blitzen then helped to push the door up even higher so that everyone had enough room to climb out. First came Blitzen, followed by the children, and last, but certainly not least, came our beloved Rudolph. When both Reindeer landed on the ground, there was a loud POOF and they promptly returned to normal size. Rudolph was very pleased to be back to his old self, but did not quite relish the idea of the Quest as much.

'Quit your whinging, Rudolph. It's going to get a lot worse,' barked Blitzen impatiently. 'We've got a lot of Christmas miles to cover and your fussing won't make it any easier.'

At this, Rudolph's lips began to quiver. 'That's fine,' he mumbled to himself in a pitiful voice. 'All I ever ask for is a little Christmas pampering once in a while. I never wanted to get roped into this Quest, but some old *Scroll* says that I've gotta come along, and I think it's downright Christmas-mean and......'

'Rudolph, come on. It's this way,' commanded Blitzen.

Rudolph, who had inadvertently begun walking back in the direction of Cinnamon Village, was now forced to turn around and follow the others.

'And don't drop the food,' ordered Blitzen, as he took the lead.

'Don't drop the food,' mimicked Rudolph, pulling a face.

'I heard that.'

To this, Rudolph merely poked out his tongue and pulled a number of faces. Fortunately, Blitzen had his back to him so that he could not see.

Then a voice came from behind them.

'Good luck, everyone,' cried Mrs Bunnie, as she stuck her head out of the trap door. She then dropped back inside and the door shut, leaving no trace of the hideout. It was as if it had never existed.

Rudolph now felt alone and cut off. Suddenly, the idea of Blitzen's company did not seem like such a bad idea, and he galloped a little way to catch up with his colleague.

*   *   *   *

To Rudolph it seemed as if they had been walking for hours. He could fly all night long if he had enough Reindeer dust, but walking wasn't exactly something he was used to.

'Hey, guys, when are we guna stop for a rest? My hooves are hurtin', and this darn bundle of food in my satchel is getting heavier by the second,' he whined.

'We've only been walking for about an hour, Rudolph. Stop complaining. We've got a lot further to go,' snapped Blitzen unsympathetically.

'Can we *please* stop in a little while? I'm in shock and I need to recover,' he continued in a nagging manner.

'Say, Red Nose. If trekking's not your thing, then why did *The Magic Scroll of Christmas* choose you to come along in the first place?' asked Michael, turning around.

'I've been asking myself the exact same question,' said Blitzen with a nod. 'I think the whole point of this Quest for Rudolph is that *The Scroll* wants him to learn something.'

'Oh, it doesn't want me to learn something, Blitzy. It just chose me because I'm a celebrity,' nodded Rudolph in earnest. 'But the thing is, I'm just not designed for this sort of thing. I hate the fear and the danger and the cold and the snow and........'

'Rudolph,' interrupted Blitzen, 'it's always cold and snowing here; this is The Kingdom of Christmas.'

'Yeah, but we're not normally out in it all day long. If I get any colder, creatures are guna start calling me *Bluedolph*. And I miss my casa, dude, - my Christmatastic Villa Noël. Hey, can we please go there on the way to the castle? Blitzy? Christmas please, with extra Reindeer dust on top?'

'Rudolph! I told you last night. It's not safe for us to go that way,' sighed Blitzen in exasperation.

'No, Blitzy. What you said was that there were Snow Wolves in the village. That doesn't mean to say that it won't be Christmasafe there today,' contended Rudolph, his nose glowing with optimism. 'Oh *please* can we go to Villa Noël on our way to the castle? Christmaplease, please, please, with extra Reindeer dust on top. It's the most Christmatastic house in the world – scrap that! In all worlds.'

'Look, I'm sorry, Rudolph. I know it means a lot to you, but we just can't risk it,' added Blitzen with a nod. 'We can't jeopardise the Quest and the chance of saving Christmas just for you to pay a visit to your house.'

'But I asked, Christmaplease, with extra Reindeer dust on top,' whimpered Rudolph, as his eyes slightly filled with tears.

'The answer's still NO, Rudolph, and you'll thank me for it in the long run. Now, we will be working our way around the basin of the forest to reach Mistletoe Falls, with a view of hanging our stockings in the conifer trees tonight and sleeping there. Now can you please just do something to entertain yourself so that you don't annoy anyone,' said Blitzen, exasperated.

'Entertain myself,' blurted Rudolph suddenly. 'Well, like how, Blitzy? What am I supposed to do? You want me to sing?'

'No!' said Blitzen quickly, and maybe a little too hastily. 'No, no, no. No *singing*, thank you, Rudolph. I still have the memory of you singing on *The X-mas Factor* last year,' added Blitzen, thinking that he had really put his hoof in it this time. 'No, I was thinking you might entertain yourself in a *quieter* manner.'

'Oh, ok. Well uh, how about a game?' ventured Rudolph, his nose lighting up slightly. 'You know how to play *Tag and Tell*?'

'*Tag and Tell*,' repeated Michael, raising his eyebrows. 'I haven't played that for ages. I used to be *really* good at it.'

'Yes, so did I,' added Sarah, her face lighting up. 'Let's play that. I think it's exactly what's needed to lighten the atmosphere around here.'

'What exactly does *Tag and Tell* entail?' asked Sergeant Squirrelseed, who was becoming quite intrigued by this little game now.

'Oh well, it's real simple, Squirreldude,' began Rudolph excitedly. 'You have to tell us the items on your Christmas list, and add one false item that you didn't ask for. We have to try to guess which is the false one, and shout out *Tag*. If we get it right, *you* have to do a forfeit. If we get it wrong, *we* have to do a forfeit.'

'Oh dear – what do you mean by a forfeit?' asked Squirrelseed, who was remarkably hopeless at anything like this.

'Oh nothing too troubling, Double S,' interrupted Michael. 'Standing on your head, hanging upside down, balancing on one foot, that sort of thing. It really is a lot of fun. Especially when Sarah here is losing.'

'Oh, shut up, Michael,' cried Sarah, as she gave her brother a nudge.

'Well, my, that does sound fun. I think I'll give it a go,' said Squirrelseed, who thought, like Sarah, that they needed *something* to take the edge off their journey. 'Are you playing, Blitzen?'

'No thank you, Sergeant. I will just keep a look out and trek quietly,' answered Blitzen, clearing his throat.

'Aw, snow way, Blitzy! Don't you wanna join in?' asked Rudolph enthusiastically.

'No thank you, Rudolph. *Someone* has to have their Christmas wits about them,' said Blitzen, wondering whether Rudolph's singing *would* have been a better alternative, after all.

'Ok then. Well, I'll go first,' suggested Rudolph, looking pleased. 'For Christmas this year I asked for:
Reindeer rollerblades
Snowmen bed sheets
An ice cream sundae maker
Pink fluffy slippers and uh, uh, oh yeah
A nose duster.'

'*Tag* on pink fluffy slippers,' shouted out Michael, confidently. 'You didn't really ask for them.'

'Aw sorry, Christmasdude. My fake item was a nose duster, cos I already have one,' said Rudolph with a beam.

'You *really* asked Santa for pink fluffly slippers?' asked Michael, looking perplexed.

'Oh yeah, Christmasdude. Pink fluffy slippers are the best,' chirped Rudolph merrily.

'They're kind of girly, Red Nose,' scoffed Michael, knitting his eyebrows together.

'Shut up, Michael. Stop teasing him. And stop trying to get out of doing your Christmas forfeit,' said Sarah, giving him a nudge.

'Yeah, Princey! I'm guna act as Forfeit Master, and I say you should...... stand on your head,' ordered Rudolph, with a playful chuckle.

'Stand on my head! How the devil am I supposed to do that? I'm already on a Reindeer,' said Michael, looking perplexed.

'Aw easy, Christmasdude. C'mon, try it. It'll be fun,' urged Rudolph, clapping his hooves together.

At this, Michael huffed, but being a good sport, he soon turned himself upside down and held himself in place by putting his hands on the saddle.

'I hope this *pleases* you, Red Nose,' said Michael, trying to keep his legs as straight as possible in the air. 'How long do I have to stay like this?'

'Oh, just until the forfeit passes to another player,' chirped Rudolph. 'Who wants to go next?'

'Oh, I'll go,' said Sarah enthusiastically.

'For Christmas this year I asked for:
An X-mas Box
A pair of ice skates....'

'*Tag* on a pair of ice skates,' interrupted Michael, without flinching.

'Michael, wait! I haven't even finished my list yet,' snapped Sarah crossly.

'So what! I *know* you didn't really ask for ice skates. You fell on the castle moat three years ago and cut your head. Why would you ask for another pair?' insisted Michael cockily.

'Ok then, fine,' said Sarah, sighing slightly. 'I didn't really ask for ice skates. Although your memory is far too good, you know, Michael.'

'I *know*. That's why I *always* win this game,' boasted Michael, now turning himself the right way up and beaming smugly.

'So what's my forfeit, Rudolph?' asked Sarah, putting her hand over Michael's face.

'Oh uh, let's see. I'm the Forfeit Master, and I name the forfeit as.... balancing on one foot on top of a Reindeer.'

'Ha ha,' chuckled Michael, poking his tongue out as Sarah's expression suddenly dropped.

'Oh, Christmas crackers,' she exclaimed as she now climbed on top of the saddle and began balancing unsteadily on her left leg, swinging more precariously than a loose pendulum.

'Rudolph, *do* please try and keep the forfeits sensible,' commanded Blitzen, who had the misfortune of carrying both the children and Sergeant Squirrelseed on his back.

'We are, Blitzen, there's no need to worry. Sarah's a dab hand at doing things cock-eyed.'

'Shut up, Michael,' snapped Sarah, giving him a shove.

She didn't want to say too much in case she lost her balance. She was actually just about to suggest that Sergeant Squirrelseed go next, when she suddenly felt a scuffling in her pocket.

'What the Christmas?' she asked, reaching in and lifting out a little ball of white fluff.

'Bunnyflower!' she exclaimed, astounded.

'Hello,' he said, smiling sheepishly up at her and then turning towards Blitzen in anticipation of a reprimand. Blitzen halted with such a sharp jerk that Sarah, Michael and Squirrelseed lost balance and fell into the snow.

'Bunnyflower! What in The Kingdom of Christmas are you doing here?' asked Blitzen, deeply annoyed. 'You're supposed to be down in the hideout with your mother.'

'Yeah, well I'm not,' he sulked. 'Dad wouldn't let me go with the others, so I had no choice but to sneak away with you guys.'

'But, Bunnyflower. I don't think you understand. This Quest will get very dangerous,' stated Squirrelseed, intervening. 'More dangerous than anything you have ever seen before.'

'So what, I'm brave,' announced Bunnyflower earnestly. 'And I wanna fight in a war. I don't wanna be stuck down the hideout while all my brothers are off helping the war effort. When we beat the Guardian and get Christmas back, I wanna say that I was a part of it.'

'Bunnyflower, such intentions are honourable, but you are much too young to come on this Quest. *The Scroll* stated specifically who it wanted, based on their skill and prowess. Why, even I will find it difficult to fight the Guardian, and I am much bigger and stronger than you. How in the name of Christmas do you think you will fare against him?' asked Blitzen.

'Well, I guess I'll just ride with you,' said the Chritsmacub, thinking of how glorious that sounded.

'Bunnyflower, that is the worst place of all for you to be. You'll be as good as Snow Wolf meat if you do that,' continued Blitzen, deeply concerned.

'Come on, Blitzy, go easy on him, Christmasdude,' said Rudolph, laxly. 'He's just a Christmacub. He didn't know any different. I think it's Christmatastic that you wanna help out, little dude.'

'Thanks,' gushed Bunnyflower, as he turned the same colour as his idol's nose.

'Well, that's just the kind of typical idiotic response I'd expect from you,' barked Blitzen scathingly. 'I mean, your brains really are in your big, shiny hooter, aren't they!'

'Hey, watch it, Blitzy. That's kind of harsh,' replied Rudolph, clearly stung.

'Yeah, Blitzen, what's the problem?' asked Michael, now entering the conversation. 'Bunnyflower wants to do an honourable thing by fighting for the Kingdom. Why are you being such a munchkin about it?'

'I'm not being a *munchkin*, Michael, as you so kindly put it. I am being realistic. This war is highly dangerous, I'll have you know, and certainly not suitable for a young Christmacub barely out of nappies,' snapped Blitzen, glowering slightly.

'Oh, come on, Blitzen, that's hardly fair. Bunnyflower is nearly 7 years old. You really are being a Stiff Ears about this. I know I said at Cosy Cottage that I was ok with you being in charge, but I think I'm pulling an intervention on this one and overruling you. Bunnyflower, pay no attention to Stiff Ears. You can come along if you want to,' confirmed Michael with a nod.

'Thanks, Prince Michael,' sighed Bunnflower, giving the Prince a hug.

'Thanks, Prince Michael, nothing!' barked Blitzen, now deeply annoyed. 'You are not overruling me on this one, Michael. You may well be the Queen's son, but that does not mean you have superior insight. And as for you, Rudolph. You have been living in this Kingdom all your life. You know full well how dangerous this Quest is going to be. You've got less sense of responsibility than a bowl of Christmas jelly.'

'Huh!' gasped Rudolph, clearly offended. 'Yeah well, you're nuthin' but an overgrown buffoon, whose feet are too big for his Reindeer hooves, Blitzy,' retorted Rudolph.

'Right, I've had just about enough of this,' announced Blitzen, now turning to face Rudolph and eyeing him angrily. 'I have to put up with nonsense from you all year long at the station, and now I'm getting nonsense from you on this Quest. Well, I'm not putting up with anymore, Rudolph,' added the Chief Reindeer, as he cleared the ground with his hooves.

'Yeah, well I'm ready for you, Chief,' replied Rudolph, who had also stopped and began jumping from side to side in the snow as though he were getting ready to enter a boxing ring.

Blitzen's nostrils flared, and without further ado, the two Reindeer charged headlong towards each other and locked antlers.

'Oh no, not Reindeer Wrestling,' cried Squirrelseed, as he suddenly jumped up to take control of the situation.

'Right! Time out, you two. Back up. Back up!' he shouted.

But the Reindeer were not listening. They were still bashing their antlers together, much to the amusement of Michael, now who jumped up to get a better look.

'Good God, Red Nose. This is a turn up for the books,' exclaimed Michael, as he tried to contain his surprise. 'Care to make it interesting, Sergeant, by putting a little money on it?'

'Oh, for Christmas sakes, Michael, you're not helping,' snapped Sergeant Squirrelseed, who continued running back and forth between the two Reindeer as he tried to reason with them. I mean, the Reindeer are here fighting, and you're here goading them on.'

'I *am not*,' objected Michael with feigned annoyance. 'They've been bickering like a pair of old Felfs since we set out on this Quest. Isn't that right, Stiff Ears?'

'Well, Rudolph has no notion of responsibility,' insisted Blitzen, grinding his teeth. 'And as his Chief, I have to teach him some.'

'Yeah, well Blitzy's insulted my celebrity, Princey. And I feel really *really* Christm-offended.'

'See. I told you,' said Michael, folding his arms semi-triumphantly and looking down at the little Squirrel in anticipation of an apology.

'Oh, Michael, that is grossly missing the point,' said Sergeant Squirrelseed, as he continued to run back and forth between the two of them. 'It doesn't matter what it's about, we just need to stop them fighting. Now can you please help me before I blow a Christmas light in my head,' he added, as torrents of sweat now raced down his face.

'Oh, alright then. Been as you asked nicely. But you owe me for this one, Double S. Alright now, Blitzen. Red Nose. Stop your antler bashing and let's get on with the Quest,' commanded Michael, as he took a step towards the two. 'Come on, Red Nose, you might break a nail.'

The Reindeer continued with their wrestling, and Michael grew quite annoyed at being ignored for once in his entire life.

'Excuse me, Stick Heads, I'm *talking* to you. I'm the Prince of this Kingdom, in case you hadn't noticed, and I've just asked you to stop fighting,' he cried, making a move for their antlers.

Michael was now just about to throw a punch, himself, when Sarah, who had taken the time to place Bunnyflower up in a conifer tree, so that he was out of the way, now hurled a large snowball at her brother and caught hold of the Reindeer by their antlers.

'For Christmas sakes,' she hollered, as they lost their footing.

'What are you? Christmacubs? There's a war on, in case you hadn't noticed, and instead of doing something constructive, you two are busy bickering and locking antlers with each other.'

The two Reindeer looked embarrassed and pulled away in shame.

'Sorry, Sarah.'

'Sorry, Christmasdude,' they chimed together.

'That's alright. But now apologise to each other,' commanded Sarah, who was really quite shocked at how authoritative she could be.

'Sorry,'

'Sorry Blitzy,' each muttered, in a strained manner.

'Well - good!' exclaimed Sarah, now turning her attention to her brother.

'And *you* ought to be more ashamed than the other two.'

'Now see here, Sarah, I....mmmmm,' cried Michael, as yet another snowball struck him, this time straight in the mouth.

'No '*see here Sarah.*' Not today!' retorted Sarah with a scowl. 'You were jolly well in the wrong, and you can take your scolding quietly. Now this isn't even about you. This is about Bunnyflower. He's the one who could be in grave danger.'

Everyone now turned and looked at Bunnyflower, whose large black eyes looked so helpless and needy that it made one's heart melt.

'You're right. Of course it is,' agreed Blitzen, feeling deeply embarrassed and clearing his throat. 'But the question now is what to do with him.'

'Well, I don't think it's wise for him to continue on this Quest with us, Blitzen,' said Squirrelseed earnestly.

'No,' said Blitzen, 'but we can't very well send him back through the forest on his own. And none of us can go back with him because then the Quest would fall apart.'

'Couldn't we all take him back and then turn around?' suggested Rudolph a little sheepishly.

'No, we'll lose too much time,' replied Blitzen firmly. 'And there could be Snow Wolves roaming around.'

'What are we going to do, then?' asked Squirrelseed flummoxed.

'I think maybe Bunnyflower should stay with us until we find a safe place to deposit him.'

'Such as where?' enquired Squirrelseed, worried for a moment that the little Bunny would be left alone.

'Maybe we could leave him with some of the Woodland Creatures who live in these parts, or in The Forest of Magic Lanterns. He will certainly be safer there than he will with us,' suggested Blitzen, with an air of finality.

'Is that alright, Bunnyflower?' asked Squirrelseed, approaching him.

Bunnyflower pulled a bit of a face, but said finally that as long as he could ride with Rudolph then it would be ok.

Rudolph was certainly pleased to have the company – especially a fan – nothing could have been more exciting for him, and soon the game of *Tag and Tell* resumed, this time with Blitzen joining in too. It certainly helped to relieve the tension, and only Sarah out of the group was momentarily distracted as she had a quick peek at the compass. Fifteen Christmas miles to the waterfall. They were over half way there and the way ahead looked pristine and clear. She smiled to herself as she joined back in the game, failing to notice the ribbon in Michael's pocket, which now flashed briefly with a faint, yet unsettling, luminous glow.

15 - What Happened at Mistletoe Falls

A few hours later, the Quest eventually reached the waterfall, and while no one had noticed the red ribbon glowing, they *did* observe something else. The key that they had received from Christmas Street Station now began to glisten as though it were alive with electricity.

'Hey, look. Look at the key. It wants to show us something,' Sarah said, as the key pulled her forwards like an invisible, yet incredibly powerful Christmas ghost. The rest of the Quest looked on in excitement and followed Sarah as it pulled her under a canopy of mistletoe which grew along the walls of the cave behind the waterfall. The canopy was deeper than it looked, and snug and cosy like a bird's nest. The key continued to pull Sarah forwards, until it led her to a magic lantern that hung on an icicle embedded in the snowy rock. The lantern cast a silver light on the ground.

Stand amidst the light and aim the key at the cross,

read a message inside the lantern that now magically appeared on the front of an envelope.

Sarah bowed obediently before placing the key to face the marking on the wall. A gleam of light appeared, and the little Princess now stood in anticipation.

Thank you, Princess Sarah, and welcome to the rest of the Quest,

read the words inside the lantern, as the envelope now opened up to reveal a full sized letter.

The lantern has identified each one of you. Congratulations on making it as far as Mistletoe Falls. The Sacred Reading lies at the top of the cave. Use your intuition to find it. You cannot remove the tablet on which it is written. You must copy it and carry the words in your heart. Be cautious and beware of false caves and deceitful traps. There are further instructions inside. Good luck, and may you succeed in returning Christmas to the Kingdom.

The message and the lantern then disappeared, and in their place now stood a large archway leading into the cave, dark and hollow like an open mouth.

'What did it mean by *beware of false caves and deceitful traps?*' asked Sarah, as the others peered into the cave.

'I dunno, but you know what, Christmasdudes. It looks kinda dark and creepy in there. I think maybe we should go back,' gulped Rudolph, as his legs began to quiver and he made a move to turn around.

'Don't be silly, Red Nose. We've made it this far. We've got to keep on going,' rallied Michael, placing his hand on Rudolph's back. 'This is what we came here to do, and if false keys and deceitful traps are what we have to tolerate, then so be it.'

The Quest, with a reluctant Rudolph, all agreed with Michael, and placed their hands and paws together before entering the cave.

They now had to walk quite some distance in the darkness along a narrow passageway that had been carved between the rocks, with only the dim light from a few fireflies up ahead to light their way. Eventually, however, the passageway ended, and the Quest now found themselves in a large, open area at the centre of the cave, surrounded by snow on all sides. It was brightly lit by a selection of candles that had been placed on little niches in the walls, and featured three small tunnels in a row. The tunnels were all raised a good Christmas foot off the ground, and each differed remarkably in its nature. The first featured a wooden sign above it, which read **Secret Chalet**, and a swarm of fireflies danced around its archway gracefully. A wooden stepladder had been placed at the bottom to assist entry, with a little mat in front saying **Welcome**. The tunnel itself was dark, yet the chirping of birds from within and the delicate sound of bells ringing certainly drew the Quest's attention to it.

The second tunnel was equally as inviting, although remarkably different from the first. Garlands of sweets formed an archway at the entrance, and a sign just above read **Sugar Grove**. A little candy cane step-way led into this tunnel, and Bunnyflower's mouth began to water, just looking at it. Indeed, the tunnel oozed delicious baking smells that would have put even his mother's cake shop to shame, and he now found himself quite inadvertently licking his lips and wagging his fluffy tail.

The third tunnel, however, was not as inviting, and was not raised off the ground as the other two were. It had been carved between jagged rock formations and featured an eerie wooden signpost, with the words **Icy Falls** scratched into it by witch's nails. A cold wind screeched restlessly inside, and this made the Quest shiver. A heavy fog, like dragon's breath, was coughed out every few seconds, rendering the passage more foreboding, and an urgent trickle, which Blitzen could only assume was the water leading to the falls, could be heard from inside this hollow coffin. Sarah shuddered, just looking at it, and now turned her attention back to the other two, in confusion.

'How are we supposed to know which one to go in?' she asked, remembering the words of the magic lantern from outside. 'I mean, I know that Icy Falls is deliberately off-putting, but it could just as easily be in the other two.'

'Good Christmas, look,' exclaimed Squirrelseed, as another envelope now materialised straight out of the air and hovered tantalisingly before the Quest.

The way to the sacred tablet lies before you. Take care to choose the right tunnel. Once you leave a tunnel, it will close up forever.

The message then evaporated, leaving the Quest nervous and bewildered.

'Well, this is inconvenient. Doesn't *The Scroll want* us to succeed in saving Christmas?' asked Michael, looking quite annoyed. 'Talk about putting a pointless succession of obstacles in our way.'

'I'm afraid, Michael, that this is what *The Scroll* does,' replied Blitzen, trying to work out which tunnel was most likely to house the key. 'The laws of magic state that every Quest must have obstacles.'

'What a *stupid* law!' spat Michael, raising his head indignantly. 'I suppose we can't *really* afford to criticise it at Christmas present, however.'

With that, Michael led the way up to the first tunnel, since it seemed as good a place as any to start.

The Quest climbed the wooden stairway and soon found themselves inside the most beautiful little chalet they had ever seen. There was a large log fire to the left of the room, decorated with an abundance of Christmas stockings that were overflowing with goodies. Comfy chairs and cushions lounged about the room, and a most inviting spread of Christmas berry cakes had been placed next to the tea set on a country style kitchen table. To Bunnyflower's surprise, a trio of robins flew about the room and twittered merrily to themselves, dancing in between the potted poinsettias and the wall paintings.

'Well, this is confusing. There are any number of places the tablet could be hidden,' vexed Squirrelseed, as he took in the multitude of teapots, drawers, sewing boxes and nooks and crannies until his head swirled in confusion.

'Could it be in here, Squirreldude?' asked Rudolph, as he now picked up a box on top of the fireplace with the words *Magic Readings* written on top of it in a beautiful silver dust.

'It's worth a try, Red Nose. Here, let me open it,' offered Michael.

The box opened with a hefty tug, but instead of a marble tablet, all it contained was a miniature snowman who began laughing ecstatically and rocking back and forth.

'What's so funny about *that*?' asked Sarah, looking cross, and trying to shut the lid on the box to make the snowman go away. To her surprise, however, the box would *not* shut, and instead of the snowman disappearing, his laugh became louder and louder, until the room started spinning around.

'What's happening, Blitzy?' asked Rudolph, as the room now turned harder and faster and everything now really did become topsy-turvy. Indeed, drawers opened and closed, the cuckoo clock wouldn't stop chiming, and the entire tea collection flew up into the air, acquiring a life of its own.

'I think this must be one of the fake tunnels,' cried Blitzen, who was now struggling to keep his balance on the floor in all of the mayhem. 'The lantern said to watch out for deceitful traps.'

'Then we have to get out of here,' cried Sarah, who was beginning to feel sick. 'Quickly, let's head for the exit.'

This wasn't as easy as she thought, since the room kept picking up speed every second, and no sooner did the exit appear than it had passed them again. However, after showering themselves with some Reindeer dust, they managed to tumble out and landed on the ground with a mighty thud.

'Well, I say, that was a bit unexpected,' murmured Squirrelseed, as his head still whirled and the tunnel to the **Secret Chalet** now sealed itself shut.

'What if the reading was in there and we missed it?' worried Sarah, now fearing that all the spinning around had been meant to put them off.

'No. The message said if the tunnel was false it would reveal itself to be so,' replied Blitzen assuredly. 'The tablet has got to be in one of the other two.'

They now approached the second tunnel, entitled **Sugar Grove**, which really did look quite delicious. The walls and ceiling of the tunnel were made of ice cream, much to the delight of Bunnyflower, with a large, chocolate waterfall cascading at the far end. An abundance of muffins lay scattered around like toadstools, and Christmas candy trees and lollipops, that were even larger than the Reindeer, rose out of the ground.

'Are we allowed to eat it?' asked Bunnyflower, who hadn't eaten much since last night in the hideout, and was suddenly overwhelmed by the bountiful goodies in front of him.

'No, Bunnyflower. You mustn't eat it. We're here to find the tablet, remember,' ordered Blitzen firmly, at which the little cub looked down dejectedly, and rather hastily placed a chunk of ice cream, which he had otherwise intended eating, back into the wall.

'Hey look, you guys. I'm Santa Claus. He he,' cried Rudolph, as he emerged from behind a lollipop, his face covered in white candyfloss. 'Ho ho ho.'

'For Christmas sakes, Rudolph,' barked Blitzen, rolling his eyes as Bunnyflower chuckled and clutched his stomach. 'Just start looking for the tablet, will you.'

Rudolph poked his tongue out at Blitzen, but as he saw the rest of the Quest breaking open the goodies, he joined in too, pawing his way through the muffins and ducking his head inside the chocolate river.

'Well, no prizes for guessing why it's called **Sugar Grove**,' remarked Squirrelseed, who was beginning to feel quite tempted, himself, by all these lovely treats.

'Yes. If only all of them could be like this,' uttered Sarah thoughtfully.

'Hey you guys. You guys, I found it!' cried Bunnyflower, bouncing forward with what appeared to be an engraved marble tablet in his paws. 'I found it inside that frozen lollipop over there. This is it, right?' cried Bunnyflower, appearing extremely chuffed with himself now as he held out his paw-sized discovery for the Quest to see.

'Let's have a look,' said Blitzen, taking the tablet and holding it up before him. The tablet certainly looked like marble. It sparkled magically and bore some very impressive Christmas words. But if it was the correct tablet, then what was it doing hidden inside a lollipop?

'It can't be the right one,' insisted Michael, looking at it sceptically. 'Some of the words have been misspelt. Sorry, Bunnyflower, but it must be a false one again.'

No sooner had Michael spoken these words than the tablet began to melt like ice, and all the food around them slowly began to turn rotten.

'Oh dear. It doesn't look so appetising now, does it?' remarked Squirrelseed, watching the ice cream turn to slush. 'I suppose we'd better get out of here.'

Snow now fell on their heads as the exit began to shrink, and as Rudolph looked down, he nearly had a Christmas fit.

'Christmas crinkly bits, everybody, look at your feet!' he cried, jumping up and down like a Jack-in-the-box. 'We're under a spell or something, Christmasdudes. We're under an evil curse.'

The Quest looked down to see, to their astonishment, that they were slowly being immersed in marshmallow. Their feet were sinking into a sea of sticky pink goo.

'Snow way, I'm sinking,' cried Bunnyflower, as the goo was fast approaching his neck. 'It's swallowing me up. Help! Help!'

'Great Crimbo, what do we do. What do we do?' cried Squirrelseed, who was now also up to his neck in marshmallow, and waved his arms around frantically for help.

Blitzen struggled mightily in a panic, and really did think that they were done for when, with that, the sea of marshmallow erupted like a volcano, and all six were flung out from **Sugar Grove** before its entrance sealed shut.

'Well, that's it then, I guess. That just leaves one tunnel left,' declared Michael, looking at its gaping mouth, and wondering what surprises *this* one had in store.

'Yes indeed,' said Squirrelseed in a bit of a fluster. 'But I can't help feeling that maybe we didn't have a good enough look inside the other two.'

'In our defence, Double S, we really weren't given much of a choice,' remarked Michael, pulling the goo from his hair.

'Uh, guys,' ventured Rudolph, as his lips began quivering. 'Sorry to break up this Christmatastic little conversation, but what in the name of Christmas is *that*?'

Everyone looked to where Rudolph was pointing and were equally stunned and intrigued by what they saw. At the entrance to the third and final cave stood a spectre, semi-transparent, and dressed from head to foot in a white hooded cloak, carrying a small white-flamed candle. The spectre had long hair, and left no footprints in the snow on which it walked.

'What is it?' whispered Sarah, who felt she must have turned as pallid as the apparition itself.

'Why - it's a ghost,' breathed Blitzen in confusion, as he watched it beckon to them before disappearing into the cave. 'A *Christmas* ghost. And it seems to want us to follow it into the tunnel.'

'Oh, I dunno, Blitzy. I mean, I was all on board when I thought we just had to go in and get the *Magic Reading*,' protested Rudolph, his eyes widening, 'but now that there's some weird little Christmas ghost guarding it, well I'm feeling kinda FREAKED OUT.'

'Come on, Red Nose. A little fright might do you good,' teased Michael, giving the Reindeer a slap on the back. 'Might take some wrinkles off your face.'

'Oh I dunno, Princey, I mean....'

'Sshhhhh, look! There it is again,' murmured Squirrelseed, as the spectre now reappeared at the tunnel's mouth and beckoned them with its ghostly finger before de-materializing again into a rapture of darkness.

'Come on! We *have* to follow it,' called Michael, pulling Rudolph by the tail, and now closely followed by the others.

This tunnel did *not* open into a cheery world. In fact, it remained very dark, and their only guide was the faint outline of the spectre. The tunnel grew colder, the further they advanced, and they heard the sound of rushing water somewhere up ahead.

'Can you hear that?' whispered Sarah, as her voice resounded around the cave like a thousand echoes.

'Yes. I think we must be approaching some kind of river,' said Blitzen, as the tunnel widened and grew lighter. 'And look! There's a sign up ahead.'

The Quest looked up to where a crude archway now stood before them, with a crooked wooden sign bearing the words **Icy Falls**. The spectre now disappeared through the archway, and as the Quest followed, they found that they were now standing on the edge of an icy pool of water which plunged into the darkness below.

'What's going on?' asked Michael, peering over the edge and listening to the violent thrashing of the waterfall. 'Surely we don't have to go down there. We'll kill ourselves,' he said, looking in alarm at the near vertical drop and descrying no safe path around it.

'There is no other way,' came a hollow voice behind him.

As the Quest looked behind them, they now saw, to their horror, that five more spectres accompanied the first, who had spoken these chilling words, all wearing white cloaks and gowns and each bearing a white-flamed candle.

'What the devil is that supposed to mean?' asked Michael, as all six of the Quest were now hovering dangerously close to the edge of the waterfall.

The spectres said nothing and stared at the Quest in chilling silence, until suddenly the first spectre blew out its candle.

'It means, Michael, that you are in for a bumpy ride.'

Without another word, all six were pushed forcefully down the waterfall and tumbled headlong at a startling pace. Their screams resounded around the tunnel and became even louder as the icy water down below hit them. But the journey didn't end there. The pool's current now carried them forwards into a second tunnel, this time thrashing them down it like a waterslide. All six of them were washed down it together, bumping into each other like drowning Rats.

'What's guna happen to us, Blitzy? We're going the wrong way,' cried Rudolph, as the waterfall spiralled downwards wildly, until it washed them up an incline, only to plunge them back down again.

'I don't know,' cried Blitzen. 'Just hang onto each other.'

The tunnel seemed to be getting narrower and steeper, and the icy water was actually getting colder.

'I don't understand how this will take us to the top of the cave,' cried Sarah, as she was now being washed sideways and kept bumping into Michael, who was travelling backwards.

'Well, if I could just spin myself around it might help. Argh, crackers,' he yelled, as they passed through a small shower of icy water.

'Wait, look up there! Could we be nearing the end?' asked Sarah, as they appeared to be heading towards a break in the tunnel.

'I don't know,' shouted Squirrelseed, who was holding on for dear life inside Sarah's coat pocket. 'But it looks like it's going to drop us into nothing.'

'Oh no! I know what's going to happen,' yelled Michael. 'Everybody hang on tight. Catch hold of each other's hands.'

The tunnel now came to an abrupt stop, flinging the Quest into an icy whirlpool down below, but no sooner were they plunged into it than a gigantic rumbling was heard that grew louder and louder until the stalactites on the ceiling began to shake.

'What's happening to us?' yelled Sarah, kicking her feet.

'Oh, this is it, Christmasdudes. This is how I'm guna die,' whispered Rudolph, shutting his eyes tightly and clutching Bunnyflower as though he were a cuddly toy.

'We're not going to die, Red Nose. Hang on. Ready? Here it comes.'

With that, a gigantic jet of water shot them up into the air so that they landed on a ledge at the top of the cave. It then washed them between a gap in the wall so that they rolled down a slope into a hidden room. The water then retreated, and when the Quest regained their senses, they couldn't believe their eyes.

'My great, good Christmas!' breathed Michael, standing up and wringing his clothes dry as he gazed around him. The entire room was snow-swept, the walls made of pure diamond, and there, perched on a ledge at the centre of it all, was a marble tablet bearing the sacred and magical words that would save the Kingdom.

Michael now walked towards it, utterly mesmerised, as the rest of the Quest trailed behind him.

'We've found it,' he cried, approaching the tablet slowly, as his hands began to sweat. 'We've found the marble tablet. It's definitely the right one this time. It looks like it was written by the Angels in Heaven.'

'Good Christmas,' gasped Sarah, spellbound, as a small silver envelope now floated before her.

Congratulations on finding the sacred tablet. Its words can save the fate of Christmas. Good Luck, and remember not to remove it.

'Good Christmas, I feel so nervous now,' trembled Sarah, as she reached for some paper and gold Reindeer dust.

The rest of the Quest had now gathered around the famous tablet and quietly read its powerful words.

Christmas is the mighty light,
A most noble cause for which to fight.
Any force which threatens its power
Must be stopped this very hour.

'It almost makes one shiver,' said Blitzen, who felt mightily touched by the sacred engraving.

'Yes, indeed it does,' added Sergeant Squirrelseed, as Sarah scribbled down the final line of the tablet.

'Hey, you guys, what's that?' asked Bunnyflower, suddenly pointing with his paw.

'What's what?' asked Michael, looking up at the Christmacub, and wondering why he was pointing at him.

'That!' asked Bunnyflower again, as he pointed at the mysterious red ribbon which had now emerged from Michael's pocket and was floating in mid-air.

Michael's face suddenly turned white as he reached out and grabbed the ribbon.

'It's nothing,' he faltered, snatching the ribbon out of mid-air and putting it back inside his pocket, only to find that it shook vibrantly and flew back out again.

'It's nothing?' contested Blitzen, walking over to him and picking up the ribbon himself. 'Michael, this is a ribbon receipt from the North Wind. When did you send a letter along it? *The Scroll* told you not to send letters at this time.'

'I didn't. Really, I didn't,' gulped Michael, feeling his face growing hotter by the second.

Michael looked around at the Quest's faces, but seeing that they looked unconvinced, he decided to come clean.

'Alright, alright. I sent it at Christmas Street Station. I couldn't resist taking a chance. I know *The Scroll* was supposed to contact my father, but that just wasn't good enough for me. I had to contact him as well, just in case it was unsuccessful - you saw how scary that frozen candle was.'

'Yes, but Michael, *The Scroll* told you not to use the North Wind for a reason. Under evil rule, it's all completely....'

'Yes I know, I know. But all that doesn't matter now, does it? The letter reached him, it must have. The wind delivered it there unhindered, else why would I be holding this red ribbon in my hands?' blurted Michael, as Blitzen's face glowered.

'But, Prince Michael, if the ribbon's from your father, why is it flickering like that?' asked Bunnyflower, now pointing to the ribbon again in complete innocence.

'Flickering! What are you talking about?' asked Michael, turning to look at the floating ribbon.

'Oh, my goodness,' exclaimed Sarah, as she saw the piece of ribbon now fill with a yellow glow, and the face of the Guardian flash over it.

At that moment the ribbon screeched and burst open, creating a blinding flash of yellow light, as if generated by a thousand Snow Wolves – so fierce in its intentions that it caused everything in the Quest's line of vision to go blank. Sarah blinked hard and fast. It took a good few minutes for her vision to return, but when it did, she stared in horror at what she now saw. She and Michael were completely surrounded by a wreath of candles, and were bound together by a frozen chain, with their hands turned to sheer ice. She did not know where the rest of the Quest were; she could not see them, but a new arresting figure now made its way towards them and stared at them vindictively.

'Why, hello Your Majesties. So brave of you to have made it this far.'

'Snooks,' spat Michael, as he saw the face of the treacherous sorcerer standing before him and began to writhe. 'Snooks, let us out of here at once. I could hang you for what you've done to this Kingdom.'

'Oh now, now, Michael, it's a little late for that. You no longer have any power here,' the sorcerer reminded him, as his snow spider crawled menacingly across his concealed wings. 'It is the Guardian who rules the Kingdom now, not you and your family, and I would advise you to curb your tongue, given it was you who got you both into this mess in the first place,' he added, nodding at Michael and his sister. 'I mean, it was you who sent the letter, was it not?'

'I sent that letter to warn my father of the attack on the Kingdom. You obviously intercepted it and used it against me, you devious little snake. What did you put in that red ribbon? A tracker, was it? You callous, obnoxious, little fiend, you. Well, it doesn't matter anyway. *The Scroll* is going to contact him too. Another letter is on its way to him as we speak. The only reason I sent mine is because I feared it wouldn't get there in time.'

'Oh Michael, you make me laugh,' cackled Snooks rather smugly. 'Do you think we didn't intercept that one too? The message sent by *The Scroll* has been destroyed. The only thing that has reached your father is a deputation of Snow Wolves, who are now holding him prisoner in The

Town of Flickering Candles until the Guardian works out what to do with him.'

'Arrgghhh, I hate you. I hate you. I despise you with every ounce of my being. And besides which, we haven't lost yet. Sarah still has the words of the engraving. I've burned them into my brain so that I won't ever forget them. Even with our hands tied up we can still save Christmas,' spat the Prince, with the fire of determination in his eye.

'Yes, well, that would be the case if you had not distributed a drop of your and your sister's blood onto the letter,' said the sorcerer, as a malicious smile saturated with smugness now crept slowly over his face. 'You were warned of the dangers of invoking *The Secret Seal of Christmas* in a time of darkness, and now it has come back to haunt you. You see, the Guardian now owns a piece of your souls, and if you want them back, so that you can try and save Christmas, then you'd better do exactly as he says.'

Michael now screamed in agony when, with that, both children were bundled into a sack, and with a simple click of Snooks' fingers, all three of them disappeared. The rest of the Quest now stood in horror at the engulfing reality, as the walls of the cave began to crumble.

16 - The Escape

The Quest looked around in fear.

'What are we supposed to do now?' cried Rudolph, as his legs shook uncontrollably.

'Well, if we don't get out of here soon, we'll be as flat as Christmas pancakes, because the ceiling is getting lower,' cried Sergeant Squirrelseed.

It certainly was, but fortunately Blitzen had an idea.

'I know a method we once used in a training exercise. Don't try to remember it, Rudolph, because you weren't there. Ok, now, when I throw this pawful of dust into the air, we've all got to chant the *Secret Message of Distress.* Do you all know what this is?' he asked, looking at them earnestly, one by one.

The creatures nodded, so Blitzen pulled them even further into the corner as the ceiling shook wildly.

'Alright then, here we go,' shouted Blitzen, throwing the pink Reindeer dust into the air. 'One, two, three:

Dust of Christmas, we're in doubt.

Use your powers to get us out,'

chanted the creatures, following the dust with their eyes, as it whirled around in the shape of a twister.

'Look, there it goes,' said Sergeant Squirrelseed, as the dust suddenly created a revolving archway in the wall.

'Is that it? Is that the way out?' asked Bunnyflower, jumping onto Rudolph's back for safety.

'Yes, it must be. Quickly, everyone, jump through,' yelled Blitzen, pushing them all towards it.

The Reindeer dust was revolving faster and faster, as all four Christma-questers stepped into the archway. It spun around even faster before producing a burst of light that suddenly transported them out of the tunnel and placed them back in the snow-covered grounds of Cinnamon Forest.

'Alright, we made it,' cried Bunnyflower, as he beamed brightly.

'Uh, Blitzen,' panicked Sergeant Squirrelseed, as he suddenly looked around them and noticed, to his horror, that they were not quite out of the woods yet.

'What is it?' asked Blitzen, pricking his ears up and looking around.

'Listen. Can't you hear that?' he cried.

'What! The thunder?' asked Rudolph dumbly, but hoping that he was correct.

'No, that. That's not thunder. It's growling. Listen,' blurted Squirrelseed, as he shook uncontrollably. Bunnyflower clutched on tightly to Rudolph as he heard the growls.

'The Snow Wolves?' he questioned, in the hope that it was not true. 'Oh no, we have to get out of here.'

But it was too late. The Snow Wolves were already in front of them and had started closing in from the sides.

'Oh, good Christmas! What do we do?' shrieked Squirrelseed.

'We fight,' said Blitzen bravely. 'We have to. If the Snow Wolves capture us, they will throw us in the castle dungeons, or worse, and then we will not be able to save the Kingdom. We must resist them at all costs. The Guardian already has the children. He cannot take us as well, otherwise the Quest will fail. If we are to succeed in this then we must infiltrate the castle ourselves, secretly, and then attack. We cannot and must not get caught. Remember why we are doing this. We are fighting for the children. And we are fighting for Christmas. And no matter what happens, we cannot let these Snow Wolves win,' declared Blitzen.

Squirrelseed obeyed and jumped off Blitzen to stand alone. The horror of the Snow Wolves confronting them was astounding.

'For Christmas and the Reindeer Honour,' declared Blitzen, putting his right hoof next to Rudolph's.

'For Christmas and the Reindeer Honour,' declared Rudolph, gulping down his fear.

'Ready! And charge!!' yelled Blitzen, as he rushed headlong to meet the Wolves in battle.

The Snow Wolves came pounding towards them, brutal and fierce. Their eyes were gleaming a blinding yellow and their tongues were a bloody red. There were at least twenty of them, each one as bloodthirsty as the next.

Blitzen was the first to feel the attack. The Wolves seemed to relish attacking the great leader of the Reindeer - but he fought strongly and bravely, and Rudolph helped to relieve the load, albeit with a great deal of complaining. Sergeant Squirrelseed was not to be toyed with. He charged at the Wolves and gnawed at their legs and necks until the pain was too much for them. Bunnyflower, in the meantime, had jumped into a nearby conifer tree for safety. The battle terrified him, and now that he was face to face with the Wolves, he understood exactly why Blitzen and the others had not wanted him to fight. He could see now how he didn't stand a chance. He clung fast to the branches of the conifer tree, shut his eyes and prayed for this dreadful battle to be over. He wished he was back on Christmas Mountain with his brothers, eating out of the giant ice cream cone. He'd even rather be back in the hideout with his mother, or helping out with a Christmas Deeds Project for Camp Christmas, but he did not want to be here. Whoever said that war was glorious had obviously never fought in one. He squeezed his eyes so tightly that tears began to roll down them, and he tightened his grip as the battle around him caused the ground to shake.

Across the way, Blitzen was beginning to lose ground. Two Wolves were viciously assaulting him, and he could not handle them both. He was pinned down by one, as another sank his teeth straight into his front leg. An agonizing scream echoed through the battlefield - one which Squirrelseed had never heard the like of before, and hoped that he never would again. Rudolph looked across to see that his friend was in grave danger.

'Oh no, Blitzy. I'm cumin', Christmasdude,' he cried, as he charged to his aid.

'Hey, Wolfy, leave him alone,' he cried rather shakily, as he tried to distract the Wolf. 'Here, come and get me instead. I'm a celebrity Reindeer.' Rudolph danced around on the spot with his best disco moves, but the Wolf merely hit him to the ground before turning his attention back to Blitzen. The red-nosed Reindeer shook his head. They were severely outnumbered on the battlefield, and the Wolves were too vicious and large for them to contend with.

'Rainbow Cakes,' muttered Rudolph to himself. 'We need some Rainbow Cakes. It's the only way we're guna win.'

Rainbow Cakes were a special concoction of pink and gold Reindeer dust infused inside a Christmas muffin.One bite of a Rainbow Cake and he had a whole range of crazy powers for two Christmas minutes.

He pulled his leather bag from around his torso and took a hefty bite into a Rainbow Cake he had stashed away. A rush of magic surged through his system, and his hooves and antlers turned pink. This done, he took off into the air, and with the extra energy – and bravery - induced by the cake, he began lifting up the Wolves with his hooves, and flung them far, far away across the forest.

'Yeah, take that and that, you big brutes. That'll teach you to mess with my Christmasbuddies. No one messes with Rainbow Rudolph when he gets going. Yeah, and that's for the Prince and Princess, you big oaf.'

He then headed straight for Blitzen - who by this time had turned pale and weak - picked him up, and flew him to safety in a wooded area nearby.

'I'll come back for you, Blitzy. Just stay here for now,' said Rudolph. 'I've gotta help the others.'

Blitzen gave a nod and a groan. Rudolph then took off again to find the others on the battlefield. Sergeant Squirrelseed found himself in serious trouble as he became cornered by three Snow Wolves. He hurled a stick at them, which managed to catch all three of them on their faces, but this was too much for him, and the sheer force knocked him over, so that he fell backwards and hit the conifer tree. At this moment Bunnyflower fell out of his hiding place and landed face down in the snow, right in front of the Wolves. Bunnyflower lay still for a moment before slowly lifting up his head. The expression on the Wolves' faces now changed, and Sergeant Squirrelseed moved completely out of their focus as all eyes were now on the bundle before them. Their eyes gleamed, like the fires of Hell, and emitted a heat that began to burn as Bunnyflower looked on helplessly and in terror.

'Pppplease,' faltered the little Bunny Rabbit. 'Ppppplease don't hurt me,' he winced, looking up at them with huge, desperate eyes. But it was too late. Snow Blood snatched the little Bunny by the scruff of his neck and shook him violently in his jaw. He then flung him headlong across the field so that the little Bunny hit a giant oak tree with a deep, hard thud. Squirrelseed cried for help, and ran over to see if he was alright, but the Wolves were already behind him and began tearing at his tail and feet. Then, as if by magic, Rudolph appeared from behind and flung them one by one across the battlefield.

'Get out of here, you brutes. You're never guna defeat my Christmabuddies,' he cried, as the last of the Wolves slunk back towards the castle.

Rudolph stood there panting for a moment, while Sergeant Squirrelseed simply shook.

'Phew, I don't ever wanna do *that* again,' he added, as his face flushed as red as his nose. Indeed, his heroism had quite surprised him.

'Are you ok, Squirreldude?' he asked, now turning to the Sergeant.

'Well yes, I'm alright. But I'm not sure about Bunnyflower.'

The woods were completely silent as they turned towards the conifer tree underneath which lay a little bundle of white fur. Sergeant Squirrelseed turned the Bunny over on his side to reveal a red patch of snow underneath his bleeding body. Bunnyflower was dead.

17 - The Forest of Magic Lanterns

The two returned to the spot where Blitzen lay in silence. Rudolph had wrapt Bunnyflower's body in a red velvet scarf so that he could be given a proper burial in Cinnamon Forest. The wounded Blitzen was absolutely devastated to hear the news.

'If only we'd taken him back to the hideout,' lamented Blitzen with a heavy heart. 'I was so stupid to think that we could make it this far without running into trouble. What will Mrs Bunnie say? How could I have let this happen?' continued the Reindeer in great distress. 'I blame myself.'

'You didn't let this happen,' said Sergeant Squirrelseed. 'The Snow Wolves came out of nowhere. The poor little Christmacub didn't stand a chance.'

'But if I hadn't been injured. If we'd taken a different route....' he continued.

'What about me, Blitzy?' interrupted Rudolph. 'If I'd gotten there a few seconds earlier I could've saved him. I hate this horrid war. That little Christmasdude was so cute.'

Here, Rudolph blew his shiny red nose as Squirrelseed patted him on the back.

'He was, Rudolph. He was,' sighed Sergeant Squirrelseed. 'But I'm afraid nothing we say now can bring him back. We have to continue to fight for The Kingdom of Christmas to ensure that his little life wasn't lost in vain.'

'You're right,' agreed Blitzen, suddenly taking hold of himself. 'We have to continue.'

With these words he tried to stand up, but his leg was still badly injured, and he faltered, falling back down in the snow again.

'Oh here, let me help you, Blitzy,' offered Rudolph, running over to lend his support.

Standing on two legs, Rudolph put Blitzen's arm around his shoulder to help him to walk.

'You know, I haven't thanked you yet for saving my life,' said Blitzen sincerely.

'Don't worry about it, Blitzy,' answered Rudolph. 'Us Reindeer have gotta stick together. Although, I've gotta say, Christmasdude, I'd never have managed it without those Rainbow Cakes. I'd never have had it in me.'

'I'm not so sure,' winked Blitzen, who for once, had been thoroughly impressed with Rudolph's behaviour.

They had not advanced far out of the clearing, when a flickering speck of light came darting through the trees and began to fly around the Quest.

'What is it?' asked Squirrelseed, squinting his eyes in confusion.

The flickering light hovered before them for a moment, before it grew into a rainbow of dazzling rays that filled the entire area of the forest and temporarily blinded the creatures. Then, as the stain of light gradually retreated from their eyes they were confronted by a beautiful Snowbelle dressed in a sparkling, white tutu, with clear, glittering wings and flossy blonde hair. It was Loretta.

'Good evening,' she said, 'and welcome to The Forest of Magic Lanterns.'

The Quest had been so spellbound by the Snowflake's sudden appearance, that they failed to notice how their surroundings had also changed. The snow-covered conifers of Cinnamon Forest had now been replaced with delicate oak trees, many of which had tiny marble cottages with sloping roofs built high up in their branches. Instead of lamps, each pixie cottage was lit with fireflies, and from every tree hung a lantern. At this moment the lanterns gave out a dim orange light, signifying that although things had gone wrong, there was a faint hope of saving the Kingdom.

Rudolph now looked at the Snowbelle, perplexed.

'Wait, when did we enter the forest, Snowdude?' he asked, scratching his head.

'When the bright light appeared before you,' she answered. 'You have been absorbed into the forest and are completely hidden from view. You see, when it chooses to be, the forest is completely invisible, and it is so now. Not even the Guardian or Snooks can find you here.'

The Quest gave a faint smile at this, feeling somewhat relieved that they were temporarily safe.

'So Clarinda managed to free the forest from the Guardian's spell then,' commented Blitzen, who was now standing upright with the help of a toadstool.

'Yes, she did,' confirmed Loretta proudly. 'She had to travel all the way to Whispering Island to get a special magic potion. The spell the Guardian placed on us was very powerful - fortunately however, we are here now and plan to assist you as best we can.'

She then turned and looked down at the red scarf which enveloped Bunnyflower.

'I am deeply sorry to hear about Bunnyflower's death,' she sympathised, bowing. 'Please, give him to us and we will ensure that he is buried in Cinnamon Forest.'

Another Snowflake now appeared, carrying a white marble chest adorned with silver swirls with the name **Bunnyflower** engraved on the top. Rudolph patted the red bundle gently, before placing it in the chest, and wiping a fresh set of tears from his eyes.

'Goodbye, Christmasdude,' he whispered gently.

The Quest bowed their heads, as the Snowflake closed the lid and curtseyed, before disappearing back into the forest.

'I'm terribly sorry to hear about what has happened to the children,' said Loretta, as the Quest finished saying their goodbyes. 'We are watching The Well of Truth closely to find out exactly what the Guardian wants to do with them. When the lanterns begin to turn red, we will know that they have reached the castle. Fortunately, we still have a bit of time to build you up before we take you there. We hear they have also taken Prince Harcourt hostage in the Northern Regions. We are trying to contact our sources there too.'

'Of course,' said Blitzen, nodding. 'And am I right in understanding that you will be providing us with reinforcements when we attack the castle?'

'Yes, you are. We will discuss logistics and attacking strategies over dinner, but first I think we'd better get that leg of yours seen to. Follow me, please. We will have to make contact with the underground hideout in order to let Mrs Bunnie know what has happened. When she discovered Bunnyflower was missing, she left and began looking for him alone. Fortunately Tristan, a refugee Snowflake who had escaped from the castle, found her and returned her to the hideout before making contact with us. He is here tonight if you wish to speak to him.' Loretta led them through the central path of the forest towards *The Snowflake Headquarters* situated in The Snowy Oak Tree.

'Did many Snowflakes manage to escape from the castle?' asked Blitzen, as he limped along.

'Very few. I hear those who didn't are being frozen and smashed in the Mountains. It is near to impossible for us to infiltrate the castle at the moment. Snooks has developed a very sophisticated charm which senses the presence of Snowflakes within the castle. Of course, he should know, being one himself.'

As they made their way to *The Snowflake Headquarters*, the true enchantment of the forest became apparent. Fireflies lit up white cottages in the trees and glistening mistletoe hung down from the branches. Snow changed colour intermittently from pink to silver, and Rudolph beamed with delight at the presence of such magic.

'Hello, Blitzen, hello, Rudolph, hello, Sergeant Squirrelseed,' called some of the Snowflakes from their tree houses.

They soon came to a snow-covered weeping willow, whose leaves hung down like a curtain, closing off the next part of the forest. Loretta pulled the sparkling white leaves back to reveal a little clearing in the forest, at the centre of which stood an oak tree with a large chalet in its branches.

'Here it is,' she stated. *'The Snowflake Headquarters.'*

Rudolph stopped and looked up in awe at the ornate, pixie-like building. He didn't remember it being *this* pretty. Indeed, the walls and roof were made of a sparkling marble, adorned with spiralling vines of mistletoe, while a holly-trimmed swing hung down from the oak tree to assist entry.

'Hey, is that a Christmas countdown?' asked Rudolph, suddenly pointing to the number 21 which was carved on the door of the chalet in delicate frost.

'Yes, it is,' replied Loretta solemnly. 'It magically changes number every day. Don't worry, we still have time, but as you can see, it is running out.'

Rudolph nodded slowly, and a jolt of nervousness shot through him. What if Christmas *couldn't* be saved? What if the Guardian *did* win? His thoughts were cut short however, as Loretta pulled on a lever that lowered the large holly trimmed swing.

'On you get. We keep it for our most special guests.'

The trio managed to squeeze on – just about - and the swing was then raised upwards as Loretta flew to the ivory balcony to greet them at the top. As they got out, two Snowflakes flew towards them, with a toadstool-shaped wheelchair to transport Blitzen.

'We'll have to treat your leg first,' said one of the Snowbelles. 'It will need some Christmas healing cream and the Kiss of Health,' she said, wheeling him away.

'Hey, do we all get the Kiss of Health for the trauma of battle?' piped Rudolph, suddenly feeling left out. 'I mean, my hooves are Christmakilling me, and my nose isn't as red as it should be. What do you say, Frosty? Have you got a little Snow Kiss for Rude the dude?' he asked, now puckering up his Reindeer lips as he leaned towards her on his tippy toes.

'You can collect one yourself from the wishing well, if you want,' smiled the pretty little Snowbelle, before entering the chalet.

'Oh, *that* kind of kiss,' muttered Rudolph, disappointed.

Loretta then opened the double doors at the front of the building and led them inside to where a group of high-ranking Snowflakes were waiting for them.

'Hey, Hansen. I haven't seen you since the slalom after-party,' shouted Rudolph across the room, pleased to see that he recognised many of the Snowflakes present, from the Magic Lantern Marvels Team.

'Yes, it is a pity we are having to meet under such difficult circumstances,' replied Hansen curtly, as the fireflies twinkled on the walls behind him.

'Yes, indeed. Please take a seat, Rudolph. Our banquet will commence shortly,' seconded Tristan, the Head of the Snowflake Secret Service, and the second racer in the slalom team.

Rudolph beamed merrily as he sat down, feeling he fitted in quite nicely here after the ordeal of the Quest. A canopy of mistletoe hung above them and scattered snow petals lay on the floor, making this setting truly beautiful and magical. Blitzen now entered too, his leg miraculously healed, and pulled up a seat next to Clarinda, whom Rudolph had not seen since the night of the Christmas concert at the Snowglobe Theatre.

'Hey, Clarry, how's it going?' he cried, waving at her across the table.

'Very well, thank you, Rudolph. It's very nice to have you here tonight,' she said, before raising her goblet and standing up.

'Let the feast begin,' she announced in a magical voice, as the entire gathering went silent.

The table, Rudolph observed, had been empty up until this point, and since he had never been to a banquet at the forest before, he didn't quite know what to expect. Happily, he was about to receive a very pleasant surprise.

'Chocolate biscuits,' said Loretta, at which a generous stack of rather large biscuits appeared on her plate.

'Christmas trifle with treacle sauce,' said Tristan greedily.

'Snow way! You can wish for whatever you want,' exclaimed Rudolph in disbelief.

'Absolutely. What else would you expect from The Forest of Magic Lanterns,' said Hansen loftily.

Rudolph's head whirled for a second while he thought about what he wanted.

'Oh, in that case I'll have cinnamon cakes with cinnamon punch, Christmas cake with extra icing, frosted fizz bites, sugared almonds, treacle pudding and oh, uh, uh, wait, there was something else. Uh, cream candy puffs,' said the overzealous Rudolph. 'Ya know, I really didn't think I was so hungry.'

'Christmas crackers, Rudolph, you know you are going to have to fit through the doors of the castle, don't you,' mocked Blitzen, who could barely see across the table, due to the amount of food Rudolph had wished for.

'Hey, it's Christma-comfort food, Blitzy. I've earned it, what with all this stress,' snapped Rudolph, tucking in.

Soon the table was overflowing with treats, both sweet and savoury, and everyone tucked into a delicious, hearty meal. After dinner the plates cleared themselves away at the click of a finger.

Discussions then began on how the attack on the castle would unfold. Tristan, being the head of the Secret Service, naturally took the lead, and much of what was said passed chiefly between him and Blitzen. The plan was for the Quest to be taken to the castle at nightfall, under cover of darkness. It was estimated it would take Snooks that long to get the children to the castle. The Quest would then break in through the North West Tower which, according to the Snowflake spies, was currently redundant under the control of the Guardian. Once they were inside, the Snowflakes would align themselves in the air for a ten-mile radius around the castle. If they flew high enough, they would be unseen by the Wolves, and would swoop down when the time came. Blitzen agreed to this plan, but said they would need extra supplies of Reindeer dust if they were going to fly in through the tower. Tristan assured him that this had already been taken care of. Rudolph was for the present time too concerned with the pretty Snowbelles either side of him to care much about tomorrow's plans, but he was quite happy to go along with whatever Blitzen thought was best.

'And what about the Elves?' asked Blitzen, knowing that this subject had to be broached sooner or later.

'What about them?' retorted Hansen, curtly.

'There are rumours that some are being tortured in the Mountains. We *have* to release them. I know there is a longstanding rift existing between you, but if you allow this to happen, then you're no better than the Guardian.'

'Now see here, Blitzen,' smarted Hansen. 'You have no right to march in here waving accusations around like that. No one ever said we wanted to torture the Elves. We just want our differences to be observed, that is all. As soon as our great friend, Lysander, returns with *The Testament of the Snowflakes*, we can be more clear about our boundaries. We cannot do anything until then.'

A picture of Lysander hung on the wall behind them, with his blue eyes glistening and his hair as blonde as a Golden Eagle's egg. He was the quintessential Snowflake. More perfect even than Hansen. More haughty and superior. He seemed to cast them down with his demeanour, yet raise them in hope all at once.

'Oh, for Christmas sakes, Hansen. Lysander is not going to return with *The Testament of the Snowflakes*,' scoffed Blitzen, sneering at the picture disdainfully, and spotting a few tears along its edges, caused by age. 'He left over 30 years ago. He would have done so by now if he had found it. Don't you think his disappearance is a sign that you should leave the book alone?'

'We do not know that he has disappeared, for a fact. According to

The Well of Truth, we may find him yet, but even if we don't, we can still send out someone else. The book exists. And if it exists we have a duty to find it.'

'Do you indeed. And what then? Even more bad blood between you and the Elves? There is enough of a rift existing between the two of you, as it is, without having the teachings of an ancient book exacerbating it. No, I think you should leave the book there and put this whole matter behind you. You are different from the Elves, but not superior. If this war has taught you anything, it proves that we should stick together. Any book which suggests otherwise should be burned into a thousand ashes.'

'How dare you!' exclaimed Loretta, clearly stung. '*The Testament* speaks an ancient law.'

'If it says what you think it says, then that law is wrong,' argued Blitzen, with an accent of finality.

There was a pause of silence after these words, as everyone stared at him.

'And it is just that,' he continued. 'Ancient. Outdated. Not fitting to our world. You cannot live like this. This book will only stand in your way.'

'Well said, Blitzen,' said Clarinda, rising. 'I believe enough time has been wasted on this book. I, like you, believe it will bring no benefit to us. When this war is over, we will improve our relations with the Elves, whether Lysander returns or not. To Christmas!' she toasted, raising her goblet.

Everyone at the table raised their glass to the toast, except Hansen, Loretta and Tristan.

Blitzen turned towards them and folded his hooves.

'I cannot just shake off my beliefs,' objected Hansen. 'And I certainly cannot give up on our search for this mighty book, especially when one of my greatest friends is out looking for it. But I *can* execute a deed for the good of Christmas.

I will arrange for a small battalion to go to the Mountains and rescue the Elves, how does that suit you, Blitzen?'

'It will do for now,' agreed Blitzen, nodding his head.

So it was decided that the Snowflakes would split their forces between the castle and the northeast. Hansen, on Blitzen's orders, would lead the battalion to the Mountains. His true willingness to form an alliance with the Elves would then truly be tested.

Following this, there was a knock at the door as Lindsay, another member of the famous slalom team, came rushing in.

'Blitzen, everyone. I'm afraid the lanterns have begun to turn red. The children must have reached the castle.'

'Already?' asked Hansen, looking at his watch, and thinking that even for a Snowflake, Snooks had managed to carry them across the boundary lands in record time.

'Yes I'm afraid so. It took them much less time than we expected. We must prepare ourselves to leave for the castle at once.'

The company agreed, and made their way across to The Well of Truth.

18-The Guardian's Bargain

At the frozen castle Snooks emptied the children onto the floor of the Courtroom and handed the Guardian the paper containing *The Sacred Reading.*

'Thank you, Snooks. You have been most helpful,' said the Guardian, placing the paper inside his pocket.

'It is of no consequence, Your Heinous. I am happy to serve you,' bowed the sorcerer unemotionally.

'Good. Then get out of my sight,' seethed the Guardian, as his expression remained unfathomable beneath the sea of darkness.

A few bolts of lightning flashed silently down the sorcerer's cloak, but he quickly managed to collect himself and withdrew his bow.

'Very well, Heinous. I will see you later.'

The sorcerer then turned on his heel and exited the Courtroom.

As the door shut, it echoed down the hall, and the children reluctantly got to their feet.

'Good evening, children. Welcome to my castle,' bowed the Guardian, with a sort of feigned humility before the little twins.

'What do you want with us?' bit Michael sullenly, as Sarah stared down in frustration at her frozen hands.

'Why, merely to make you feel welcome here, Michael,' returned the Guardian with feigned light-heartedness. 'And to get to know you both a little better.'

'To get to know us a little better. You've got to be kidding me. We came here to defeat you, you faceless brute. You've kidnapped my mother. You've kidnapped my father, and now you've kidnapped my sister and me. All you're getting from *me* is the slap of death. And you can untie this frozen chain while you're at it,' glowered Michael, as he pulled away sharply from his sister, the effect of which merely strengthened the binding ice and forced him closer to Sarah. Michael scrunched up his face in despair.

'Why, Michael, that is not a nice way to speak of the bond I have given you and your sister,' continued the Guardian, whose expression remained hidden, and a mystery. 'As twins, you share so many things in life. This chain has always had an invisible presence.'

'You have bound us on purpose, to our own disadvantage, and we both just want to be free. Now give us back the missing pieces of our souls, and let's make this a fair fight,' spat Michael, whose hands were now as lifeless as a rotting corpse.

The Guardian seemed somewhat amused by Michael's rant, while

Sarah was growing impatient with her brother. She felt the ice was turning her blood somewhat colder, and she would have to be as calculating as the Guardian if they were going to get out of this.

'Be quiet, Michael. Let me do the talking,' she said, shooting him a reproachful glance. 'You still haven't answered my brother's question,' she continued, looking boldly at the Guardian. 'Snooks told us that if we want the stolen pieces of our soul back, we have to do as you say. What exactly is it that you want us to do?'

The Guardian chuckled for a moment beneath his cloak, before tapping his talon-like fingers together like a cunning bird of prey.

'You know that you can only save the Kingdom if your souls are completely intact; that you must have shed not one jot of *The Essence of Christmas* from it; and at darkness present that is not the case. Of course, this is a pity - you both have such striking souls. Have you ever seen your souls?' asked the Guardian, now leaning forward slightly on his throne in a manipulative manner.

'No,' said Sarah, struck. 'No, we have never seen them.'

'Ho, well, my *dear* children, I think it is time for you to take a look.'

The children said nothing as the Guardian waved the Staff and Altra at them, thus generating a stream of golden light. The children now lit up and filled with a white light as their souls suddenly became visible through their skin. They looked like Heavenly angels, and both children suddenly gasped in astonishment as their souls stepped outside their bodies and stood before them. At first glance, they appeared to be the children in perfect form - lighter, brighter, whiter, blinding and ethereal-looking, astoundingly reverential and surrounded by a glowing halo that looked as if it had been placed there by the hands of Heaven. Yet as they looked again, they noticed that the left hand on each soul was maggot-ridden and decrepit. This clearly was the hand from which they had drawn a drop of blood.

'I see that you are looking at your hands, children - that is the part of your soul which I possess. Indeed, you might say it spoils them, really,' taunted the Guardian, twirling the letter in front of them like a tantalising document.

'Why are you showing us this?' asked Michael, feeling his stomach twist and knot as though it were all somehow his fault. After all, it was he who had sent the letter. 'Are you just trying to brag?'

'On the contrary, Michael, I am just trying to show you what spectacular souls your error has tarnished. For they *are* spectacular souls, are they not? Why, I myself have never seen two souls so bright and glittering. It is no wonder you were chosen for this Quest. And since you have made it this far, I feel it would be a great shame if you should leave this castle without having a sporting chance.'

'A sporting chance?' he asked, as his eyebrows knotted in confusion. 'A sporting chance at what?'

'Why – at separating the Staff and Altra, of course. That is *why* you came here, is it not?'

'Why, yes, of course it is,' fumbled Michael, wondering why in the universe the Guardian would be giving them this opportunity.

'Why, yes, of course it is,' repeated the Guardian ambivalently. 'And I understand that in order to do that I will have to return – or at least return temporarily – the stolen pieces of your soul. That is why I have devised a little game for us to play,'

'A game?' asked Sarah, raising her eyebrows in distrust.

'Yes, Sarah. A game. You like playing games, don't you, children?'

'If they're fun to play – yes,' added Michael, feeling bewildered. 'But I don't...'

'But nothing, Michael. You said you like playing games, therefore I shall entreat you to play *my* little game. I am more reasonable than you have been led to believe.

Now as you know, all games have rules, and in my game it is no different. This is how it shall work. I will place the Staff and Altra at the centre of the room at exactly 3 feet away from us all, alongside *The Sacred Reading*. I will be seated 3 feet to the north of the table. You will be standing 3 feet to the south. I will then count to three, and whoever reaches the objects first, invariably wins the game. How does that sound to you?'

'It sounds fairly reasonable,' replied Sarah, wondering if there was a catch. 'But as you said, you will have to return the missing pieces of our soul first, so that *The Essence of Christmas* is reignited, and you'll have to untie and unfreeze our hands.'

'Oh, *of course, of course*, Sarah. Consider it done,' said the Guardian, who at the click of a finger returned the children's hands to normal and snapped the frozen chain in half.

'Why would you put yourself at such a risk?' asked Michael, as his eyes narrowed in distrust of this supreme fiend. 'Why would you risk giving up your life and power? It just doesn't make sense.'

'It makes perfect sense, Michael, if you yourself are a bit of a gambler, and the risk is what makes it exciting. There is, however, one thing which I must ask of you if you are to play this little game. You, if you win, of course seek to gain everything, however, if I win, I stand to gain no more than what I already started with, and for me that is not really a viable gamble. In fact, it is not really a gamble at all.'

'So what exactly are you suggesting, then?' asked Michael, catching sight of the clock above the Guardian's throne.

'I am suggesting that we strike a bargain, Michael – an agreement of mutual understanding - whereby if you lose at this game, I take more back from you than I already had, and since, in order to play this game, I am returning a piece of your soul to you, I find it fair that if you lose, then I get to take even more of your soul than I returned.'

'How *much* more?' asked Sarah, feeling a lump stick in her throat. 'How much more of it do you want to take?'

'All of it,' said the Guardian, without even flinching. 'If you lose, I want to possess *all* of your soul.'

The children's souls – still standing at the side of them - shook their heads, as though advising against this dubious proposal.

'No way – absolutely not. *The Essence of Christmas* won't just stop *working* that way - it'll be destroyed,' cried Michael, looking back at the Guardian and turning red. 'If you take our souls, then that's it. We're done for. Kaput! Feral rodents possessing no *Essence of Christmas* at all, with no hope of ever rescuing the fate of this Kingdom. We may as well be in league with the devil.'

'That is eloquently put, Michael, but if you don't agree to this bargain then you will have *failed* in the Quest you so earnestly agreed to, and betrayed your entire Kingdom. Is that the sort of behaviour you've been taught in your Princely classes, Michael, or have you been taught to be more bold?' enquired the Guardian, as his eyes flashed slightly and his head tilted forwards. 'You must have always known this Quest would be difficult, and I do not *have* to give you this opportunity. I already own a piece of your souls, and I could just as easily have thrown you both in prison and denied you this opportunity altogether.'

The children knew that he was right. This was their only chance. Their only opportunity of saving the fate of Christmas in the Kingdom and on Earth. They *had* to take it and play this hand. And they *had* to ensure that they won.

'Alright, we'll do it,' agreed Michael, reluctantly, after he had exchanged a look of accordance with his sister. 'We'll play your game. You can have our entire souls if we lose.'

'Excellent,' breathed the Guardian, as his eyes emitted a faint, yellow light, and Snow Blood now carried a piece of paper over to each of them. 'I am afraid you will have to sign a document, just to make it official. Without your signatures your promise can never be binding.'

Michael looked at his soul before him and sighed, before glancing across at the Guardian.

'I think you should give us the missing pieces of our souls first, before we sign this,' he said, as beads of sweat formed on his forehead.

'No, no, Michael. This is the correct way to handle such a matter. Sign the document first and you can have the missing pieces upon signature,' said the Guardian, tapping his fingers.

The children drew a deep breath and read the document.

I solemnly declare ownership of my entire soul to pass to the Guardian of the Mountains, or whoever the bearer of the Staff and Altra shall be, should I fail in this little game.

Michael signed his name first, followed by Sarah, and to their surprise, the Guardian did not double cross them on this point, but did exactly as he promised and released the missing pieces of their souls.

Their souls were now completely clear, white, and more importantly, *The Essence of Christmas* – that elusive chain of silver particles – danced through their veins and along their fingertips – thus empowering them with the ability to bring life to the words of the tablet.

The letter to their father in the meantime disintegrated, as though it had never existed, and as though Michael had never placed the fateful *Seal of Christmas* in a drop of their blood.

'Thank you, children. I told you I am a creature of my word,' said the Guardian, as Snow Blood handed him the reluctantly signed document.

A large frozen table, circular in shape, then rose out of the Courtroom floor at the exact middle point between the Guardian and the children, and the Guardian took out the Staff and Altra and the piece of paper containing *The Sacred Reading*.

'Place these objects on the table, please, Snow Blood, and when I ask, you must wait outside. It is my wish to play this little game alone, you understand me, don't you?' stated the Guardian, as he handed the objects to the Snow Wolf.

The Snow Wolf bowed as the innocent souls standing before the children looked on, helpless to the situation they were being put in. The clock continued to tick loudly, in sharp, brutal jabs, and Snow Blood now placed the two objects on the table as the Guardian had promised. Snow Blood then walked towards the door and awaited the Guardian's cue.

'There we are now, children. I hope you are both feeling lucky.'

Michael nodded towards the piece of paper before nodding sharply at Sarah. She nodded back, understanding, and felt her adrenaline course through her body. This was the ultimate test. The moment the entire Quest boiled down to. And it was exactly like *Hansel and Gretel*. The power of good times two versus evil. They had to use their superior numbers to win this. Michael would get the Staff and Altra. Sarah would get *The Sacred Reading*. That way they couldn't lose, and it wouldn't matter about the document they had signed then. It wouldn't have any bearing. It couldn't harm them because they would have won the game. Still the clock continued to tick. If they managed to separate the Staff and Altra, the Guardian would be defeated. It didn't make any sense to Michael why the Guardian would risk so much. His entire life was at stake here. Then again, psychopaths were known to be reckless - if indeed he *was* a psychopath - and this was clearly the Guardian's reckless moment. He was clearly underestimating the children's potential, and even now he sat back, relaxed on his throne.

'Are you ready, children? Please leave us, Snow Blood,' said the Guardian calmly, as the children's hands felt wet and clammy.

The door to the Courtroom slammed shut, and the Guardian placed his hands inside his cloak.

'On your marks, children. Get set. Three, two, one, Go!'

The table spun around, the children dived forward, and somewhere in this moment the Guardian pulled an object out of his pocket. In the frenzy, the children failed to notice however, and each managed to grab their allotted object from the table. Sarah had seized the paper, Michael had throttled the neck of the Staff and Altra, and each now ran a safe distance away from the Guardian.

'Quickly, Michael, quickly we've got it, we've got it,' yelled Sarah, as her hand shook and she held the paper up so they could see it.

'Quickly, steady your voice so that we can read it.'

Michael held the weapon firmly, and on the count of three the children went to read the words on the document.

But their vocal chords failed them. Nothing came out, and Sarah felt now as if she were trapped in a different fairy tale involving a naive mermaid and a manipulative sea witch.

'What's happening? Why aren't the words coming out of my mouth?' asked Sarah, who attempted to speak only to find her voice failed her.

'I don't know. My vocal chords aren't working properly either. How can we be speaking now but not when we try to read the document?'

The children tried to read the words again, but again only silence came out as though someone had completely stolen their voices from their bodies.

'How can this be happening?' cried Michael, as he tried listening for the sound of the clock. 'How can this be happening?'

He still could not hear the clock ticking, and as he looked up, horror now struck him as he caught sight of what the Guardian was holding in his hands.

'Ha ha ha ha ha ha ha ha ha,' he chuckled in a malevolent voice that wrapt its way around the air particles and carried up to every angle of the frozen Courtroom.

'Did you really think I was going to let you win that easily?'

Sarah and Michael both froze as their eyes locked in on the Guardian's object, which was none other than a frozen candle, he had set in motion at the exact moment they had run from the table. As they looked around the room they saw that the clock had now stopped and the door to the Courtroom, normally wooden, was now sealed tightly shut by thick, black ice.

'You tricked us,' yelled Michael, as the Staff and Altra went flying out of his hands alongside the words from the marble tablet, in much the same way as the cup and saucer had done at Christmas Street Station. 'You planned to place us in a time trap all along. You *knew* we couldn't win if you used that candle. *That candle* prohibits *all* consequential action; the reading was doomed to failure.'

'Yes, Michael. Of course I did. And I would not have had it any other way.'

Michael screamed in horror and went to dart forwards to attack the Guardian, when, with that, the door to the Courtroom was thrown open by Snow Blood, thus breaking the stalemate, and the frozen candle shattered into nothing. The children's hands were once again tied together, and the Guardian stepped forward to retrieve the mighty weapon. They had lost another two minutes of their lives.

'You tricked us,' yelled Michael, kicking and screaming, as the clock began to tick again and a glass dome now formed around the children. 'You evil, malevolent, coward!'

'Yes, I did, Michael,' confirmed the Guardian, as a frost began to form on this glass prison. 'And thanks to that little document you signed, your souls now belong to me. By the time I have finished with you, you'll want to steal the Staff and Altra for your own gain, and you will never, ever be able to save Christmas.'

The children yelled and screamed as they kicked against the glass - trapped entirely, like two ferrets in a cage.

'Oh, good Christmas. Our souls! Michael, look, look! Look at your arms and your body,' cried Sarah, as she stared at her own self in horror.

Michael looked but could do nothing but scream; their souls had now stepped back inside them and were being eaten by maggots and turned into a mass of sores and blisters.

'Let us out of here, you monster. Let us out of here,' screamed Sarah, as the Guardian turned indifferently from the children to speak to his assistant, Snow Blood.

'Snow Blood, I want you to send for Snooks. Given that their souls are so special, it will take a half hour longer than usual to destroy them completely. I place the time of complete destruction at first break of daylight, and I want him here to witness the delicious wasteland that remains.'

Snow Blood bowed and exited the Courtroom, taking the pieces of the shattered candle with him.

Meanwhile, down in the prisons, Snooks was preparing to leave for the Courtroom, when suddenly the Christmacreatures called to him.

'You don't know, do you?' shouted Dora, sticking her head through the bars and looking at the lofty Snowflake. 'You don't know about this.'

Here, she held out the mysterious mirror she had discovered in the Guardian's chamber, which was still crying out for help.

'What are you talking about, you little Troll. What is it?' asked Snooks, as the jewel on the mirror lit up, and the writing once again formed on the glass, crying in distant gasps.

'It is communicating with Lysander, the Snowflake who went out in search of the cursed *Testament*. Or at least – it is communicating with a *part* of him,' she added, as the cries continued and the frost formed on the ice in an eerie and chilling manner.

'What are you talking about? How can it only be communicating with a part of him?'

'Because a part of him is trapped inside the mirror. Sit down, Snooks. There's something you should know before you go back up to the Court. I've got something else here for you to look at, too.'

Snooks narrowed his eyes suspiciously, but sat down and listened all the same.

19-Into the Castle

Back at The Forest of Magic Lanterns, Blitzen stared in horror as the lanterns were fast turning from the danger code of red to the deep despair of purple.

'How long do we have before their souls are entirely destroyed?'

'An hour,' replied Lindsay, his voice dripping with worry. 'It takes half an hour for a normal soul to erode, but because the children's souls contain *The Essence of Christmas*, it will take twice as long - that leaves us very little time to rescue them. It's a full hour until sunlight. At first ray of dawn it'll be too late.'

'Then we must hurry. Are the Snowflake troops all rallied?' asked Blitzen anxiously.

'Yes, they are gathering in the clearing as we speak. There is one more thing, however. The Well has received a message from The Town of Flickering Candles. Prince Harcourt appears to be in great distress.'

'What kind of distress?' asked Blitzen, looking rather alarmed.

'Well, we're not sure exactly. All that we know is this:'

The water in the Well now flickered, as an image of a human man, uncannily resembling Michael, appeared, bound and desperate, in a terrible prison.

'Please - help me. My time runs out. Please - help me. You don't know what he's done.'

The Prince coughed and spluttered as he struggled with his restraints before the water in the Well then bubbled and dissolved the image.

'What does the Prince mean by his 'time runs out?' What exactly has the Guardian done to him?' asked Blitzen, now looking distraught.

'We don't know exactly. We're trying to unravel this as quickly as possible. A group of Snowflakes have already been sent up there. We're hoping that by saving the children we can save the Prince too.'

'I hope you're right,' said Blitzen, as Clarinda now appeared in the clearing, bedecked with a bow and case of arrows.

'Is everything alright in here, Blitzen? We need to get going soon.'

'Yes, of course,' confirmed Blitzen, glancing at the Well again. 'I hope your operation is successful, Lindsay. We can't afford to lose our entire royal family in one swoop.'

'Everything will be ok, Blitzen. You'll see,' added Clarinda with a faint smile.

'Are you quite clear on how the attack is going to materialise?' she continued, as they moved slowly away from the Well.

'Yes. The forest will disguise us for as long as possible. We will fly through the North West Tower and break into the castle that way. You will then patrol the air invisibly until the time is right to attack,' said Blitzen, remembering all the details they had discussed at the banquet.

'That's right,' nodded Clarinda.

'And the battalion of Snowflakes that are going to the Mountains?' asked Blitzen with an enquiring eye. 'Are they ready, too?'

'Yes, they are ready and they will depart the same time as we do,' replied Clarinda.

'Led by Hansen?' asked Blitzen, demanding nothing but an answer in the affirmative.

'Led by Hansen,' she confirmed. 'But before we go, there is just one last thing I wish you to see. It'll only take a minute.'

Clarinda then led Blitzen down the central path, through a few twists and turns in the forest and on towards *Snowflake Village*. When they reached a white sparkling toadstool, she pushed open a little door and led him inside. The room was snug and cosy, filled with delicious baking smells, and there was a large open window at the back that looked out onto another realm. Angels flew about the clouds of this realm, and who should be seated on a cloud in the midst of them but Bunnyflower, or rather, Bunnyflower's ghost.

'Why, Bunnyflower!' exclaimed Blitzen, walking towards the window. 'You're settling in well.'

'Yep. I'm feeling a whole lot better. I can come back and visit for one whole day every year,' said the little Christmacub, looking chuffed. 'And I got an Angel blanket.'

An angel blanket was a special blanket made by the hands of Angels, and was stitched together by their kisses. It contained special powers that helped to make the transition into Heaven easier.

'That's wonderful,' smiled Blitzen.

'Are you going to rescue Prince Michael and Princess Sarah now?' asked the Rabbit, as he picked a piece of muffin off the bed and nibbled it.

'Yes. We're going into the castle now. And we are going to win back Christmas,' said Blitzen confidently.

'I wish you a stocking full of Christmas luck, Blitzen. Tell Michael and Sarah that I'm sorry I can't be with them.'

'That's alright, Bunnyflower. I'm sure they'll understand,' added Blitzen, smiling. 'I'll see you when we've won Christmas back,' he added with a wink.

Clarinda then led Blitzen back up the path and into a large clearing in the middle of the forest. As she pulled back the branches, Blitzen was overwhelmed by what he saw. There were thousands of Snowflakes standing there in their regiments, armoured and ready to do battle. At the front stood Rudolph, who looked exceedingly nervous, and Sergeant Squirrelseed, who looked incredibly brave.

'Hello, Blitzen,' said Squirrelseed, who bowed slightly before the Chief. 'It seems the Snowflakes can be ready at the drop of a hat.'

'Oh, we can,' agreed Clarinda with a smile. The Snowbelle then turned to face the forces.

'Snowflakes, Reindeer, Woodland Creatures, folk from every corner of this most magical of realms, we are gathered here today for one reason - to save our mighty Kingdom of Christmas from the despicable hands of the enemy.'

At the mention of this, there was a mighty cheer that reverberated through the trees and caused the whole ground to shake with fear and excitement.

'And we will fight for it. We will fight to save Christmas, to save our Queen and her children, and to save our great Father of Christmas, Santa Claus.

Christmas will not be wiped out like some ancient uncivilised nation. It will endure. It will continue to spread goodness and happiness throughout the world. And we will not fail it.'

Another great roar, a hundred times louder than the first, now erupted up to the Heavens. Rudolph, in particular, seemed to be thoroughly enjoying the crowd mentality. When the crowd had died down, Clarinda raised her hand.

'Fellows of the Kingdom, make way for the great Quest who will save us.'

At these words, the Snowflakes parted to create a pathway leading all the way to the front of the clearing.

'Go, I will follow behind,' said Clarinda.

Blitzen went first, followed by a nifty-moving Sergeant Squirrelseed and an incredibly chuffed-looking Rudolph. The Snowflakes once again dipped into a solemn bow. As they reached the front of the army, the gap closed, and all the Snowflakes now stood upright to attention.

'Our time has come. Let the forest take us to the castle.'

'What happens now, Blitzy?' asked Rudolph, whose excitement was wearing off slightly at the mention of the Guardian's abode.

'Do you remember when we first saw the forest? It was just a sparkle, no bigger than a firefly.'

'I sure do,' answered Rudolph rather dreamily. It seemed like a lifetime ago.

'That is what we look like at the moment to anyone outside of the forest - a tiny flicker of light that you will miss in the blink of an eye.'

'So how will we get to the castle,' asked Rudolph, perplexed.

'The flicker will simply fly up there and take us to the tower. No one will ever see us,' assured Blitzen.

'Thank Christmas for that,' sighed Rudolph, wiping his brow dry. 'But where are we now, then?'

'We are hidden deep in the forest.'

Rudolph looked around thinking it was Christmacool that he was only the size of a flicker, but not quite so Christmacool that he was going to have to confront the Guardian. He began cooking up an excuse to stay behind, when Blitzen turned around and spoke.

'You'd better hold on to something, Rudolph. The forest can travel quite fast. You don't want to fall over and injure yourself.'

Rudolph gulped loudly and grabbed hold of a twig that was sticking out of the snow nearby. There was then a strong wind as the ground began to rush forward. Thousands of brightly-coloured lights passed over the sky like a bohemian kaleidoscope. They were travelling forwards to the castle. It was exhilarating, truly thrilling, thought Rudolph, almost like riding a roller coaster.

Then the ground stopped moving, the coloured lights retreated and all was still.

'We are outside the tower,' announced Clarinda dramatically.

'What do we do now, Snowdude?' asked Rudolph, starting to shake.

'Just fly straight up and you will emerge just outside the tower window,' said Clarinda.

'For Christmas,' she said, holding out her hand as though she were sealing a pact.

'For Christmas,' repeated the Quest, placing, paws and hooves together.

Clarinda then reached into a silver purse and showered them with gold Reindeer dust until they looked like they'd been coated with a thousand droplets of magic. With that, Blitzen, followed closely by Rudolph, flew into the sky, towards the highest point of the forest. As they climbed higher the air started to become terribly cold and sharp.

'Good Christmas, it's freezing up here,' stammered Squirrelseed, shivering as he held onto Blitzen's back.

'That's because we're nearing the edge of the forest,' replied Blitzen.

Suddenly, they were engulfed by a dense, choking mist which temporarily blinded them. When they emerged, they were high in the air, directly outside the castle window, and a flag, bearing a silhouette of the Guardian, shook violently on the tower roof. Rudolph's heart pounded with horror as he saw how close he was to evil.

'Don't look down,' whispered Squirrelseed. 'It will rattle your nerves.'

Rudolph gulped, yet could not help but steal a quick glimpse down far, far below to where hundreds of faint yellow dots gleamed on the frozen moat as the Snow Wolves fiercely fought and guarded the castle.

Blitzen turned his head and whispered as quietly as he could to Rudolph, 'I'm going inside. Make sure you come in directly behind me.'

He then disappeared through the narrow slit and was directly followed by Rudolph. They were inside the tower. The two Reindeer now stood at the centre of the room, awash with fear and fateful anticipation. The room was completely frozen, as was to be expected, and looked as if it had been carved out of a thick layer of ice. A few snow-dusted cobwebs hung, blade like, in the corner, and were peopled by a few deadly-looking snow spiders. Other than that, the room was empty, and apart from a frozen wind which clawed its way in from every window, scratching at their necks and heads and any other part of their bodies it could find, it was completely silent. Not even a whisper or an echo of a growl carried into the frozen tower. This unnerved Squirrelseed, who felt that danger could erupt from any corner at any minute.

'What happens now?' he whispered, his voice quivering absurdly.

Rudolph, whose eyes hadn't stopped flickering since they had arrived, replied, 'I say we hide, Christmasdudes,' covering his eyes with his ear flaps.

At this, he received a knock on the head from Blitzen.

'Don't be so pathetic, Rudolph. We're here now. We have to do this. You want Villa Noël back, don't you?' urged Blitzen.

'Uh-huh,' nodded Rudolph, his legs shaking as violently as his head.

'Well, come on then, pull yourself together,' ordered Blitzen.

'But how exactly are we going to rescue the children and reclaim the Altra?' asked Squirrelseed. 'We can't just walk in. They'll set Snooks onto us. And how are we supposed to know where the children are?'

'We go looking for them first!' stated Blitzen boldly.

'But won't they be with the Guardian?' cried Rudolph, firmly in the grip of panic. 'He's not guna let them out of his sight.'

'That's a chance we're just going to have to take,' replied Blitzen, as he made a move towards the open door.

As he did so, however, a small silver butterfly flew into the room and fluttered around the Quest.

'*What is that?*' breathed Sergeant Squirrelseed, as he admired its beauty. 'Do you think the Snowflakes have sent it to help us?'

Blitzen narrowed his eyes suspiciously, when all of a sudden, the butterfly expanded into a pallid Snowflake who looked as white as a ghost.

'Follow me,' breathed the Snowbelle in an airy voice, as she held out her arm towards them. 'Take my hand.'

Her breath was cold - colder than the air outside even - and her voice was flat and deadly.

'Don't touch her,' yelled Blitzen, suddenly panicking. 'I think I know what she might be.'

The head Reindeer then picked up a small piece of jagged ice which had evidently broken off from the tower and threw it at her. She instantly rippled, before dissolving into a cloud of smoke.

'She was an illusion!' breathed Squirrelseed, as his tail began shaking. 'How did you know that, Blitzen?'

'Too much experience of Snooks,' grunted Blitzen, now looking around cautiously.

The smoke was now reassembling to form what appeared to be a dagger made out of sheer ice. It was floating in mid-air, pointing downwards, and began to spin, slowly at first, but then it picked up speed and moved faster and faster in the centre of the room. What the Quest did not realise was that it was in fact a *frozen kiss*, and if it touched them, any one of them, their plan was doomed.

'Quickly, let's get out of here,' commanded Blitzen, 'before it starts attacking us.'

The dagger was now in pursuit of them, and the Quest quickly rushed out of the room and slammed the door shut, leaving the illusion still floating inside. Blitzen than bolted it and sighed as the Quest shook in fear.

'Were those illusions intended to harm us, Blitzy?' asked Rudolph, who had now turned white.

'Undoubtedly,' returned Blitzen. 'Snooks probably created them to protect the castle, so keep your eyes peeled for any more. But now we have to go. The longer we linger around, the more danger we are likely to get into.'

The Quest looked around. They were now at the top of a spiralling staircase which led down to the main area of the castle. The steps were incredibly narrow and were covered in sheer ice which was so cold that a dense, white haze hovered above it. This *did* provide some light for their footing but, other than that, the staircase was in complete darkness. Fortunately for them, however, Rudolph's nose reacted to such situations and lit up like a red Christmas bulb, emitting a warm glow around it.

'I suppose you'd better go first,' suggested Blitzen.

Rudolph looked a little glum at this, but simply flashed his gnashers and stepped onto the stairs. Blitzen and Sergeant Squirrelseed followed. They trod carefully on each step, trying desperately not to make any noise. They were so silent they could hear one another breathing. As they turned the second corner down the never-ending spiral, Sergeant Squirrelseed lost his grip and he slipped and fell backwards.

'Whoa, whoa, whoa, what was that?' yelped Rudolph, as he jumped up into Blitzen's arms, clinging onto his neck for dear life.

'Get off, for Christmas sakes,' whispered Blitzen, pushing Rudolph away with his hooves. 'The Sergeant fell, and you're the one making a fuss. Are you ok, Sergeant?'

'Yes, I'm alright, thank you,' muttered Squirrelseed, his teeth chattering and his tail shaking like a rattlesnake. 'It's a little slippery.'

'Does anyone else fancy taking the lead?' asked Rudolph with an endearing smile.

'Nope. You are the one blessed with the red nose,' answered Blitzen. 'I think this fate befalls you. Anyway, why are you making such a fuss? You fought those Snow Wolves honourably in the woods earlier.'

'Yeah, I know, Blitzy, but this is the *Guardian*,' whimpered Rudolph, his head going dizzy at the thought of this.

'Just think of him as a big Snow Wolf then, if it helps,' suggested Blitzen, pushing Rudolph forward.

'Right ok,' said Rudolph, descending the steps and taking in deep, shaky breaths as though he were ready to hyperventilate.

'The Guardian is a Wolf,' he began chanting to himself. 'The Guardian is a Wolf.'

This continued for a while until they saw a light down below at the next turning, beyond which stood a door.

'Stop,' whispered Blitzen, as everyone quickly came to a sharp halt.

They stood in silence, trying to detect what the sound was. There was muffled talking, interspersed with the odd cheer, and what sounded like fists banging on a table. Blitzen took a few steps forward to hear more clearly. As he drew closer to the door he could hear clearly the voices of Snow Wolves, engaged in what sounded like a poker game.

'5 chips and a Rat,' spat one Wolf.

'No way, this Rat is mine. Take one from the pile. You get your own slaves here.'

A scuffle followed, and what sounded like a chair was thrown across the room.

'Damn you, Snow Thorn. You'll go to Hell.'

The door suddenly opened as one Wolf tried to push the other down the stairs. The fight then took another turn and the door slammed shut again.

'Quickly, hurry,' commanded Blitzen. 'While they are otherwise engaged.'

The Quest hurried past as quickly as they could, trying not to linger any longer outside the door than they needed to.

The Quest continued down the stairs until they could no longer hear the Wolves.

'What were they doing?' asked the Sergeant.

'Gambling for Rats,' explained Blitzen.

'For Rats?' he asked, looking horrified.

'Yes. If they win the bet, they win a Rat and keep him as their slave.'

'Good Christmas, how awful.'

'It won't be long now until we are out of here. We've been descending for ages. We should be coming to the main section of the castle soon and we'll have to be very, very quiet,' remarked Blitzen.

They turned a few more corners around the never-ending spiral staircase. The floor and walls were still frozen, so it made them feel as if they were trapped inside an icicle. Tiny snow spiders still ran across the walls and on the floor across their feet. Then, at last, they began to see light - not the light of a warm, glowing candle or a snug hearth fire, but merely the light of an open room, illuminating their way at the foot of the tower.

'We're here, Christmasdudes,' whispered Rudolph, now stopping dead before he came to the final turn in the tower. Just around the corner was the main hallway, from which every part of the castle could be reached. Rudolph could not go first. He was too scared, and besides, he no longer needed to, since they now had the light from the hallway to guide them. In here he would be too conspicuous unless he hid behind the others. Thankfully for him, Blitzen took the lead, reaching the archway of the staircase and peering around the corner slowly and carefully. The hallway looked bare, empty, silent, except for a faint murmur coming from down the corridor. Blitzen stepped out slowly, followed by the other two. The floor was a cold stone, with piles of snow in the corners, blown in through the broken windows. To their left were the frozen stairs which led down to the front entrance of the castle, and even further, into the dungeons. In front of them was an archway which led into what was once the Queen's private Christmas parlour. Now it was ruined, smashed up by the weather and the bitterness that was destroying the Kingdom. A cold air thrashed through it and out through the archway into the hallway. Along the hallway to the right were several other rooms which had once epitomised Christmas splendour and beauty. Now they were empty, frozen shells. At the far right stood a tiny archway leading to Snooks' tower, while adjacent to it there lay the great Court of Christmas, now the torturous abode of the Guardian.

'There it is,' exclaimed Blitzen, pointing towards the Court with his hoof. 'The Court of Christmas, or anti-Christmas, as it now is. That's where the Guardian is, and that is probably where he is keeping the children.'

'What are we going to do?' asked Sergeant Squirrelseed.

'I have a plan,' announced Blitzen. 'Gather around so our voices don't carry.' The Quest formed a circle so that Blitzen could tell them how the situation was to unfold. 'Sergeant Squirrelseed, I want you to go into the Court through the upstairs entrance to ensure that the Guardian and the children are there. I want you to get onto the minstrel balcony and make your observations. You will then come back and report to me. I will enter the Court through the main door which we can see from here. My presence should be sufficient to unsettle and distract the Guardian. He has, after all, been looking for me since the attack. Now listen, this bit is very important. Rudolph, in the meantime you will go into the Queen's Christmas parlour next to the Court. As the windows are broken in the parlour you will hear everything. When you hear me enter, you fly in through the window of the Court. You pick up the children and the Staff attached to the Altra - I will fend off the Guardian. Sergeant Squirrelseed, I want you to distract the Guardian so that I can catch him off guard. The children cannot get their souls back until the Guardian is dead. Is this understood?'

'With perfect clarity,' came a voice from behind them.

'Snooks!' winced Blitzen.

Before the group could turn around, they were shoved into a brown sack and dragged down the stairs towards the prison cells.

The prison door creaked and jerked as it was flung open, and Snooks entered, carrying the brown sack over his shoulder. He did not look left or right at the cells as he strode to the end of the corridor to where the other Reindeer lay. He turned the key, drew back the iron barred gate and flung the sack on the floor. He then locked the cell obsessively and tugged at the bars to ensure that they were secure. He did not look back as he turned on his heel and strode back down the corridor, slamming the prison door behind him.

20-The Fight for Christmas

The door to the Courtroom opened, as the long anticipated figure strode in.

'You are late, Snooks,' scolded the Guardian. 'The children's souls are almost destroyed.'

Snooks glared disdainfully at the glass dome, as the children continued to try and find a way out.

'I ran into a few surprises, Heinous,' answered Snooks, feeling for the mirror in his pocket and advancing closer towards the throne. 'Indeed, it seems I am running into surprises all over the place tonight, so I thought I might confront you before I run into anymore.'

'What are you talking about?' asked the Guardian uncomfortably, as his eyes flashed and held the sorcerer in their focus.

'I am talking about a mystery. A mystery which has long plagued this Kingdom. Long even before *you* arrived here.

A mystery which is connected to this mirror here and which conveniently is all written down in this diary,' he added, revealing the second item that Dora had found in the chamber.

'But what is it? Why, it is the diary of a Snowflake named Lysander. A Snowflake who, I must inform you, went out in search of *The Testament of the Snowflakes* over 30 years ago and who now, in part, resides in a tormented state inside this glass mirror.'

The mirror here began to cry again, and for the first time a small image of the blonde haired, blue eyed Snowflake appeared in the glass, accompanying the voice and the etchings as the pink jewel glowed.

'It is fascinating, isn't it, to think that only a small part of him is contained here. This is not his soul, I must point out, but merely a fragment of his being - of his entire being, with both its good and bad, all inside this mirror for a terrible purpose, which, I assure you, I am coming to. It glows pink when he is upset, and yellow when he is annoyed.

But this mirror leaves us with a problem, doesn't it?' continued Snooks, now looking up at the Guardian as he sat amidst the icy air. 'For if this mirror here contains only a part of Lysander, where is the rest of him? Where indeed, I ask myself, for I have looked all over the castle.

Did he perish on his Quest for *The Testament*? Did you, Heinous, run into him on his journey and destroy him almost entirely, keeping one little speck of him alive as a sort of grim trophy to satisfy your psychopathy?

Certainly that option is tempting – but the answer of course is *no*.

What actually happened is recorded here in this diary. A very angry diary for the most part, I must say, but an informative one all the same, and I should like to read a section from it, if I may. It is dated several weeks after he departed on his journey over 30 years ago. I am sure you won't mind listening to it, Heinous.'

The Guardian's eyes flashed a bitter yellow, but he bowed his head slowly and waited.

January 20th

I have almost uncovered The Testament. Its great teachings can be ours at last. It lies just ahead in the hidden caves on the Icy Plains, and I shall descend into them tomorrow. I cannot wait to unearth it entirely and become the ultimate hero to the Snowflakes. One thing that troubles me though is that there is a second pair of footprints in the snow behind me. I believe I am being followed, yet I have yet to spot the creature. I hope this is not an attempt by another Snowflake to deny me my prize. I intend to confront the creature tomorrow if I see him.

January 21st

I entered the first stretch of cave this morning, only to find there was an avalanche blocking the way. This will add to my journey, but I am determined to press on ahead. I have a hefty supply of magic at my disposal. I am well equipped to succeed.

As I was about to leave, a strange-looking Elf stood in the archway, pointing towards me with a mysterious and quivering hand. His body was wrapped in chains, and he was covered in sores and bruises.

'Do not remove The Testament,' he warned, in a voice more careworn than I wish to remember. 'Its teachings are more hideous than you think. It wishes the Snowflakes to enslave the Elves. It can only result in misery.'

I walked past him, grunting, and said that I owed it to the Snowflakes to release The Testament. What could an Elf possibly know about its teachings? It is more important than life. Still, his presence troubled me slightly, and I tossed and turned all night.

January 22nd

After clearing away the avalanche this morning, another one fell this afternoon, and I was once again confronted by the Elf. He had more chains around him this time, and his eyes were even seeping blood.

'Do not remove The Testament,' he commanded again, his voice much more foreboding today. 'This is your second and final warning. It will destroy The Kingdom of Christmas. All the Elves will become like me.'

Once again I laughed him off, brushing past him to set about another night's rest.

January 23rd

........Oh woe is me! Oh horror of horrors! The Elf has put a spell on me that has destroyed me completely and utterly. He was really a Winter Witch and the Protector of The Testament of the Snowflakes. He, or rather she, had a sworn duty to keep it locked up. Oh, Hell and Damnation rain upon me – it cannot be worse than this. I can never belong anywhere now. I can never return to the Kingdom. My friends, the Snowflakes, will disown me. Everyone I ever look upon will disown me. Oh woe is me that I ever tried to find that damnable book.

Only a small part of who I was, remains, and he, the Elf, has trapped it in a mirror, to torture me and to remind me of who I once was. It cries out to me all the time, begging me to save it, but alas, it is no use. The spell is irreversible and I am doomed to look like this forever.

The shadows shall be my realm from now on. The shadows and the margins. I curse the day that ever I set out in search of The Testament of the Snowflakes.

'And what did the Protector of *The Testament* turn him into?' asked Snooks, looking up now to see that the Guardian was still listening. 'Not a monster as you might think, for that would have been too easy. No – she turned him into a creature so precarious in its origins that he could not really belong anywhere. A creature who – as he said, could only now live amidst the shadows, watching the Kingdom from a distance and hating, first himself for his fangled form, but eventually, the beliefs of the Kingdom that rendered his existence so monstrous.

He grew to hate The Kingdom of Christmas for housing the Snowflakes. He began to see it as downright hypocritical. Bitterness got the better of him as his very soul fell away, and in his own words he vowed,

To hurt, to burn, to harm you all.
My fate is sealed, the world must fall.

It really is quite a story, is it not, Heinous? One certainly that succeeded in shocking me. But it was certainly very clever of you, I must say. For I would never have guessed in a million years of darkness who you really were. Who it is that I blindly and foolishly serve.

Heinous, for the past 10 years I believed you to be some Alendrian Fairy who, for reasons concerning power or hatred, sought out the Staff and Altra.

But this was all a smokescreen, just like your cloak. You - the Guardian - are no Fairy. You have never even been to Alendria. You could barely even bring yourself to set foot inside the Kingdom in which you were born, because *you*, the Guardian, are Lysander. You were from the Kingdom all along.'

The Guardian sat there in silence for a moment as the room went deathly cold. The children expected him to refute this somehow but, to their horror, he now rose from his throne and pulled his mighty hood back from his head before allowing his entire cloak to drop to the floor.

At first glance he resembled a monster, but on closer inspection he was not quite so easily categorized. He had the face of a fallen Snowflake, yet the ears of a demonic Goblin. His arms were feathered like Eagles, and his hands, mere talons. He had the feet of a bitten Snow Fawn, and legs like a crippled Fairy. He had the tail of a Rat covered in Lice, and the breast of a matted Ferret. He possessed the parts of 1000 creatures altogether, making him all creatures and none all at once. Occasionally a different part of him metamorphosed, just to ensure his continued insecurity. As he looked now, quite painfully, at his unveiler, his hair changed to a barrel of Serpents, and his nose snubbed upwards like an Elf.

'Yes, Snooks. What a clever little Flake you are. I am Lysander. Or I once was,' admitted the Guardian, whose features were now picked up by the light. 'I was turned into the most marginal creature the world has known – a mixture of a thousand creatures. Not quite one or another – never quite belonging to one particular group – just a continual outcast, and a monster, my features constantly changing just to ensure my marginalisation.'

Something twisted in the children's stomachs and the world seemed to turn even colder. All those years the Kingdom's faceless enemy had actually been someone they knew.

'When I uncovered this, I did even more research,' added Snooks, shutting the diary so that a plume of dust flew up in front of him. 'You sought out the Staff of Evil and spent many years mastering its powers. You planned your revenge meticulously, but you still despised the way you looked. Your fallen soul had rendered you even more hideous, so you began hiding yourself beneath a hood of darkness, taking residence in the caves of the Northern Mountains and observing the Kingdom intently. It was at that point that you began referring to yourself as *The Guardian*.'

'I suppose, in part, that is true. But that was not the only reason I fashioned the dark persona. I needed a new identity. Do you really think if I had turned up in the Kingdom looking like *this*, I would have acquired any followers? The Snow Wolves would never have obeyed me, *you* certainly would not have helped me – not a single creature in the Kingdom would have felt an iota of fear. Behind this cloak I had them eating out of my hands. They were petrified of me. And it all worked down to a T.'

'But you *lied*,' cried Snooks, who was now growing more acerbic by the second, while Lysander seemed to be gaining more colour. 'You *lied* about who you were.'

'I did not lie, Snooks, I just did not tell you the truth,' corrected Lysander, as the shadows of deceit hung heavily on his face. 'You never asked who I was, and I never told you. You are merely angry at yourself for not working it out sooner.'

'But to think that I could have served you – *you*, a corruption of my superior species. A mish-mash of a thousand creatures and a walking deformity. I thought at the very least I was serving an Alendrian Fairy or a rebellious Snowflake,' writhed Snooks, as the colour quite literally ran from his face.

'Well, more fool you for underestimating me, you little Snake. You Snowflakes are all the same, you always were, regardless of what side of Christmas your allegiances fall. But I wouldn't take it to heart, Snooks. You're not going to be around long enough to let it destroy you,' threatened Lysander, as he now removed the deadly weapon of the Staff and Altra from beneath his black cloak.

'What do you mean?' asked Snooks, staggering back slightly as he caught the coldness in the demon's eyes. 'What do you mean, I won't be around long enough?'

'Because you found out my truth, Snooks. You found out my secret. And my reputation as the phantom figure of all Evil can never survive if any creature knows who I really am.'

'But, Your Heinous. You can't be serious. You can't be......'

'I have never been more serious in my life,' insisted Lysander, as he pulled his black hood back up and now shot a fatal blow at the cowering Snowflake.

'Huh! Why you monster you, guh, guh, guh. Huh, you evil little monster,' struggled Snooks, as the attacking bolts knocked him to the floor.

'Oh, I'm sorry, Snooks, was that an insult? A plea for your life? You should have realised by now that I have evolved past the point of mercy.'

With these words Lysander shot the Staff directly at Snooks, who was thrown across the room in a blaze of light. His whole body shook, and a purple smoke seeped out from beneath his cloak until he landed on the floor like a crumpled rag doll.

Lysander looked carelessly at the dead Snowflake before reaching down and collecting the diary that had proved the traitorous author of his true identity.

He then walked over to the windows and tore them open in a glorious manner, letting the cold wind rush over him, re-affirming his status as Master of the dark and distorted forces of all worlds.

'Citizens of this fallen world. Destroyers of The Kingdom of Christmas. Predators of this burned-out land. Hear me!' he bellowed, as the Snow Wolves now looked up to behold their terrible master. 'News has reached me tonight of the fearful treachery of my sorcerer, Snooks – a creature whom I believed to be my friend, a creature whom I believed to be my accomplice. None of that was true, and in honour of this, I hereby give you his body to feast on,' he cried, as he now flung the body of the Snowflake through the window so that it landed on the frozen lake with a sickening thud. The Snow Wolves immediately attacked the corpse, with howling nerve shattering cries that carried up the castle walls and back down again.

'You may feast on this for now,' continued Lysander still posing as the supreme evil force of indestructibility. 'But when you have finished, the time has come to end it all. I have waited long enough. You may go forth. In honour of this revelation I want every inch of this Kingdom burned to the ground. Leave not a house or a tree standing.'

The Snow Wolves obeyed, and some now turned eagerly from the frozen lake as the Snowflakes, hiding behind the bushes, gasped in astonishment. How had Snooks betrayed the Guardian? Something about this did not seem right. Both of them hated The Kingdom of Christmas in equal amounts.

In the Courtroom the glass dome suddenly shattered, as the children finally managed to smash their way out.

'Here, quickly, give me your coat,' insisted Sarah, pulling hers off. 'We might be able to use them to climb out of a window or something.'

'Are our souls completely destroyed yet?' asked Michael, as he looked outside to see that the Kingdom was still in darkness.

Sarah looked down at her arms and body - her soul inside was barely glowing now; it was almost entirely covered in sores. When the corruption was complete it would collapse into nothing more than a pile of silver dust, and *The Essence of Christmas* would be lost forever. But they still had 15 minutes until sunrise, and there was a small chance they could save their souls yet. *The Essence of Christmas* still flickered faintly within, and seeing this, gave Sarah a surge of determination.

'There's still time,' she insisted, scurrying hastily towards the exit. 'We have to hurry to get the others.'

'You go,' said Michael, letting go of her hand. 'I have to stay here and fight. I can't *believe* that a creature from The Kingdom of Christmas has done this to us.'

Sarah was already over the threshold, but attempted to grab her brother's hand again.

'Michael, don't be ridiculous, you can't stay here alone. We need the help of the others!'

She went to pull her brother out of the Courtroom, but before she could, a bolt was suddenly shot forth from the Staff and Altra, forcing the door shut and freezing it into thick black ice.

'I don't think so, Michael,' said Lysander, now turning his full attention on the boy who was locked inside, alone. The sky outside was still black, and the moon illuminated the room, casting two dark shadows on the ill-fated figures.

* * * *

Downstairs in the prison the new arrivals had been causing quite a commotion.

'Who do you think it can be?' asked Comet, as he tried to make sense of the shape of the sack.

'Maybe it's Mrs Claus, or more of the Elves?' suggested Cupid.

'Or another bag of Snowflakes,' guessed Dancer, pushing his nose up to the bag to get a better look. They did not need to speculate for long however, for out of the bag popped a red shiny nose, sniffing its way to safety.

'Rudolph?' murmured Vixen, utterly astounded. 'Rudolph? Hey, it's Rudolph. Man, I thought you would have left for Earth,' he added sarcastically.

Rudolph, looking completely dazed, emerged fully from the sack, closely followed by Blitzen and Sergeant Squirrelseed.

'Blitzen? Sergeant? Oh great Christmas, what happened?' asked Donner, looking alarmed.

'It's a very long story,' said Blitzen. 'In a butternut shell, Snooks has ruined our chances of saving Christmas.'

'It might not be as bad as you think,' responded Cupid hurriedly. 'You see, we found out who the Guardian really is, and let's say, the truth hasn't gone down well with Snooks.'

'What do you mean?' asked Blitzen, looking shocked. 'Who *is* the Guardian? I thought he was a Fairy from Alendria.'

'So did we. You'll be as shocked by the revelation as we all were,' continued Donner, as the Quest's eyes now widened. 'You see, the Guardian is Lysander!'

'What!'

'Yes – apparently he had a hideous spell put on him by an Elf who guards *The Testament of the Snowflakes*. Snooks was so angry when he found out, he just stormed out of here and went straight to the Court to confront him.'

'Good Christmas! That must be where he was going when he ran into us,' Blitzen speculated, struggling to take it all in.

'What about the children, Blitzen?' asked Dora, who was growing concerned about the little dears' safety.

'Well, the Guardian, I mean, Lysander, is in the process of stealing their souls. We need to get out of here at once, because by sunrise it'll be too late,' Blitzen informed them, looking around frantically.

'You can't!' stated Vixen, as negative as ever. 'It's impossible to break out through these bars. We can't reach the key. It's over there on the hook.'

'Well, we have to get out somehow,' cried Sergeant Squirrelseed. 'Maybe the Snowflakes will come for us. They're bound to sense that something is up when we don't give them the signal to attack.'

'Sergeant, control yourself. We'll find a way out of here,' assured Blitzen. 'I think if we all charge at the gate with our antlers, it's bound to loosen it. What do you say, Reindeer?' suggested Blitzen, automatically assuming his role as Chief once more.

'I'm with you, Chief,' declared Donner, standing at his side, ready to charge.

The other Reindeer, including Rudolph, soon joined them and charged straight at the gate, but it didn't budge.

'Don't lose heart, guys, try again!' rallied Dancer. 'Ready, one, two, three.'

Again, the Reindeer rushed at the bars, only to fail.

'We could pick the lock,' suggested the Sergeant.

He then tried the piece of holly from his pocket, but it snapped.

'This is a nightmare!' he cried. 'We were this close, *this close*, and that vile wretch, Snooks, had to ruin it for us, and now, who knows where he's gone, or what he's got in store for us and the children, and....' He suddenly stopped talking. The slab next to him was shaking and trying to force its way up.

'What the devil,' he cried. 'Is there an earthquake?'

Everyone stood back while the slab shook more violently, until it was raised in the air and flew across the cell.

'Shhhh, I think we're here. I'll just check it out,' came a familiar voice.

Then the head of Mr Bunnie popped up alongside a firefly stick and he pulled the rest of his body out of the tunnel.

'Hello, everyone. Good Christmas, Blitzen, Rudolph, Squirrelseed, what are you doing here? Christmas crackers, has the Quest failed?'

'Not now,' smiled Blitzen, happily.

There was then a loud rumble from the hole as a sprightly Patch, Hopper and Carrot Top came bouncing out into the cell.

'Thank Christmas for that,' cried Hopper, shaking the dust from his tail.

'Yeah, I thought we'd never get out from the underground,' added Patch, coughing.

'I have so much dirt in my mouth, I'm choking,' spluttered a now rather dusty-coloured Carrot Top.

Mr Badger and Mr Prickles soon joined the group, all voicing their pleasure to have made it to the castle and to be back above ground. The Reindeer were greatly thrilled to see them, and were about to launch into an escape plan when Blitzen suddenly spoke.

'I'm afraid we have some bad news, Mr Bunnie,' pressed Blitzen gently.

'Bad news. What bad news?' asked Mr Bunnie, looking confused. He felt they'd had all the bad news they could get.

'It's about Bunnyflower,' he replied solemnly.

'Bunnyflower, what about him, he's safe in the hideout with our mother, isn't he?' interrupted Patch.

'He's not still mad at us for leaving him behind, is he?' asked Hopper, looking slightly alarmed.

The tension froze. Blitzen related the events leading to the tragedy, of how he had been brutally killed by the Snow Wolves in the battle, but would be able to come back and visit them once a year.

'But - dead?' breathed Mr Bunnie in disbelief. 'My youngest son - *dead!* How is this possible? My dear, dear son.'

Silence ensued as the little Rabbits stared into the air, searching for consolation from their grief, and tears rolled down their dusty cheeks as they mourned their younger brother.

'If we'd have snuck him out like he asked us to, then this never would have happened,' sobbed Carrot Top, wiping his eyes.

'I kn-kn-kn-now,' stuttered Hopper in between tears. 'What will we do now? How are we supposed to manage only seeing him once a year?'

Mr Bunnie wiped his tears from his eyes and collected himself before looking up.

'We fight back,' he declared, clearing his throat. 'That's what we do. We fight back. The Wolves have taken my son from me. They have taken away one of the most important things in my life. So now I am going to make them pay for it. Come on, everyone. Let's get them. Let's chase those slobbering, callous brutes out of our Kingdom!!'

A cheer erupted around the room as everyone vowed to take revenge on the Snow Wolves and gain justice for Bunnyflower's death. Then, Mr Bunnie, along with Mr Badger and Mr Prickles, soon began tunnelling under the iron bars, and after a considerable number of minutes they eventually reached the other side.

'The keys, the keys,' fumbled Mr Prickles. 'Where are they?'

'Up there, look,' shouted Comet, pointing towards a large, rusty iron key that hung on the back of the wooden door.

Mr Bunnie leapt towards it, grabbed it and turned the rusty key in the lock. With a jerk, the jail door was open.

'Hurraaaayyyy,' cried everyone, jumping up and down and running out of the cell. 'We're free.'

'Not quite. Not yet,' returned Blitzen, taking command. 'We still have to get past the Snow Wolves and rescue the children.

'What's the plan, Chief?' asked Comet who, after days of being locked in a cell, was ready to fight the enemy and was jumping keenly from side to side.

'I say we split up into teams. *We'll* make our way to the Court, while *you* fend off the Snow Wolves,' commanded Blitzen.

'Can't I just hide in here, Blitzy?' cried Rudolph, who was exhausted and now whimpering again at the thought of another assault.

'No, Rudolph. You're part of the Quest. And the Quest stays together. We all need to stay together to destroy the Guardian and Snooks and......'

'Snooks is dead,' announced a voice at the prison door.

The whole room shook with fear at his new arrival.

'Sarah?' gasped Blitzen, looking horrified at the extent of her sores.

'Yes, it's me,' began Sarah, who now resembled a ragged, little, orphan child. She stepped into the cell followed by three Snowflakes whom she had met as she fled the Courtroom.

'I don't understand,' began Sergeant Squirrelseed. 'Why is Snooks dead? And what's happened to your brother?'

'Lysander killed Snooks because he discovered his true identity,' she explained, as she began to shake and shiver. 'Michael and I managed to break out of our glass prison, but then Michael pursued him. If he kills him we can get our souls back and save Christmas, but I'm worried it won't turn out like that.'

'What about the Snowflakes?' asked Dasher, leaning towards them.

'We were in the bushes ready to attack the frozen lake when Snooks' body was thrown from the Court window. We returned immediately, sensing something was amiss, before consequently running into Sarah.'

'Oh, good Christmas. We have to get out of here. We have to get to Prince Michael *now*. There's only 10 minutes until sunrise.'

'Just a minute, Sergeant, this strategy will be dangerous. We must be very careful how we go about it,' advised Blitzen, looking at the Christmacreatures in earnest. 'We will have to encircle the Courtroom slowly and back Lysander into a corner. It's the only way we can reach Prince Michael without getting him or ourselves killed.'

The creatures all nodded in agreement and then disbanded to their allotted targets.

*   *   *   *

Back in the Courtroom the real battle was about to begin, as Michael's life was in grave danger. Lysander was shooting Michael across the room with the Staff and Altra, and Michael was struggling to recover his footing.

'It can really sink its teeth into you, can't it, Michael,' spat Lysander, as he grimaced wildly at Michael's pain. 'And you thought your sores were painful. Perhaps now you can finally understand what it's like to endure a living Hell.'

'A living Hell,' cried Michael, as he tried to find his feet. 'Is that your excuse for what you've done? I could endure a thousand of these Hells and I would never have turned evil like you. Your excuse is pathetic.'

'It's not an excuse, it is fate. My soul fell away from me. What was I supposed to do?' added Lysander, as he shot another bolt from the deadly weapon.

'You were supposed to fight it like I am,' insisted Michael, who was determined to resist the temptations of the Staff and Altra. 'I can't *believe* that you were actually born inside this Kingdom. You're an utter disgrace to its very existence. If *I* had been turned into a monster like you, *I* wouldn't have used it as an excuse to become evil.'

'Oh, that is rich, given that you are just minutes away from being an out and out little savage. I would like to see you try and resist evil then,' scoffed Lysander, smugly.

Michael swallowed and panted. 'As long as I have my breath in my body I will fight you,' he declared, as he clenched his teeth and charged headlong towards the fiend. 'Do not speak to me about the laws of fate.'

But Lysander once again knocked him off his feet, and Michael now lay face down on the ice, as blood fell thickly from his head. The room swirled slightly and he felt a hard kick in his side.

'Get up,' taunted Lysander, as he brandished the Staff and Altra in the air.

'Get up!' he growled, kicking him once again, this time much harder as Michael groaned.

Lysander was sweating now and was desperate for the kill.

'Get up, you coward!'

'No. You're the coward!' declared Michael, trying to fight back verbally as his head hurt. 'And there was me thinking you were a true warrior. Well, how wrong I was about that. Drop the Staff, Lysander, and fight me like a man.'

'I am no man. I am a demon, and therefore I fight like one,' growled Lysander, kicking Michael.

'No! You are a coward who is hiding behind his own magic,' challenged Michael. 'You think that you are powerful now that you have the Staff, but you are still nothing! A hideous mesh of 'otherness', just like the Winter Witch intended. You will never amount to anything anymore.'

Lysander stopped as a surge of hatred jolted through him.

'Alright then, Michael. What do you suggest?'

'We both fight with daggers,' returned Michael boldly. 'No magic, no Staff, just hand to hand combat based on our own physical prowess.'

Lysander paused for a moment before making up his mind.

'Alright then, Michael. I'll not have anyone calling me a coward. If you are foolish enough to challenge my dagger-fighting prowess, then so be it. Come at me if you dare.'

Michael watched as the misshapen fiend pulled a dagger from beneath his cloak, before placing the Staff and Altra on the ground behind him.

'I hope you know what you've done,' grimaced Lysander evilly.

'Oh, I think I do,' declared Michael, sweating determination, but still looking alarmingly feral.

He got to his feet, his dagger was swung, and the fight was once again set in motion.

Lysander's eyes were ablaze, now brighter than they had ever been before. So bright, in fact, that they illuminated the entire room. He was swishing his dagger through the air, and looked crazier than ever as his very eyes seemed to be advancing forwards. Michael was struggling to keep up. The sores on his body were causing him immense pain, stinging him to his very core, the sight of which caused Lysander to laugh wildly.

'Come on now, Michael, don't grin and bear it all so nobly. Why don't you scream and let the pain out. Didn't anyone ever tell you there is a nobility in mental agony,' he taunted, lunging forwards. 'It might put some life back into that feral face of yours. Still, it puzzles me why you wish to fight me. You have always had such a curiosity for the dark side.'

'I have *never* possessed such curiosity,' cried Michael, as his hands began to shake. 'I am the Prince of *Christmas*. I was *born* good and I will *die* good, because that is the will of my existence.'

'And that is the *only* will of your existence, is it?' cried Lysander, as he howled smugly. 'How do you explain that little letter then, Michael? The one you were instructed not to send to your father? Or even the fact that you launched snowballs at me in the Mountains for years, forever keeping me in your focus.

You are not so innocent deep down as you like to think. You have an unconscious desire to shake the foundations of your own system right through to its very core, as much, if not more so than I do. Why, you are 'part of the devil's party without knowing it'. 4 One might even argue that for you to possess this desire is even worse, given your social standing. At least I was deliberately cast as your system's misfit. You have been cast as its Prince and saviour. Now how about that for an uncanny and vicious twist of fate.'

'You are talking absolute rubbish and psychobabble,' cried Michael, as his face contorted into an expression of anguish. 'I sent that letter to my father with honourable intentions. You and Snooks were the ones who took it and corrupted its meaning. And I am dearly sorry it led to his capture. I wanted to *save* my father. To protect him. You can only see evil in everything because you are evil to your very core.'

'Be that as it may, Michael, it still led to his capture. And, incidentally, his impending downfall in more ways than you can realise.'

'What are you talking about? What impending downfall? You told me that my father was being held captive in The Town of Flickering Candles,' panicked Michael, as a wave of fear now shimmered across his body. 'What have you done with him then? Was Snooks lying?'

'Oh, so now you want something from me, do you?' sneered Lysander, splicing the air with his dagger so that it just missed Michael. 'And yet just minutes ago you wished to kill me.'

'What have you done with him?' shrieked Michael, now thrusting his dagger more recklessly. 'Tell me what impending danger he is in! What vicious plot have you set in motion?'

'Hahahahahaha' continued Lysander, enjoying the immense power afforded him at this particular moment. He could keep him dangling like a dried worm gut on the end of a fish hook all night long, and it would pleasure him immensely.

'Tell me!' screamed Michael, now seething with anger and worry. 'Tell me, and so help me God, I might spare you an ounce of pain.'

He felt something terrible coming on and squeezed the dagger

---

4 *The Marriage of Heaven and Hell*, William Blake.

handle even more tightly to counteract the pain.

'Alright,' said Lysander theatrically. 'If you must have it, it was hidden in that little document you signed – the one conceding ownership of your and your sister's souls. It was printed at the bottom in invisible ink.'

'Arrrgghhhh, you villain. What did it say?'

'Hahahaha,' cackled Lysander again. 'Patience never was one of your virtues, was it, Michael? That is apparent from your behaviour on this Quest. But since you relinquished a drop of your sister's and your blood, it was almost too easy then for me to place a curse upon your father. He is, after all, part of you and your sister. I could not do it with your mother. She can only be killed inside the Frozen Mirror. But your father's fate was just too good to resist.'

'You still haven't told me what you have done to him,' yelled Michael, feeling he would never get to the bottom of this. Lysander was leading him a merry dance. 'You tell me, or I'll yell your secret out somehow.'

'Be my guest, Michael. I'll see you dead before you even get to that. But since you have been so dearly persistent, I may as well spit it out. Your father's fate is tied to your own. The minute your souls pass entirely to me, your father's breath will give out, and he will die like the mortal little fool that he is.'

Michael trembled for a moment. He was almost entirely plastered in sores. There was very little of his soul left.

'You haven't,' he cried, feeling now that he had almost been checkmated. 'You couldn't possibly have.'

'Oh, believe me, I could. I have no mercy left in my body, remember. I am all strangeness and otherness, like you said. Any last requests, Your Majesty?'

Michael, now seething with hurt, could contain himself no longer. Completely driven by anger and the guilt that pervaded him for having endangered his father and the entire Kingdom, he ran directly forwards towards Lysander, screaming, and thrust the dagger straight into his side. Lysander's hood fell back, and his expression fell from one of pure smugness and almost realised victory, to one of horror. He fell slowly and macabrely to the ground, the tarnished letter to Prince Harcourt and *The Sacred Reading* from the Falls, dropping to the ice as he did so. Michael walked over to Lysander's body. Blood rushed out from a solitary wound – an evil, luminous, yellow blood, with an eerie smoke rising from it. He drew a few difficult breaths and gave a slight nod in acknowledgement of his impending death.

'It was.... always meant to be so,' he staggered. 'I am free.... of my hatred.'

His eyes then shut and his breath gave out. Lysander was dead.

Michael shook, still holding the jewelled dagger, now blood stained and tarnished. He began to weep as his chest hurt with the weight of the events that had unfolded around him. He was puffy and worn, sick of death and murders, and nauseatingly plagued by worry about his father. He placed his hands over his head to try and stop the rays of the Staff and Altra from penetrating him, when a voice suddenly cut up his thoughts.

'Michael,' came the voice, as he buried his face in his knees. 'Michael, over here.'

He heard her, but his thoughts were still traumatised, and he could not bear to look at her after what had just happened.

'Michael,' cried the voice again. 'Michael, it's ok now. It's nearly over. By killing the Guardian you've given us back our souls.'

Michael sat up suddenly as he looked down at his hands. His soul was shining through from within, sore-free, as though an angel were living inside of him, and as Sarah approached him, he could see that her innocence too had returned.

'Does this mean that our father is safe?' he asked, barely able to catch his breath as he tried to wipe away his tears.

'Yes, yes, the Guardian's curse didn't work. And *The Essence of Christmas* has returned.'

He looked again at his hands to see the silver thread dancing restlessly around, before turning his eyes to the window.

The sky was alight with Snowflakes, and now the Reindeer, the Bunnies, Mr Badger and Mr Prickles all entered the room.

'You have been very brave, Michael. You have done very well,' said the reassuring voice of Blitzen. 'But there is still one more thing you have to do in order to fully restore Christmas.'

The children nodded and looked across the room to where the Staff and Altra lay. It gleamed fiercely like an evil beacon, emitting a luminous glow and betraying two golden slithers inside the corrupted Altra itself. Sarah and Michael slowly walked over to the formidable weapon. It was time to execute the deed they had been brought there to do.

'Ready, Michael?' said Sarah, as she picked up the words of *The Sacred Reading* from the floor.

'Ready, Sarah,' replied Michael, placing the Staff and the Altra on the floor in front of them.

The two then held *The Sacred Reading*, and on a silent count of three, they began:

Christmas is the mighty light,
A most worthy cause for which to fight.
Any force, which threatens its power

Must be destroyed this very hour.

A blinding, white light suddenly drenched the room, causing the Staff of Evil to crumble, whilst absorbing the dead bodies of the fallen axis. The light then turned into showers and showers of glittering dust that swirled around the room like little drops of magic. The dust began to change colour and shape, before finally settling and dispelling to reveal jovial old Santa Claus and the beautiful Queen.

'Christmatastic, it worked!' yelled Rudolph, running forward to hug Santa.

'Good Christmas. Hello, Rudolph. It's very nice to see you too.'

All the Reindeer were soon flocking towards Santa Claus to pay their respects, before bowing before the elegantly restored Queen Krystiana. Her hair shone radiantly, and the red jewel in her crown sparkled in the frozen room. Her red velvet dress draped along the floor like a regal carpet, and her sapphire eyes glinted as she smiled.

'Hello, Mother,' said Prince Michael, rather sheepishly, as Sarah rushed forward to hug her.

'Oh Michael,' sighed his mother, holding out her arms. 'There's no need to look so modest. You are the one who has saved the Kingdom.'

Michael smiled faintly as he stepped forward and wiped away another tear.

'Oh, there, there, now, my darling, the war is over now. I do think you need some rest, however. I think this Quest has really taken it out of you. But first,' she said, turning towards the Altra, which was no longer attached to the Staff, and lay abandoned on the floor of the frozen room. 'It is time to restore Christmas to this Kingdom.' She held out her hands, and at this command, the Altra floated into her palm. As the Queen's hands closed in on it, a rich golden glow formed around it and washed the room. When it subsided, The Kingdom of Christmas had returned to its normal state. The walls of the castle were now alabaster and gold, with a crimson carpet along the floor, and the diamond-patterned glass returned to the windows. The large, sparkling Christmas tree reappeared in the Courtroom, and the stairs were once again an elegant swish marble, that always reminded Santa Claus of a Neapolitan ice cream. Outside, the Kingdom returned to its magical splendour. Christmas Mountain sparkled with a pink glow, while down to the south of the castle, Winterland Village lit up with Christmas lights and looked delectable again. Mistletown looked spotless and ready for Christmas, and Gingerbread Lane was given a facelift so that it no longer looked tumble-down and eerie. Sarah stood by the window with Blitzen, admiring the restored Kingdom and its endless promises of wonder and excitement. Michael was still quivering, and was comforted by his mother as he struggled to overcome his trial. Then Blitzen was suddenly struck by movement coming from the Mountains of the North.

'Well, I'll be,' he muttered, quickly turning and galloping out of the Court, down the marble staircase and out onto the causeway. The others followed, including Krystiana, who held Michael in her arms. They all stopped behind Blitzen. In front of them strode a large battalion of Snowflakes leading the Elves to freedom. Unshackled and unbound, the Elves, led by Snooks' former assistant Edgar, slowly walked beside the Snowflakes, up to where Blitzen stood.

'Well, this is magnificent,' Blitzen proudly declared, as he smiled at the group of Snowflakes. 'Truly magnificent.'

The Snowflakes, led by Hansen, said nothing, but dipped their heads rather sheepishly and stood aside. They were still struggling with the truth, and it would take a while to sink in. The Guardian had been one of them, motivated and defeated by their precious book. For now they were speechless and just took comfort in the fact that the war was over.

A flickering glow now appeared in the sky, just to the right of the castle.

'Look,' whispered Squirrelseed to Sarah. 'It's The Forest of Magic Lanterns. It's returned to the ground. That means that the war is over and the Kingdom is safe.'

Sarah looked dreamily at it. But her attention was soon diverted to a small group running across the snow towards where they stood.

'Santa, Santa,' cried a voice, waving its arms frantically in the air.

Santa, who had been busy pondering when his next meal would be coming - since it was long, long overdue - looked towards the crowd to see a figure shaped exactly like a Christmas pudding running towards him.

'Ho ho ho,' he cried, slapping his hands on his stomach. 'Mrs Claus.'

As Mrs Claus approached her husband, she gave him a big, fat, jolly Christmas hug, followed by a little handkerchief full of cookies.

'I knew you'd be hungry, pudding,' she remarked.

'Ho ho ho,' he chuckled. 'I've never been hungrier.'

'Hello, Santa, good to see you back. You too, Your Majesty,' came a quiet little voice from behind Santa.

'Mum,' yelled the three little Bunnies, as they came bouncing down the drawbridge.

'Hello, boys,' she cried, holding out her arms to them. 'Oh dear,' she added, as she burst into tears.

'Mum, Bunnyflower is.....' began Patch.

'.....I know, I know,' she sobbed, her eyes squinting through the tears to see her husband coming towards her. 'I know. The Snowflakes brought him home. He's buried in Cinnamon Forest.' Here, she again broke down.

'There, there, dear,' said Mr Bunnie, putting his paw on her shoulder. 'We're all upset. I thought I........ wouldn't be able to go on when I heard.'

'Who told you?' she asked.

'Blitzen, my love. He told me everything.'

The three little Bunnies were now looking up at their parents with heavy eyes, searching for some kind of answer or absolution. Mr Bunnie pulled them all close to him as they wept. 'We must now stay strong,' he said. 'We must be strong.'

Krystiana took this cue to speak.

'Creatures of the realm. Messengers of Christmas. Snowflakes, Elves, Reindeer, Woodland Creatures, and children. We have endured a terrible war. We have lost cherished and irreplaceable loved ones. We have endured injuries, both physical and mental, and we have seen our Kingdom sink into ruin. But we have it back. The evil is gone. We have defeated it. *You* have defeated it, by working together. By helping each other. By forming bonds. The enemy failed because they could not work together. They were not held together by love and friendship, they were held together by hatred, and those bonds cracked and broke at the critical minute. I will have more to say about Lysander later, but for now let us rejoice together. We now have our beloved Christmas and this magical of all Kingdoms returned to us, and we must work doubly hard to ensure that the Christmas love and spirit is spread throughout those other worlds, where it is needed most. Let us all meet together for a feast at the castle in memory of those we have lost, and in celebration of what we have regained.'

A cheer went through the crowd at the thought of the Christmas banquet. Sarah smiled and raised her eyes up to the skies and across to the northeast. The skies were clear, the Mountains were still, and far across the snowy plains a brave Prince was getting ready to come home.

21 – A Christmas Feast

The children took several days to recover, and were nursed preciously by the Queen for each and every one of them. Dora too was there, and together they helped the children through their nightmares, until they were declared strong enough to return to society again. Michael was the more badly affected of the two; it really seemed to have damaged a part of him, learning that the Guardian had been Lysander all along, and he talked about this incessantly. The Christmas feast the Queen had promised was postponed, and eventually set to take place on Christmas Eve. At around six o'clock on this evening the Queen entered the children's chamber.

'Hello, my darlings. How are you feeling today?' she enquired, as her glistening, white dress trailed behind her.

The walls in the children's nursery were pure marble and decorated with garlands of holly. Covering the floor was a soft crimson carpet into which the Queen's feet sank as she walked across it.

'I'm not *too* bad,' replied Michael, sitting up in his sleigh-shaped bed, having now regained some colour after his ordeal. 'The nightmares are retreating slowly.'

'Yes – and the scars from my sores are all gone,' added Sarah, feeling along her arms and cheeks.

'Well, that's wonderful,' smiled the Queen in a restrained manner, as she squeezed her daughter's hand. 'Now then, before we go downstairs, I have a little surprise for you, but first you have to close your eyes.'

The children looked bewildered at first, but shut their eyes tightly, on which cue the Queen called out, 'Ready,' and the door to the nursery opened. Some gentle, yet very deliberate footsteps were heard along the marble floor of the hallway, approaching their room, until the children sensed a presence close to them.

'You may open your eyes now, children,' permitted the Queen, in a very gleeful voice.

Sarah and Michael opened their eyes slowly, and what they saw now caused them to jump up in complete elation.

'Dad,' they both cried, as they rushed forward to hug their father.

'Well, good, great Christmas,' smiled the Prince, who was almost knocked over by their enthusiasm. 'I didn't think you'd be *that* pleased to see me,' he added, as he hugged them both and sat down next to them on the bed.

'Dad, we thought you were done for,' cried Michael, as a knot turned in his stomach. 'It's been completely crazy here. There was the annex, then I sent you a letter, then the Guardian - well Lysander actually - intercepted that letter. Then there was this big glass dome that housed us while it stole our souls, all because the Guardian tricked us with a frozen candle and.....'

'And yet you still managed to defeat it all and bring Christmas back to us,' smiled their father, full of pride.

Michael paused for a moment and suddenly straightened his jumper. 'Well, yes, I did,' he replied, beginning for the first time in over a fortnight to feel quite pleased with himself again. 'Actually, *we* did,' he added, giving Sarah a shove. 'We made a pretty good team in the end.'

'Yes, we did, Michael – although it was you who eventually killed the Guardian and saved our souls. You should never forget that,' she said, with a gentle smile. 'How were the Northern Regions, Father? Apart from The Town of Flickering Candles, of course.'

'Well, they were really quite an experience, actually,' replied Prince Harcourt, putting his arms around his children. 'I have a great many stories about them to relay to you, but first I believe there is a feast waiting for us downstairs.'

'Why, yes there is,' confirmed the Queen with a smile. 'And this year we've got an extra special surprise.'

The children smiled, and with Michael clutching his father's hand, and Sarah clutching her mother's, the family of Christmas made their way down the winding stairs that led them into the Great Hall of Christmas. As they descended the stairway into the corridor, they were greeted with the most delicious cooking smells that came wafting along the air, serving as sensual invites to the great feast. A few Elves who worked at the castle could be seen hurrying along the corridor, carrying jugs of punch, and various other concoctions.

'Hello, Your Majesty,' said an Elf named Avery, as he struggled to carry a large pot of potatoes that was at least half his size.

'Do you need a hand?' she asked, as he staggered sideways, almost dropping the potatoes.

'No, no. I'm fine,' he replied, falling sideways through the archway into the hall and just making it to the table. Inside, the hall was as splendid as the rest of the castle. Flakes of snow fell from the ceiling onto a doughnut-shaped banqueting table in time.

'Where's the Christmas surprise?' asked Michael, who had been accustomed to all sorts of things positioned at the middle of the table in his time; from giant twenty-tiered Christmas cakes to a whole edible Christmas village and ski slope.

'Well, Michael, if I told you, it would spoil the surprise,' answered the Queen with a wink.

Along the back wall, a parade of arched-shaped windows were lit up with fireflies, whilst a group of Elfin musicians sat on a fluffy cloud that floated around the room.

As the children and the Queen stepped inside the room, the mix of chatter and clatter ceased, and the entire Hall stood up and applauded. Michael and Sarah both gushed as the Queen smiled at everyone and led them to the round table.

'Please be seated,' she said, as she pulled out her seat, but remained standing as everyone else sat down. 'I am thrilled that you have all made it here tonight, but before we begin, I must say a few words about the war this Kingdom has endured.'

The entire room now bowed their heads as they listened to the Queen's words.

'As you know, for many years we had a problem with a creature we called the Guardian. We bravely resisted his attacks, and I was personally forced to lock him inside the Mountains. We all believed him to be a creature from a faraway place - some demonic creature, perhaps from Alendria - or even something darker. We all expected to be shocked by what lay beneath that cloak. In the end we were more shocked than we could possibly have imagined, for we learnt that he was someone we knew.'

The Queen paused for a moment as silence swept the hall. The Elves and the Snowflakes looked down in shame, and some of them even wiped a few tears from their eyes. They were seated together this evening, and that at least was a new beginning.

'We do not know what Lysander would have been like had he not been raised under the bigotry of the Snowflakes. We do not know what he would have been like if *The Testament* did not exist. Perhaps his curse of deformity was intended to open his eyes and not shut them tighter, but we do not know this for sure. What we do know is that the war in this Kingdom was begun in this Kingdom by another war that already existed within it. *The Testament of the Snowflakes* is evil. The Winter Witch said so herself. And for any of you who wish to continue with your stubborn notions, I ask you this – was this war really worth it? Were all the Christmacreatures we've lost worth less than your beliefs?

I would sincerely hope not.

We are The Kingdom of Christmas, my dear creatures. We must never forget this! If *we* can't have harmony, then where can? We must learn from Lysander, *not* condemn him. We must learn from his colossal mistake, in the hope that no creature ever makes it again.

Now, will you please raise your glasses, as I propose a toast to this Kingdom - to the *new* Kingdom, where every creature loves and respects each other, regardless of *what* they are.

To Christmas!'

'To Christmas,' repeated the Great Hall, some more sheepishly than others, while Hansen and some of the more senior Snowflakes continued to hide their faces in shame.

'Very good,' said the Queen, now relaxing her expression a little. 'Now, let the feast begin.'

The entire Hall now looked on in anticipation, as an enormous, edible Christmas tree rose out of the centre of the table, stretching a full twenty feet to the ceiling. It was made entirely of icing and featured chocolate baubles and gingerbread men, in addition to stockings filled with Wish Biscuits and sugar-bread loaves. White, chocolate butterflies flew around it, and dustings of sugar flakes fell from the branches.

'Oh wow, this is the best Christmas feast ever,' cried Hopper, jumping on the table to get a better look.

'Please feel free to climb the Christmas tree,' announced her Majesty, as she joined her Kingdom and sat down. 'There is a chocolate fountain at the centre for those of you who wish to tunnel through.'

The cubs immediately set to work on this, and collected so many trimmings to put on their plates that they had to eat a few before they could make it back down.

Michael, who normally would have been up there with them, opted for a quieter dinner and merely picked a handful of gingerbread men from a nearby branch.

'Ho ho ho, well isn't this nice,' remarked Santa, mincing his hands together as he set to work on a large dish of Christmas trifle.

'You betcha, Santa,' beamed Rudolph, who held a ridiculously over-trimmed Christmacocktail in his hoof. 'All of us Christmasdudes together.'

'Yes, and on Christmas Eve too,' winked Santa, spraying spots of trifle over Squirrelseed.

'Santa, pudding, mind you manners!' snapped Mrs Claus, slapping his wrist as the little Squirrel gushed and wiped his fur clean.

Sarah smiled to herself as she began heaping her plate with a mixture of food that was inevitably going to make her sick later on. She had mince pies, Christmas gâteaux, whipped cream, Reindeer-shaped biscuits, custard and white sauce swirl and a large dollop of snow cream.

'Sarah, are you not going to have anything healthy?' asked her mother, pointing towards the roast turkey and vegetable platters.

'Oh, uh, in a minute,' replied Sarah, tucking greedily into her plate of goodies.

'I say, Santa, what's going to happen to Snook's shop now? I mean, who is going to brew your Reindeer Dust for you?' asked the Squirrel, leaning over the table.

'Ahem. Did you say Snook's shop?' asked Rudolph, clearing his throat and leaning over the table, flashing his great white teeth at the Squirrel.

'Yes, that's right,' replied Squirrelseed.

'Why, you're looking at him, Squirreldude,' smiled Rudolph, striking a great pose as if he were ready to have his picture taken.

The table suddenly stopped and looked towards Rudolph in amazement.

'*You!*' exclaimed Blitzen in astonishment. '*You* are in charge of the most important, most secretive shop in the Kingdom.'

'Hey, watch it, Blitzy, I'm a lot better than that cross-eyed, double-crossing, slimy little anti-Christmas geezer who had it before me.'

'But you're not............'

Santa had just gulped down a glass of Christmas wine and jumped in just in time.

'Alright now, boys, let's not get too carried away. Yes, Rudolph is the new shopkeeper of the Shop of Christmas Wonders.'

There was an explosive roar from the rest of the Reindeer as hooves were banged on the table in protest.

'Yes,' stated Santa firmly. 'Krystiana and I have decided it. Rudolph was getting bored at the station.'

'He was never at the station,' blurted Vixen.

'Well, now he can serve Christmas in a way more suited to him,' confirmed Santa.

'So he's not guna be flying with us anymore?' asked Dancer, looking confused.

'Yeah, I will. I'm not giving up *that*,' interrupted Rudolph. 'I just won't be doing any of the Christmaboring patrolling nonsense that you lot do. I get to mix potions all day,' he grinned. 'Hey, wanna try one I mixed earlier?' he asked Dancer, reaching into his bag and pulling out a little brown bag that shook and sparkled and could barely sit still.

'Hey, I'll try it,' volunteered Hopper, leaping out of his seat and snatching it out of Rudolph's hoof.

'Rudolph, let's not get carried away,' began Krystiana, eyeing the bag suspiciously.

'Oh it's fine, Your Majesty. Watch this.'

Hopper opened the bag and caught a very excitable green dust in his paw. He sprinkled it over himself and then began to wriggle incessantly.

'Hey, what's happening?' he asked in a warbling voice.

'It's ok, little dude. It'll turn you into a Reindeer in a minute. Wait for it, wait, wait....'

Hopper continued to shimmy and shake until he shot straight up to the ceiling like a rocket, followed by a trail of green dust. He then landed back on the table, splattered in green and singed. There was a roar of laughter from the table, except from Hopper, who looked most put out, and from Rudolph, who couldn't quite understand why his potion hadn't worked.

'Well, Rudolph. A little work is needed on your potions, I think,' suggested Krystiana kindly.

'Maybe I could set up a bar there instead. I'm good at making Christmacocktails,' said Rudolph, scratching his head.

'Rudolph, Rudolph,' sighed Santa, shaking his head. 'Come now, have some more pudding.'

Rudolph happily stuffed his face, in between arranging an after-party at Villa Noël, and fighting off jokes and jibes from the other Reindeer. Dinner was followed by some festive dancing at the Court and some magical excitement after an incredible batch of Wish Biscuits. Glitter and snow fell simultaneously from the hallway ceiling, and the little Christmacubs enjoyed themselves immensely by dancing on top of the tables.

As the clock approached 9 pm however, Santa suddenly stood up.

'Well then, boys. The time is now upon us. Have you eaten enough to last you all night?'

'You betcha, Santa,' replied Comet, nibbling his last carrot stick. 'I've never been so stuffed in all my life.'

'Should we tell the children yet, Santa, or shall we keep it a surprise?' asked Blitzen, wiping his mouth with a serviette and standing up.

'Oh, let's keep it a surprise,' chuckled Santa. 'They'll enjoy it more that way.'

'Alright then, Michael, Sarah,' began Blitzen, turning to the children. 'Can you follow me, please. Santa and the Reindeer have got a surprise for you.'

'A surprise, Stiff Ears? What the devil do you mean?' asked Michael, taking his party hat off his head.

'Well now, if I told you, it wouldn't be a surprise, would it?' remarked Blitzen with a wink.

The two children looked at each other before looking at their mother in confusion.

'That's right, you two. Follow Blitzen now. You've definitely earned this treat,' assured their mother with a smile.

Michael and Sarah looked around to see that the other Reindeer had now left with Santa, leaving only Blitzen in the Great Hall.

'Ok then,' said Michael, now following Blitzen, with Sarah close behind. 'It's not another Quest is it, Stiff Ears? I've had enough of those for one winter.'

'Not exactly,' answered Blitzen, leading them up to the Queen's private parlour and out through the glass doors, onto the balcony. 'Not one in which you have to fight against evil, anyway.'

'What could it possibly be?' asked Sarah, as Blitzen drew open the balcony doors.

'Oh good Christmas!' gasped Michael in astonishment, as a wave of joy rushed over him.

Sarah beamed too, to see Santa seated in his sleigh with the Reindeer all linked up to it. The sleigh was stacked full of Christmas presents that were ready to be delivered that evening to all those good girls and boys throughout the world.

'You mean, we're actually allowed to come with you,' cried Michael, tearing forwards towards the sleigh.

'Yes, that's right,' chuckled Santa, as he sat on his big, red seat. 'It's the least I could offer after you saved my life.'

'Oh my God, this is absolutely Christmatastic! I wish I'd rescued the Kingdom long ago if *this* is the reward I'd get for it,' beamed Michael, jumping aboard.

Sarah too now climbed in next to them, looking up to observe a new star in the skies of Christmas looking down on her. *The Scroll* was happy. That *had* to be it. It was gleaming next to the Star of Christmas, as though it were somehow watching over and protecting them.

'See, pigtails, I *told* you it was going to be the best Christmas ever. Old Red Nose got it right in the first place,' said Michael with a smile.

'Ho ho ho. Well it will certainly take some beating,' chuckled Santa, grabbing the reigns. 'Hold on tight now. Alright, boys. Here we go.'

Rudolph heaved backwards.

'Merry Christmas, everyone. It's guna be a good one.'

With that, the sleigh left the castle and climbed high into the air, rising higher and higher above the clouds until it veered left towards the Gates of the Air like a train of magic wishes.

Glossary

The North Pole: situated at the very tip of Earth. It is the gateway to the magical Kingdom of Christmas.

The Kingdom of Christmas: the magical setting for our story and the home of Santa Claus, The Spirit of Christmas and the Reindeer, amongst others.

The Mountains of the North: a formidable domain to the northeast of the Kingdom.

The Enchantment of Christmas Castle: the glamorous abode of The Spirit of Christmas, Prince Harcourt, Prince Michael and Princess Sarah.

The Forest of Magic Lanterns: home to the Snowflakes. The forest has strange magical properties and is able to shrink, fly and even render itself invisible.

Cinnamon Forest: home to the Woodland Creatures. It covers the entire southern side of the Kingdom and extends up through the centre of the Kingdom, as far as The Enchantment of Christmas Castle.

Winterland Village: home to Santa Claus, the Elves and the Reindeer. It is a small village located at the very centre of the Kingdom.

Mistletown: the commercial centre of the Kingdom, featuring an array of shops, the bank, the press office and, of course, Santa's Workshop.

Christmas Mountain: a pink, sparkling mountain to the west of the Kingdom, featuring a theme park, ski slopes and toboggan tracks. A Christmas Festival is held here annually on the first night of Advent.

Christmas Street Station: a floating station on the clouds from which neighbouring lands can be reached.

Mistletoe Falls: a frozen waterfall deep within Cinnamon Forest.

Reindeer Station One: the Reindeer headquarters and training grounds.

The Northern Regions: a collection of small villages located to the far north of the Kingdom.

Whispering Island: a floating island outside the Kingdom.

Queen Krystiana - The Spirit of Christmas: the ruler of the Kingdom. On certain nights she travels to Earth and blows a kiss of Christmas joy through the keyhole of every household.

Santa Claus: Santa is responsible for delivering toys and checking the Naughty and Nice Lists. Next to the Queen, he is the most important person in the Kingdom.

Mrs Claus: Santa's wife. She is able to see partially into the past, the present and the future through her Magic Mixing Bowl.

The Guardian of the Mountains: a prisoner of the Mountains who derives his powers from his magical Staff. He hates Christmas and wishes to destroy it.

The Reindeer: Santa's personal chauffeurs and the Kingdom's official police force. The Reindeer work in conjunction with the Snowflakes and the Woodland Creatures to ensure the Kingdom's safety and stability.

The Woodland Creatures: an eclectic mix of Rabbits, Hedgehogs, Badgers and Squirrels - these live in Cinnamon Forest in the south of the Kingdom. They contribute to the spread of Christmas cheer within the Kingdom and help to protect and police the realm. They have no intrinsic ability to perform magic, but certain individuals amongst them have mastered humble charms and enchantments.

Christmacubs: young Woodland Creatures.

Elves: the workforce of the Kingdom - they manufacture the toys at Santa's Workshop. Elves are small creatures with large noses, pointed ears and black hair. They have no ability to fly or do magic.

The Snowflakes: Protectors of the Realm and the Queen's Secret Service. The Snowflakes inhabit the highest social strata in the Kingdom. They are an athletic build, with sapphire eyes, blonde hair and large, clear, glittering wings. They have magical powers and are able to change their size from that of an adult to that of a thumbnail. They also travel to Earth to observe every child's behaviour before presenting a list to Santa.

Fairies: these do not actually live in The Kingdom of Christmas, but we are told of their existence in the magical world of Alendria. Like Snowflakes, they are an athletic build but they have emerald eyes, brown or black hair and green leaf-like wings. They have magical powers and, like the Snowflakes, are able to alter their size.

The Snow Wolves: these roam the Mountains of the North and join forces with the Guardian. They are brutal, evil and greatly feared by every creature in the Kingdom.

The Papa Ratzi: the press. The Papa Ratzi work for a newspaper called The X-mas Times.

The Altra: the source of Queen Krystiana's powers. Whoever commands the Altra is ruler of the entire Kingdom. It is neither good nor bad, but responds to the desires of its ruler. When it is joined to the Staff of Evil, it becomes the most powerful weapon of all worlds.

The Staff of Evil: the source of the Guardian's powers. When it is joined with the Altra it becomes the most powerful device in the Kingdom, capable of unknown destruction.

The Testament of the Snowflakes: an ancient book allegedly declaring the Snowflakes to be the greatest and most superior race ever created. The book has been lost for centuries, yet its apparent teachings continue to fuel the ongoing feud between the Snowflakes and the Elves.

Reindeer Dust: magic dust. Gold Reindeer dust enables the individual to fly. Pink Reindeer dust enables creatures to travel into the next world.

The Magic Scroll of Christmas: an Oracle that tells the creatures what to do in times of darkness.

The Secret Seal of Christmas: a drop of blood placed on a letter to show that the subject matter is serious.

The North Wind: delivers letters to and from the Kingdom.

A Frozen Candle: an ancient weapon of northern torture, which has the ability to freeze time.

Magic Lanterns: a feature of the Snowflake forest. These are filled with fireflies and change colour to warn of Hope, Glory, Danger or Despair by changing Orange, Gold, Red or Purple, respectively.

Wish Biscuits: a variety of wishing biscuits of various shapes and colours. These are an enchanting delicacy and a particular favourite with the folk of the Kingdom.